THE
Sage
AFTER
Rain

By Jaclyn M. Hawkes

Spirit
Dance
Books

Be sure to read Jaclyn's other books
Journey of Honor A love story
An entertaining historical romance set in
1848 in the American West

The Outer Edge of Heaven
A rollicking contemporary love story set
on a beautiful Montana ranch

The Most Important Catch
A tender and intense modern day story
of devotion set against a backdrop of
pro football in North Carolina

Healing Creek
A heartfelt and fun tale of love and trust

Rockland Ranch Series
The epic saga of a Wyoming ranch family
Peace River
Above Rubies
Once Enchanted

Warrior's Moon
An intrepid tale of adventure and devotion set in the
medieval kingdom of Monciere'

What readers are saying about Jaclyn's books:

I have just one thing to say about Jaclyn M. Hawkes' book **The Outer Edge of Heaven**! I absolutely love, Love, LOVE it! Okay, really, I actually do have more to say about it. . . I never wanted it to end, and when it did, I wanted more. Debbie Davis

I have to say that as a writer, I think Jaclyn M. Hawkes has hit her stride. I enjoyed every moment of this story as I laughed, cried, and even went for my own bag of Oreos and glass of milk. Jaclyn M. Hawkes has found her place in clean, contemporary fiction. I would love to see more stories like this one from her. Cheryl Christensen A Good Day to Read

Wow! I absolutely LOVED this book. I could not put it down, not to do homework, not to sleep, not to clean house, nada! Fantastic book! Tamera Westhoff

This book is a fast read and one that you really won't want to put down. You will fall in love with the characters and not want the story to end. I enjoy Jaclyn's writing and hope to read even more books from her. Sheila Staley

Killer dialogue, and the hero was well worth the wait. It was definitely a fun read. Heather Justesen

The Sage After Rain

By Jaclyn M. Hawkes

Published and distributed by Spirit Dance Books. Spiritdancebooks.com
855-648-5559

Cover design by Roland Ali Pantin
Printed in USA
First Printing December 2013
LOC 2013955627
ISBN: 0-9851648-6-7
ISBN-13: 978-0-9851648-6-7

Acknowledgements

Thanks to my team. There is no way I could be successful without you. Thanks to all the readers and editors—even when you're brutally honest. And thanks to Roland for his exquisite artwork. Thanks to Amanda for not getting testy when I admit I hate marketing. Thanks to my younger children for still doing their chores, even when Mom is buried finishing a book. Thanks to the seismic crew that I watched get off the helicopter one sunny day in Sigurd. Thanks to Phil Sharer of Houston Texas for helping me research this book. And most of all, thanks to my husband— for everything, but especially for supporting my need to write. He encouraged me even when at first it seemed a little wacko. But then, he's always been the most uplifting man I know.

Dedication

This book is dedicated to my husband. Like the hero of this book, he is a gentle man. He has that wonderful, soft spoken sense of who he is and because of it, you don't feel the need to question his wisdom or his counsel. You just know that under his care it's all going to be okay. As a wife in a world that can sometimes be more eventful than you expected, that is a priceless gift. He is definitely my hero and the love of my life.

Chapter 1

Baltimore Maryland

Taya Kaye gave her elegant hair and make up one last glance in the reflection of the glass door as she stepped into John's office and greeted her parents. They were definitely two of the beautiful people of the world in their evening wear. John was beautiful himself in a tux leaning on his desk, talking on the phone, but Taya realized immediately he was in a bad mood as she listened to the way he was speaking to whoever was on the other end. Something, somewhere in his world wasn't going the way he wanted it to this evening.

He got off the phone and stood up to approach her and gave her a smile that didn't entirely erase the scowl around his eyes and said, "Taya, you look magnificent tonight. People will come from near and far to donate to the campaign the moment they see you. Don't you agree Stan? Evelyn?"

"You do look wonderful, Taya, honey." Her mom walked toward her. "I love the hair, and the jewelry is perfect, but why don't you lose the little jacket. You have such pretty shoulders, and the jacket almost covers that exquisite necklace. The jacket is too matronly for you. Go ahead and slip it off."

With a sigh, Taya replied, "Mother we've been through this a hundred times. Not tonight. I don't want to argue. You know I'm not going to go anywhere strapless, so don't even start."

1

Her father opened his mouth to say something, but John interrupted, "Just this once, Taya. Listen to your mother. She's right, and you're so pretty I want to show you off." His phone rang and interrupted whatever he had been going to say next.

He turned aside to take the call and Taya's father came close and whispered, "Do as he asks, Taya. He's already in a temper and you need to help him relax before this evening. It's a huge night for him. There are millions of dollars of campaign funds on the line here. The strapless dress might even help with the fundraising, you never know. You get some of these wealthy old men drinking and they might take one look at you and hand over their billfolds." He wasn't smiling as he spoke and Taya began to wonder what was going on.

Her mom put in as well, "It's a wife's place to help ease the strain on a busy and successful husband, Taya. Or in this case, a fiancée's. You need to do whatever it takes to help him relax for this party."

John's voice raised a few decibels in the back ground and she heard him use an expletive she'd never heard him use before and she quietly asked, "What's he so upset about?"

"I'm not sure, Taya, honey, but he's spitting nails. Something about his opponent insinuating corrupt dealings with some highway contractors. It lit him up fast, I can tell you. You need to help him calm down."

"He's a grown man, Mother. I'm sure he'll be fine. He would have never made it to congressman if he wasn't capable of calming himself down."

He finally got off the phone and approached the three of them. "We're late. Let's head out to the car. Taya, take off the jacket and let's go. There are a lot of people waiting for me."

He went to undo the little button at her throat and she pulled away. "I'm not taking off the jacket, John. It's part of the dress."

He shook his head without smiling. "Come on, Taya. It's a fundraiser. The better you look, the more money I'll get." He picked up his phone and a sheaf of papers from his desk and turned toward the door. "We're late. Quit messing around and take it off."

Turning with him to go, she said, "No. I'm not taking it off. It's not modest without it."

He stopped so abruptly she almost walked into him. She could hear him breathing deeply in front of her for the merest second and then he back handed her so suddenly and so explosively that she never even saw the blow coming.

The phone in his hand impacted with her head on the point of her brow and almost instantly blood spattered across the papers on his desk as she collided with his chair. It rolled as she hit it and she careened into the corner of the desk before slamming into the wall and then to the floor beside it.

The humongous diamond solitaire from her engagement ring had somehow tangled in the beads of her dress and her hand was between her body and the desk when she smashed into it. Then it was bent back under her when she fell as she tried to catch herself.

Pain ripped through her whole left hand as she lay there, stunned and trying to breathe after the impact of her landing. Lights sparkled in her vision, and it took her a moment to even understand what had just happened. He had hit her! John Channing, her own fiancé' had hit her!

White hot anger spurted through her and was the only thing that kept her from crying out from the excruciating pain of her hand. The blood dripping from her head onto the carpeting of his office floor didn't even register through the agony that radiated from her ring finger all the way up through her wrist.

Slowly, she turned her head to look up, but John wasn't even looking at her. He was swearing viciously over the fact that she had gotten blood on his white tuxedo shirt.

Picking up the office phone, he barked an order for whoever picked up on the other end to meet him with another one. He hung up and threw a venomous glance over his shoulder at her and swore again, then said, "Now look what you've done! I needed your help tonight!" He picked up his tuxedo jacket and stalked out the door.

Taya's father came over to stand above her and she couldn't believe her ears when she heard him say, "Someday, girl, you're going to figure out just where your bread is buttered." He turned to his wife. "Let's go, Evelyn. We're late." They walked out the door as well and Taya laid her head back down on the bloody carpet unable to even comprehend what had just occurred here. John had always been a perfect gentleman to her. She'd never dreamed he was capable of something like this.

She was in too much pain to even look up when she heard the door open again, but the sudden intake of breath prompted her to drag her head up to see who had come in. John's private secretary advanced toward her across the room and said, "Oh my stars! Taya, what happened? Was that crash I just heard, you?"

Tiredly, Taya answered, "In the flesh, Judy. John apparently didn't like my dress." She struggled to her knees in the beaded evening gown and began to try to extricate what remained of the ring on her finger from the fabric of her dress as blood ran down the side of her eye from above her brow bone. Seeing the condition of her hand made her want to be sick. She hadn't ever even wanted the huge diamond. She'd wanted a plain gold band, but John had insisted. Calmly she asked, "Judy is there any way I could trouble you for some ice?"

Judy was standing there with her mouth agape. "Are you telling me John did this?" Taya nodded. "And then he walked out and left you like this?"

Bitterness dripped from Taya's voice as she added, "That was just before my parents followed him. Would you mind calling me a cab?"

Judy finally got past her shock enough to jump into action. She tore a handful of tissues out of the box on the shelf against the wall and bent to put pressure on the cut on Taya's brow. Taya groaned at the touch. She was still trying to untangle the prongs from the ring and her dress one handedly. The eight carat diamond was completely broken off and she had no idea where it had landed.

Judy pushed her hand away gently and finished untangling it. She made a sympathetic sound with her mouth as she looked up into Taya's watering eyes. "Oh, honey I'm so sorry. I'm afraid your finger is pretty well shattered. I'll go get that ice."

She helped Taya to her feet and to the nearby office chair, where she helped her hold pressure on the cut on her brow and then picked up the phone and punched in a zero for the switchboard operator. "Hello. This is Judy in John Channing's office. I need you to send security, and a janitor with a tool box as soon as possible! Yes! Hurry!" She hung up and then dialed again and asked for an ambulance and the police and then headed out the front door of the office at a jog.

Jaclyn M. Hawkes

Chapter 2

Western Colorado

There was the most striking woman at the gas station in Halloran as Matt Maylon filled up his Jeep on the way back to Steamboat Springs and he couldn't help but notice her, but then he felt guilty for thinking she was exquisite. All he did was see a beautiful girl at the next gas pump, but it felt somehow disloyal to Stacy. Stacy. How had he gotten into this mess of a relationship with Stacy?

All the way back to Steamboat and his office and then to his apartment, he worried about dealing with Stacy again. When he finally got home, he knew he was indeed in trouble the moment he walked in the door to see her standing in the kitchen in the outfit she usually wore to go out dancing and with a beer in her hand. Dead tired, he had to be back at the project site two and a half hours away at eight o'clock in the morning and he really wasn't up to going out tonight. He wasn't up to dealing with Stacy at all. He wouldn't have even come back here to his apartment except that he needed clean clothes and was honestly too tired to drive back to the site tonight.

Stacy looked up as he came in the door, gave him a hesitant smile and said, "Hi, Matt. I wondered if I'd see you tonight. How is the project going these days?" At least she asked this time. Glancing at her, he noticed her hair was a yellower blonde than it had been the last time he'd seen her.

Tossing his keys on the counter, he went across to give her a half-hearted hug. He had absolutely no interest in kissing her, especially when she'd already started drinking by herself at seven-thirty in the evening. He didn't remember her drinking that much before she moved in here five weeks ago, but then if he was honest, he hadn't known her all that well.

He felt like he knew her even less now. His work was insanely busy, and except for checking in with his office, he'd made it a point to be out of town constantly from the day he'd woken up hung over and realized that somehow, in the one time he had blown it and gotten smashed drunk, she had moved in with him. He still had no clue how that had come about, because he couldn't imagine himself asking her, or any girl, to do something like that, even if he had been completely comatose. He just wasn't that kind of a guy.

It sounded terrible, but sometimes he wondered if he even had invited her, or if she had simply used his moment of complete stupidity drinking to move in as her way of dealing with a housing shortage. When he considered that, he felt guilty again for wondering if she was really that shallow. She'd seemed like a nice girl when he'd first met her. At any rate he hadn't quite figured out how a decent guy handled a situation like this. The whole fiasco was so awkward that he'd been hesitant to even deal with it, even though Stacy seemed perfectly content with living here except for her inevitable comments about him working so much.

It hadn't mattered anyway. The fact was, he was in the middle of a nightmare work project that he didn't have the option of backing out of. He wasn't really even living here except to come home, do a load or two of laundry, grab a bite and head back out to his job site. He certainly wasn't going to come home to sleep with her. Still . . .

He should have known hanging out with Justin and his friends would screw up his life. Nothing good had come of the friendship with a hellion like Justin. Well, one good thing. After that night, Matt knew he'd never touch another drop of alcohol in his life.

Going back to Stacy's question about his project, he answered her almost warily, "It's going okay. How was work?" She immediately assumed a pouty look and he wished he could take his question back, but was saved from having to listen to her go on about some injustice at the store by her phone ringing.

Rubbing the back of his neck, he stretched and automatically walked to the fridge to open it. Stacy hadn't been eating in this week apparently. The fridge was mostly empty except for the leftovers from the grilled chicken he'd made last Sunday when he'd stopped by the apartment before going back to the project. He reached in to check out the chicken, noticed it was growing and dumped it down the disposal, then rinsed the dish. This time he went to the freezer in hopes of finding food he didn't have to either go somewhere to get, or order on the phone. After living out of a hotel for months, he wanted something cooked on his own stove.

He halfheartedly moved two frozen pizzas and a pile of Lean Cuisines. He had pork chops and a package of crumbled bacon. The pork chops would take too long, but the bacon had potential. He opened the fridge back up to see what there was in the way of fresh vegetables for an omelet.

He turned on some mellow background music and was happily cutting onion, zucchini, and bell peppers when Stacy ended her phone call and came over to see what he was doing and then wrinkled her nose at the bell pepper and said, "I thought maybe you'd take me out to dinner since this is the first night you've been home in ages. What do you say?" She went to take his hand and he deftly avoided her by reaching into the drawer to find a sauté pan.

"Not tonight, Stace. I'm going to eat, take a shower, and sleep for twelve full hours before I have to be back out in the desert tomorrow morning. You want an omelet?"

Her tentative smile disappeared and she said, "No. And I don't want to hear any more about that stupid project you're pouring your life into either. You never have a spare moment for me. It's always just your project. Can't you put it aside for one weekend?" Her voice brightened and she went on, "Justin and Jenna and I are talking about taking a fast trip to Vegas. Come go with us. We'll leave tomorrow night and fly back Monday morning. Or Monday afternoon probably, knowing us." She laughed. "We probably better get an afternoon flight, since it is Vegas. The City of Sin." She laughed again and put a hand on his arm as he turned to look at her. *Who was this girl?* She was so different from the pretty, happy, fun person he had once thought he was starting to have feelings for. He didn't think her joke about the City of Sin was funny.

Shrugging off her hand, he said, "I can't go to Las Vegas this weekend, Stacy. I couldn't afford to even if I wanted to. Which I don't. You and Jenna and Justin go without me, but thanks for the invite."

"Oh c'mon, Matt. Stop being all responsible. Call in sick and spend some of your savings and lighten up for a change. You've gotten so serious that you're not even fun anymore."

Not even fun anymore were the exact words he could use for her. How had he ever gotten into this mess? "I don't think using my savings to gamble with would be all that great of an idea. Especially the way this project is going. Are you sure you don't want an omelet?" He took his plate to the table.

Stacy went on, "That project—hey, Carla at work was telling me her boyfriend makes gobs of money being a bartender downtown. He was telling her the more drinks he can get people to buy, the more tips he makes and the drunker they are the bigger the tips. Maybe you could quit this project and go do something like that. Carla says Jose' brings home wads of cash!"

Taking another bite, he looked at her while he chewed. He didn't think that one even merited an answer. He was unbelievably glad she hadn't agreed to marry him when he'd tried to get her to after realizing they were, in fact, living together. He'd been trying to be honorable, because he was so not a live-in kind of a guy, but she'd said no. Man was he glad. The thought of being stuck in this for life was completely depressing.

He took another bite and then felt guilty for that thought. He needed to fix this mess. Patching up their relationship was as much his responsibility as hers. Maybe more. He was the one who was out of town nonstop. He tried to make an overture. "How about a movie tonight, Stacy? You and me. No Jenna, no beer. I'll even watch a chick flick."

"What do you mean a movie? We're going dancing aren't we? Didn't you just hear me make plans on the phone?"

"I'm sorry, I wasn't listening."

"That's the problem, Matt. You weren't listening. You can't listen when you're gone, and you don't listen when you're here."

Remaining calm, he replied, "Stacy, it was your phone call. Remember? Eavesdropping isn't polite."

"Don't split hairs, Matt," she snapped, "And no, I'm not watching a movie with you. I'm going dancing! With or without you!" She tossed her empty can into the garbage that he'd noticed already held several and picked up her purse and keys.

He immediately got up and pulled the keys out of her hand and sat back down. "How many beers have you had tonight, Stace?"

She turned on him angrily. "Don't even go there, Mr. holier than thou. How many beers I've had is none of your business!"

"Tell me how many you've had or I'm not going to give you your keys back." He kept his voice calm and matter-of-fact.

The calmer he stayed the madder she got sometimes. This was one of those times. She must have had a couple or three already because she said, "I have another set, and you can't stop me!"

"Stacy, you go out that door and climb into your car and drive off and I'll call the cops on you. And I won't come bail you out of jail." She glared at him, apparently understanding he'd do just exactly what he'd said he would.

"Fine! Justin or Jenna can drive." She turned away from him and went into the bedroom where he could hear her talking on the phone again. He continued to eat the omelet that had begun to taste like cardboard after this conversation. A few minutes later, she came out of the bedroom and went out the front door, closing it with a resounding slam. The neighbors downstairs were probably going to call the manager again.

He watched her climb into Justin's little truck in the parking lot. Jenna wasn't in the cab with them and he wondered if his best friend was taking his girlfriend dancing, just the two of them. Either way it was a relief to be rid of her for the night. Justin deserved her. It was him who had helped get him into this situation. Matt realized the tone his thoughts had taken and reminded himself that Stacy moving in here was nobody's fault but his own. Just because he didn't remember inviting her was no excuse. He was the one who had been drinking that night. He'd known better, and could only blame himself. He'd made this mess. He was the one who was going to have to clean it up.

He tried to tell himself that as he straightened the kitchen, but it still didn't make him want to be here when she got home, even though it was his apartment. He debated whether to go in and go to bed and deal with her when she came in drunk in the middle of the night, or leave tonight to head back to the project site two and a half hours away and deal with the men there who weren't going to be a whole lot better. He finally rationalized that at least the guys weren't going to come get in bed with him like she would and he loaded up some clean clothes and went out and climbed back into his Jeep. He wished he had listened to his mother more when she tried to encourage him to get away from Justin. He'd have never messed things up like this.

As he pulled out of his apartment complex, he shook his tired head and sighed. Geez, he needed to quit feeling so guilty about this and just tell her to leave, although who knew what kind of theatrics she'd go into?

The next morning he wondered if he'd made the right choice after all. One of the guys hadn't even come back from wherever it was they'd been partying and the other two were hung over and surly beyond belief. None of the three ended up going out to work and it was just Matt and the helicopter pilot again when they took off. He was never going to be able to pull this thing out by the project deadline by himself.

He was the office guy anyway. He was only supposed to analyze the data, not have to gather it too. His boss, the main contractor, was lying in there in that two bit motel nursing a hangover, while Matt was out here doing their jobs and his too. He'd been pouring his heart and soul into this deal, at first in hopes of making a lot of money. Now he merely hoped he would be able to make anything for all the ridiculous hours he had put in trying to keep the project on the table.

Just then the helicopter topped the ridge to reveal a breathtaking pink and orange sunrise that reflected all across the valley floor. It filled the whole front window of the chopper with fiery color, and erased his black mood instantly. If he'd been stuck in some office back in Steamboat, he'd never have been able to see something like that as he flew in a helicopter across the desert. He dug his camera out and photographed it and reminded himself that he had a lot to be thankful for. He wished he could pray again just to say thanks when he saw things like this, but there was no way he could pray when he was living the way he was.

Chapter 3

Before she even knew she was waking up, Taya became overwhelmed with a confusing mix of emotion and pain. She was sad, and confused, and frightened, and oh man did her left hand hurt. She fought through the disjointed images and struggled to open her eyes and even when she got them opened, something was wrong. The one wasn't working very well. It felt fat and her vision was distorted.

The pain in her left hand was over the top and she lifted her hand to cradle it to her body and realized it was completely swallowed in a cumbersome cast and wrapping. She felt herself grimace in pain and confusion. Then it started to come back to her. John had hit her. The police had come and talked to her for what seemed like hours. She'd had to have emergency surgery.

Tears welled in her eyes as she looked around in confusion, wondering where she was and hoping that the memory of her parents leaving her bleeding on John's office floor was simply a nightmare. A vivid, heartbreaking nightmare.

Even as she hoped that, she knew somehow beyond her fuzzy head and swollen eye that it was all too real. Her parents really had walked out on her last night. She settled the cast on her left hand onto the bed in front of her and closed her eyes again, feeling the tears seep out. Her own parents really had left her lying there and had gone with John, even with her hand shattered and her head bleeding.

She heard a sound and opened her eyes again to see her dear friend Madeline leaning over her bed, a sad smile on her face as she said, "Good morning, lazy bones. Are you finally going to wake up?" She wrapped a soft hand beneath Taya's neck and gave her a gentle partial hug. "Hi, princess. It's good to see those pretty blue eyes."

Madeline pulled back and looked down at Taya and added, "Okay, well, so only one of your eyes is pretty, but the other one will come around in a few days. Welcome to Colorado."

Taya grimaced again and asked in a voice that made her throat hurt, "Colorado? You're kidding How did you get involved in this mess?"

Shaking her head, Madeline said, "You put me down as the emergency contact at the hospital. And no, I'm not kidding. For once, I wish I was, girl. You've had quite a couple of days. But it is wonderful to see you. I just wish it wasn't under these circumstances. How are you feeling?"

Taya groaned. "Rough. Couple of days? Really? What day is it?"

"Monday. All day." Madeline reached for a pill bottle that sat on the table next to the bed. "Some pain medication will help. I was supposed to give you one of these a couple of hours ago, but you didn't wake up. They'd given you some pretty stiff stuff to last you through the flights and ride here and you've been mostly zonked. I was beginning to worry." She handed Taya a pill and then a glass of water and said, "Take this and I'll go get you something to eat with it or it might make you sick. You want to sit up some?"

Taya struggled to sit up and Madeline propped pillows behind her and then left the room and Taya looked all around. She didn't recognize the room and wondered where Madeline's husband and children were. She yawned and sighed and closed her one pretty and one swollen eyes. What was she doing in Colorado? She couldn't even remember making arrangements to come here.

****

"The witness protection program? Like the federal witness protection program? Like the FBI or something? And my father was indicted too?" Taya couldn't believe what she was hearing.

The slightly balding man with the power issues standing in front of her in the guest room of Madeline's in-laws' cabin simply took a step toward her and extended a small wallet. He flipped it open to reveal an official looking badge and said drily, "Just like the FBI or something. That shouldn't surprise you after the kinds of things your hotshot fiancé was involved in. And yes, your slick conniving father. It's either hide and testify. Or you go down with them."

Taya's eyebrows shot up at his attitude and it made her swollen eye hurt, but she sat up straighter and said firmly, "Don't you even dare threaten me, Mr. hotshot FBI agent. I don't care if you're one of the Royal Canadian Mounties. This is still America, buddy, no matter how much we mess it up, and we still live by the Constitution. I've done nothing. I am innocent—until proven guilty in a court of law and one little badge doesn't make you . . ."

The other man in the room held up a calming hand and said to the badge holder, "Back off, Reid. She was the victim. Remember? We wouldn't even be here if it wasn't for her. She's the one who called us in. And was willing to press charges. Just because she was engaged to him, doesn't make her an accomplice. She's right. This is America. And as of yet, she looks clean."

Under his breath, Reid said, "Too clean if you ask me. Mormon, really? That's a set-up if I've ever seen one."

The other man rolled his eyes and to Taya he said, "Sorry, Ms. Kaye. And yes, the witness protection program. Your fiancé was into some thoroughly deep stuff with some truly dangerous people. If you saw anything at all of what he was into, you probably already have a contract out on your life. Mr. Channing played with the big dogs. And if you follow through with your assault charges, it won't matter what you saw. They've been using him to sway legislation and if he loses this election they're sunk. They'll need you out of the way. You'd be wise to let us put you in the program."

Taya shook her head silently, still troubled by the whole idea. How could she really matter either way? Sure, she'd seen a couple things that had seemed weird at the time, but they hadn't seemed that dastardly—unless you factored in that John had apparently been wheeling and dealing with big labor, and the waterfront boys and even the very highway contractors he'd been fuming about that night.

At least that's what they were saying they had found on his phone and paperwork. But there was no question about whether she'd press assault charges. She didn't feel she even had a choice. She'd believed her whole life that you either stood up for right or you caved and right couldn't prevail. It was a matter of principle. There was no way around it if she wanted to keep her self respect, danger or no. There were worse things than sacrificing personal safety—like sacrificing the decency of society.

It was indeed frightening. She hoped part of that fear was just that she was on pain medication and a little out of it. The most troubling thing of all was that when she glanced back at the FBI agent Reid, she was nearly as anxious about him as she was about John's questionable contacts. Just the thought of voluntarily walking into a life of having to trust strangers like him made her mentally put on all kinds of brakes.

Suddenly, she was painfully tired. She closed her eyes and leaned her head back as she considered and then opened them to ask, "Are there any other options"

The kinder man nodded slowly. "Of course. You can not go into the program and take your chances on your own. We would still help you with whatever you wanted as far as staying under the radar. But I have to tell you, the odds are, you won't be able to stay away from them. You have no experience in knowing how to disappear. We're professionals at this. If they find you, you're probably dead. At that point, John Channing might walk."

"Do I have to decide on this right this second? Can I have a while to think about it?"

Reid made a sound of disgust that grated on Taya's nerves and made her hesitate even more and his partner threw him a stony glare and said, "Take as long as you need. But keep in mind that the longer you stay, here, the more likely they are to find you and put your friend and her family at risk. And don't try to contact anyone by phone or electronically. Just assume that if you leave any kind of a footprint, they're gonna to get hold of it. And definitely no Facebook and Tweeting and Pinning photos. That kind of thing is how people get caught every time, both the good guys and the bad guys. You'll get somebody killed. You need to basically fall off the face of the planet. I know that sounds harsh, but we're talking about your life here. And the lives of your friends and co-workers."

Taya sighed, "Geez, you weren't kidding about falling off the planet. I'm not huge into social media anyway, but what about my company? You want me to just walk away from it? With no friends or family, how am I to stay sane? And we've worked hard to build up our firm. Walking away would destroy it."

The amiable agent asked, "Do you have to send everything on-line? Can't you work off-line and ship your engineered plans by snail mail?"

"Of course. The plans have to be stamped anyway. But how can I ship anything without leaving a trail?"

"Just send it through your contact at the Bureau. And remember, it's not forever. We just need to keep you safe long enough to get through both of John Channing's trials and his re-election bid. At that point, you get your life back. Once the trial and election are over, you won't be a threat to them and there'll be no reason to pay a contract on you. And even organized crime works around the money." He gave her an apologetic look. "Sorry, I know that sounds horrible when you put it that way. But it's true."

She shook her head, fighting the sadness that was burying her and said, "It's okay. I understand." Her life back. Her entire life as she knew it had already disintegrated the moment John hit her and her parents walked out. How did you get anything back from that? What would you want back from that? At this point, wasn't it simply a matter of coming to terms with the fact that apparently what she'd thought was her life hadn't been *her* life at all. To her fiancé and her parents, she was obviously the disposable portion of the situation. She couldn't help the tears that welled in her eyes.

The kinder agent looked across at Reid and said, "Let's let her rest. She's still recovering from surgery, remember?"

Still glowering, Reid followed his partner out the door and Taya looked up at Madeline and shook her head. "What do I do now? How did a nice girl like me get into a mess like this?"

Madeline grinned. "I haven't got a clue—about either one. I'd suggest you get on your knees and ask for inspiration. And then stay where it's quiet enough that you can listen for God's answer. Or go where it's quiet enough. With Reid around, here might not be the best place for pondering. Take Zan up on his offer to take you out to see the sheepherders. It doesn't get any more peaceful than that."

Chapter 4

Fourteen days after arriving in Colorado Taya stood facing west and watched a helicopter fly over as the last rays of the sun painted the evening sky mauve and gold above the rocky desert below. Turning, she settled into a canvas chair beside her fire with a satisfied sigh, looked around her camp and thought back on her life. In two short weeks, she'd gone from being engaged to a U.S. congressman in Maryland, to literally camping in the high desert of western Colorado. It was as opposite a lifestyle as she could imagine.

She had gone from being a structural engineer who owned half of an engineering firm to the near unbelievable situation of now hiding out as a nomadic sheepherder. It was crazy enough that it felt brilliant. No one who knew her before would ever suspect she'd do something like this. It was an incredible and yet completely refreshing change of lifestyle.

When the FBI had tried to force her to go into the witness protection program—which had been absolutely frightening, recovering from surgery as she had been, somehow, she hadn't been able to feel comfortable about it. Every time she'd considered it, she'd felt it was the wrong decision. In the end, she'd followed what she believed to be a prompting to "fall off the planet" this way instead.

She and Madeline had met their sophomore year of high school at a youth leadership camp and were now more like sisters. Taya had told off some girls who were teasing Madeline because she was half Navajo Indian and it had begun a life changing friendship that had strengthened with the years. Their completely different personalities complemented each other beautifully. Madeline had given Taya roots and had introduced her to God and Taya had given Madeline wings and encouraged her to go for things she wouldn't have dared try for earlier.

Being with Madeline again those few days had been positively therapeutic. Under her sweet, solicitous care, Taya had been able to deal with both the physical injury and the heartbreak of that awful night. And watching Madeline and her husband and children together had made Taya grateful she hadn't gone as far as actually marrying John. Even if he hadn't turned out to be violent and corrupt, marrying someone she wasn't in love with would have been a huge mistake. She realized that now.

The day Madeline's brother Zan had invited her on a day trip to get out and see some of the surrounding country was the turning point. Although he was the consummate educated business man who worked for the Navajo Nation, and in fact, handled their most delicate and demanding business dealings, he was also involved in the more basic, close to the earth lifestyle many of the natives lived because his father, Joseph employed a number of them in his farming operations.

Zan had remembered that the nomadic sheepherders had fascinated Taya years ago when she'd first come to Colorado to visit, and offered to take her out to see them again. She had wondered if it was just an excuse to be with her, but she wanted to see them and agreed to go. That complete unworldly serenity was incredibly evocative and watching the herders and the dogs bring the sheep around and move them exactly where they wanted was thrilling to her every time.

That day it had stormed and the smell of the sage after the rain had been like a drug. The sheepherder's nomadic lifestyle and the sense of peace that permeated the open country they lived in had done something to her very soul. It was so totally and completely opposite from the high profile and worldly life she had been living that it really did feet like another planet and it made her realize that she not only needed time to ponder what she was going to do about the FBI, she also needed some time for personal introspection about her life in general.

On the ride back home through the broken, high desert she'd begun to get an idea and it had stayed with her and grown until she finally decided to seriously check into it. Although it at first seemed crazy, she knew it would be far less difficult to stay off the radar here than in any kind of safe house situation. After doggedly working at it, she talked Madeline's father, Joseph Bear into letting her try going to work for him as a sheepherder.

Odd as it was, the scenario was perfect. She could stay out near the Bear family so she wouldn't be completely alone, but not be where she would put them in any danger. She would be away from people and have the time to herself that she truly felt she needed right now, but she'd still be able to do some engineering on her laptop in the sheep trailer after settling the sheep for the night. It would take some serious security measures, but that was doable. She'd have a home of sorts and stay busy, and the best part of all, no one in Washington D.C. would ever dream she would do something this far removed from the black tie party world she had so recently walked away from.

Both Madeline and Zan had tried to talk her out of it over and over, telling her it wouldn't work and that she would be too lonely and the nights would frighten her, but Taya knew this was the right thing for right now. She had a peace when she prayed about her decision that left her with no doubts. Once she had the FBI's blessing and their agreement to facilitate shipping her plans back and forth, and an insanely technical secure new cell phone in case of an emergency that made her feel like some kind of Navy Seal, she threw herself into her idea with enthusiasm.

Joseph had arranged for her to stay with his oldest and best herder for several days so she could learn how to work the dogs and handle the sheep and how everything in the trailer worked, and Taya had felt like she was on the grandest adventure of her life. It took her most of two days to learn to whistle right, but she finally got it down, and felt like she had been awarded a new college degree when the old Indian gave her a toothless grin.

All of it was new and strange, but the only thing she was going to truly struggle with was the personal hygiene issue. The old sheepherder smelled just like an old sheepherder and the woman in Taya who still sported her last manicure, demanded that the engineer in her figure out an answer to that dilemma.

She had enlisted Zan's help and with a little ingenuity, constructed a strange looking shower set up that consisted of two fifty five gallon plastic garbage cans she painted black and set on a pipe frame with a shower head below. From the garbage cans to the nearby creek she ran a small water line hooked to a ram-jet pump that worked off the smallest of currents in the creek and siphoned about a quarter of a cup of water per second up the hose and into the garbage can tanks. It would take a good portion of a day to fill and heat from the sun, but she was thrilled with it when she was done.

She strung a shower curtain on a heavy wire around it and put a small chemical toilet just inside, and hoped she wouldn't begin to smell like an old sheepherder by the end of the summer. The whole rig could be taken apart and put back together in minutes so moving her trailer every few days to a new grazing area wouldn't be that big of a deal, which was important because she was still essentially one handed.

Knowing that living in the desert was going to be miserably hot, she also talked Zan into helping her rig up a porch swing of sorts that she'd be able to sit on outside the trailer at times. They attached brackets to the trailer that she hooked to lengths of chain to support a small futon like seat that could be folded out flat into a small bed if she wanted.

Although she'd ridden quite a bit, Zan had spent one whole day teaching her how to saddle and care for a horse in more depth, and then given her three different kinds of guns and taught her how to use them until her ears rang and her shoulder ached. She had a twenty gauge shotgun, and a lever action thirty thirty for four legged threats, and a twenty two caliber pistol with a clip should she encounter the two legged kind. Both she and Zan were pleasantly surprised to find she was a natural crack shot.

At the end of the day, her left hand was tired enough from trying to grip the barrels with her cast that she decided it would take a major emergency to get her to shoot at least the shotgun again any time soon.

The next day Zan had taken her into town to have her stitches removed and her hand checked and then on the way home he presented her with an exquisite black Appaloosa mare with a stark white blanket on her rump. She was gentle and sweet and Taya loved her on sight.

After her apprenticeship, Joseph and Zan took her out one day to meet her own new herd of sheep and the three dogs she would be working with. Two were black and white Border Collies that did the actual herding and one was a huge, white Great Pyrenees named Zeus that was the guardian of the bunch. When he was out with the sheep it was hard to even tell he wasn't just another one of them, but he made the rounds of the herd and kept any threatening predators at bay.

Joseph and Zan stayed with her throughout the day and then helped her bed the sheep down for the night before pulling out. Now, seated near her campfire, Taya was pleasantly surprised that she truly wasn't afraid to be by herself this far out in the wilderness with just a bunch of animals and a couple of guns to keep her company. The remoteness was actually very comforting. The only ones in the world who could contact her were the Bears and the FBI and this was like living on another planet.

She looked around her at the last light in the western sky that silhouetted the rugged hills, and the glow of the fire that reflected from the beat up old pickup truck Zan had laughingly said was named Lancaster and the sheep camp trailer that was hooked to it. A smile of satisfaction slipped across her face and she decided the only other thing she needed was an old cowboy sitting by the fire singing mellow country songs.

It was the most unbelievable sequence of events she could ever imagine, but as she settled down for the first night she was alone, she knew somehow that this was right where she was supposed to be

Chapter 5

Three days later she had decided there were a few other things she needed and when Zan called to tell her he was coming to check on her, she asked him to bring a list full. He laughed when she told him the shower worked great, but that she needed a better way to heat it.

And it had only taken her two days to realize she was going to have to find a more reliable way than the old truck Lancaster to charge up her laptop battery and IPod. The old truck battery wasn't up to powering anything but the old truck. She still hadn't figured out what to do, short of a heavy and noisy generator, so she struggled through the process of placing a secure call to let Joshua know her first plans were going to take longer than she thought. Zan brought her a little battery operated radio to tide her over until she figured the electrical shortage out and she had never been so grateful in her life.

Over the next few days she designed a minimal solar power system that would use two photo voltaic panels she could attach to the roof of her sheep trailer. In the strong desert sunshine, it would produce more than enough power barring any lasting overcast spells, to charge up her computer, phone and IPod and even to heat her shower water to what she hoped would be a heavenly warmth.

Zan brought her the parts she requested and stayed to watch as she put it all together. He appeared to be a bit mystified that she was capable of designing it and building it, and his expression as he watched made her laugh and say,

"What? What's that face? Don't you trust me to get it up and running?" She loved this kind of thing and probably should have become a mechanical engineer instead of a structural one.

Zan only smiled his enigmatic Native American smile and said, "I don't doubt that you can do anything you set your mind to, Taya Kaye."

Years ago Zan had thought himself in love with her, but she'd never given him a drop of encouragement, and now although he still looked at her with those deep, dark, native eyes occasionally, they had reached an easy friendship that felt more like a brother and sister. Before he left he asked her, "What's up with Zeus? How come he's here and not out with the sheep?"

She grinned. "I can't get him to leave me. He takes a spin out through them from time to time, but mostly he just haunts me." She petted the huge dog's shaggy head. "He makes me feel incredibly loved, don't you buddy?"

Zan looked at her like she was losing it, and asked, "Aren't you too lonely?"

She shrugged. "With the dogs and sheep and horse, and a little music in the evenings, I'm loving this. This is the ultimate way to have inner peace."

Zan shook his head and climbed into his truck. "I never dreamed you would actually go through with this. See you later, Taya. Keep in touch better now that you have more reliable electricity."

When he was gone, she looked around her again. She went inside and began to get her dinner smiling to herself at the thought that if John or her parents could see her now they'd never believe it.

****

By the fourth of July, she was completely at ease with her nomadic life. She was nearly as brown as the native herders and other than her left hand; she was in better

28

physical shape than she'd ever been. Taking the time to cook much just for herself sometimes didn't seem worth it, so she ate a lot of fresh fruit and yogurt, and it made for a slender strength she hadn't felt since high school lacrosse.

There was something about living so close to the land and the animals that was very calming, and she was developing an inner stillness that made things like pondering and prayer come much more easily. Even though she'd only been to church three times in five weeks, she felt like she was closer to her Father in Heaven than she had ever been except for the fact that she was having such a hard time forgiving her parents. She knew she was hurting herself more than them, but it was a battle she hadn't learned how to win yet. She had been able to get over John easily enough that she was incredibly grateful to him for stopping her from making the huge mistake of marrying him, but the betrayal of her parents still weighed on her like a rock. Theirs was a much more powerful hurt that she was struggling to come to terms with.

Zeus had become her shadow and she had learned to read his reactions to what was going on around her like a book. Three times she had heard him growl and then heard coyotes in the night and had been able to go out into the sheep to go after them without being afraid. At first she had wondered how she would react to a situation where she had to use one of her guns, but it had only taken finding one of her lambs mangled by coyotes to erase any qualms she had about gunning for the sneaking dogs.

Her solar panels worked like a charm and she'd been able to get a surprising amount of work done in the evenings after it got dark, and she'd gotten to the point that she could pack up so she could move her camp in literally minutes.

There were times, like at dusk or when she smelled the sage after the desert rain that she wondered if she'd ever want to go back.

Joseph had told her to keep the sheep moving so they could find new food and she was steadily migrating down the wide valley the stream ran through. It was a rough and broken land and at times she had to call in to Joseph or Zan to find out where to take the sheep through or around obstacles. She only let the sheep graze close by the trailer on those times about every eight or ten days when she bumped the old truck back over the rugged terrain to take her projects into town to be shipped after she stamped them. She had only been into town six times in eight weeks and although there were occasional houses near where she grazed the sheep, there was not much civilization. As backward as it seemed, it was very comforting.

Finally, one evening in late July, she came back to camp and realized she was lonely. She took Zeus and went out to talk to the horse she had affectionately named Horse, and stood looking up at the stars wondering what to do about this feeling she hadn't experienced since she was an emotional young teenager. At least this time, even the loneliness was reassuring.

Two days later, she topped a ridge with the sheep and not far away off to the south was the highway and what looked like a small motel or shop of some kind with a service station out in front. It was hard to tell exactly what it was from this distance. The rocky desert valley necked down somewhat and became much more rugged. It was intersected by another stream coming in from the west, and she recognized this as the place Joseph had told her about that would require taking the sheep over a series of small bridges that spanned several ravines in the area. He'd told her that when she reached this area the summer grazing would be about half over.

She thought about that as she sat on the ridge and looked over the beautiful, high desert below her in the purple light of dusk. She hadn't planned for life after sheep herding yet. Finding somewhere to stay safe was a bit intimidating and right now there was no plan out there on the horizon, and no direction she felt terribly inclined to go. That wasn't like her. She turned her horse back toward camp, telling herself she'd better start thinking. When she was through here, she was going to need something to throw herself into.

****

Washington D.C.

In his opulent office comfortably removed from the Washington beltway, Mario Salvatore hung up the phone and rubbed his hands together with a self satisfied smile. Finally, after more than two months of looking, he had a trace of information about where to find Taya Kaye. If John Channing lost his senate seat over this broad's stupid assault charge, he'd lose more money than she'd ever seen in her life and just the thought made him want to assault her himself. Hopefully, now he'd found her and could make her disappear long before she could testify at any trial.

He'd known money would talk and one of the other engineers at her work had been able to find a set of plans she had shipped to her boss via the FBI that still had an attached post mark from some Podunk place in the desert of western Colorado. It was a good cover. He never would have thought to look there, even after thoroughly checking into her friend in Denver. They'd watched the friend and even the friend's extended family, but no one had seen anything of her in months. It had been a good hiding place, but now it was just a matter of time. She was too strikingly pretty to be inconspicuous for long.

For just a second he hesitated. John Channing would kill him himself if he knew what he had in mind. Even after she'd had him indicted he was still nuts over her. Mario made a mental note to make sure John never figured out she'd been found.

Jaclyn M. Hawkes

Chapter 6

Matt stood on the flat curve of the ridge wondering if the helicopter pilot had baled on him now too. The pilot had been the only one of the whole field crew who had stayed on task, but he had never been this late to pick him up at the end of the day. For a little while, Matt had been enjoying the chance to do the more physical part of this seismic study. It had been a refreshing change of pace to start out with, but between being overwhelmed with the huge workload, and struggling to manage all the hats he was trying to fill, it was threatening to chew him up and spit him out.

He was usually involved with only processing the data that was collected by the linemen and the shooters. But since the field crew had gone MIA into the little bar at the motel, Matt was now not only trying to run all the lines and shoot the charges, but he was having to do all the pick up work after shooting the holes as well. It was a behemoth undertaking for one mere mortal, but if he didn't find a way to pull this project out and soon, he was going to lose more than five months worth of income.

He took out his binoculars to glass the direction he would be taking the lines the next day. The route was becoming more and more rugged and there were times Matt wondered if he was going to have to find a way to string them from the air. Some of those little canyons and cliffs looked impossible.

As he stood there in the last light of the day, he thought he heard whistling. He turned to see if he could hear better and realized that there was a sheepherder and a herd of sheep coming up the valley from the east on the other side of the creek. He watched for a minute in fascination as the herder on the black Appy whistled and directed the dogs with hand signals and the dogs in turn moved the whole herd that flowed over the hills and washes like a living wave.

It was incredible to see the precision and teamwork of the herder and dogs. They took the herd down to water and then as it got darker, he could see the herd move like a gray cloud back up the hill and begin to bunch and lay down in a group. He could barely make out the black sheep dogs circling around and around them as they settled in.

Once when he'd been hunting high in the mountains above Steamboat Springs he'd come upon a sheepherder's trailer. It was set up in one of the most beautiful valleys he had ever seen, and the peace of the setting felt like it had touched his very soul. He'd been in the middle of the hardest quarter of all of his college, and that sheepherder's life had looked truly tempting. That was about as down to earth and unworldly as you could get.

The helicopter finally came to pick him up and as they lifted off, Matt looked back down toward the sheep and noticed the first small flickers of a campfire that soon blazed brightly. The glow reflected off the sheep camp trailer he hadn't been able to see from his vantage point on the hill. What would it be like to settle down for the night in the middle of no where with no one?

When he got back to the motel to find the other members of the team already about half soused in the little adjoining bar, that lonely nomadic lifestyle was looking better and better. They waved him over as he came in the front door of the motel with his load of gear. Trying to keep already strained relations as amiable as possible, he walked over to their table. There were the three guys and four women with them who were the roughest looking females he had ever seen.

34

His boss hailed him with a long necked bottle. "Hey, Maylon. Drop that load and come sit with us for awhile!" He spoke with the barest hint of a slur. "These ladies want to know all about what we do." He gave a great guffaw. "Since you're the one doing all the work, you ought to tell them your side of the story." He leaned over to the women and said, "Matt's actually the computer guy, but since we have better things to do . . . Hah!" He slapped the table like he'd said the funniest thing ever. "He's helping out. Aren't you, Matt? Come have a brew with us, buddy, what do ya say? You can meet these lovely, local ladies." He waved a hand.

"Thanks, Hyatt, but I'm bushed. I'm gonna shower and eat and hit the hay. We've got another big day ahead of us tomorrow." He optimistically tried to give them a subtle hint with the "we", and picked up the backpack he had set down at his feet.

"That's too bad, isn't it girls? Because we have a big night ahead of us first!" Hyatt gave another belly laugh that ended with a belch they all busted up over. Matt gave a bemused grin and turned around to head up to the room. *Lovely ladies and girls?* He shook his head again. Those probably weren't the terms he'd have used personally, but whatever. He wondered if Hyatt ever bothered to remember he had a wife and kids back home in the city.

Matt showered and was back down in the little cafe off the lobby trying to saw his way through a gristly steak when he saw them all go up the stairs. All of them except one of the women. She saw Matt and came across to his table. "Hey, cowboy. We missed you at our little party. Why don't you come on up? We're going to be playing some cards."

He finished his bite. "Uh, I don't think so. Not tonight. I'm terrible at cards. Go ahead without me." He indicated his laptop across the table. "When I'm through eating I have to process some data anyway, but thanks." She headed on up the stairs and he went back to his meal, hoping the "ladies" didn't end up staying over.

When he finally made his way up an hour later, he opened the door to realize pretty much instantly that they were playing strip poker. *Oh, brother!* He set his laptop down in the open doorway and went inside far enough to retrieve his own bag and then headed back outside. He went back down to the front desk and arranged for another room at his own expense. There went more money lost on this mess.

When he finally laid down that night, he decided the peace and privacy and better atmosphere was worth the money and that his attitude stunk. He wasn't typically this negative, but his thoughts had been in the basement all week. They'd been a little off when he'd gone back to Steamboat last week to process data on the mainframe, but they'd taken a turn for the worse with that little episode with Stacy, and had all gone down hill from there. His negative attitude was exacerbating a bad situation into a worse one. He reminded himself to choose happy. He knew he could have a better attitude no matter what was going on with this contract or his personal life.

He looked at the Gideon Bible on the nightstand, and made a decision. He was going to start right now putting his life back in order as much as he possibly could and then having a better attitude about the things he couldn't change. He needed to fix this deal with Stacy, one way or the other, and made a mental note to make a trip home here as soon as he could to start patching things up. He didn't believe in living together before marriage. He didn't. Exactly how he'd gotten into this situation still wasn't clear, but he was in it and he needed to make things right and get back to where he was living within his value system.

If he couldn't get things to the point that he thought he could marry Stacy then he needed to move out or move her out, but he needed to get it done now. He dreaded going to his own apartment. Moreover, he needed to feel like he could pray. He needed that help and companionship in his life. And he didn't really think God wanted to visit with him right now in the situation he was in.

If there was one good thing to come out of this time of dealing with Stacy and this project, it was that he was going to quit dabbling in the important things and buckle down. His parents had taught him he should have priorities and that God should be the biggest one because everything else was founded on Him, But of course he had had to rebel. Just enough to make a huge mess of his life.

He hadn't even bothered wondering if the others would show up the next day and put in a grueling day by himself again. He saw the sheepherder a couple of times and once when he was close enough, he realized it was a woman. That shocked him. None of the women he knew could have lived out here by themselves like that.

He was even more surprised when he was glassing that afternoon to figure out his next day's plan and caught a closer up view of her. She was beautiful! Not just a little beautiful, but exquisitely beautiful. Drop dead beautiful.

It was the same woman he'd seen that day at the service station who had been so incredibly striking that he'd not been able to put her face out of his mind. He put down the field glasses and dug in his pack for his camera. That face had to be immortalized didn't it? He went to put on a bigger lens and then stopped himself. Was that like a form of voyeurism or something? To want to photograph a girl he didn't know? And what about Stacy? Somehow it didn't seem loyal to be taking another woman's picture.

He put the camera away, but the fascination with the sheepherder increased throughout the day, and when she sat her horse on the ridge in the purple haze of dusk as she watered the sheep, he couldn't help himself. That was definitely the purest form of art. He dug out his camera and attached a big lens and snapped several photos of her that she wasn't even aware of. How had a girl who looked like that escaped being caught up by some modeling agency or movie tycoon? The Indian men were brain dead to let her end up in a sheep camp in the middle of the desert.

When he got back to the motel, he considered that it was Saturday evening. The helicopter wouldn't be around tomorrow and rather than hang out working on Sunday, he decided to make a fast trip home to see if he could patch it up some with Stacy. He drove faster than he probably should have, a habit he had gotten into on this project, and arrived at his apartment complex a little before eleven thirty. He saw Stacy's car in the parking lot and was glad he'd caught her home. He'd about half expected her to be gone out somewhere with Jenna.

Unlocking the door, he stepped in and tossed his keys on the counter as he called her name. He got no answer, but the stereo was on in the living room and he knew she probably couldn't hear him and went in search of her.

He found her.

He'd pushed open the bedroom door that stood ajar and got the shock of his life! Justin was supposed to be his best friend! And in his own place, no less!

He just stood there for a second, too stunned to even react. Finally, he came to his senses enough to turn back around and pull the door closed behind him as he strode to the counter and grabbed his keys and let himself back out of his own apartment. He was in his Jeep and driving before he had a clue where he was driving to, so he just drove around Steamboat Springs for a while, thinking, trying to figure things out. He'd wanted to get things with Stacy settled. Well, they were.

He realized with a tinge of guilt that he was infinitely relieved. Justin was another matter. He wanted to go hit the guy just for the principal of the thing. Although the more he thought about it, the more he realized Justin had been the worst thing that had ever happened to him. It was when he started hanging out with Justin that his behavior and his life had started to go south. It wasn't Justin's fault. He was honest enough to admit that he had been responsible for his own decisions, but Justin had certainly encouraged him to do things he wouldn't necessarily have done without the egging on.

His mother would be thrilled to know that both Justin and Stacy were out of his life for good. He thought about his mom. He hadn't been to see her in a couple months because he was too ashamed to face her when he was living with someone. And he'd been busy, but that wasn't the reason and he knew it. It was after midnight, but he headed toward his parents' anyway. He could crash in one of the empty hunting cabins for the night, and spend some time with them in the morning before he headed back to the desert, refreshingly unencumbered by a live-in girl friend.

As he drove through the second set of locked gates on his parents' hunting preserve, he was relieved they hadn't changed the codes since he'd last been here. He drove into the compound and was just about to drive into the guest cabin area when he saw someone sitting on the porch swing of his mom's house. Pulling around in front, he shut off the Jeep and took the steps two at a time.

It was his mother in the porch swing, slowly rocking back and forth, the slight breeze blowing the skirt of her night gown and robe, and he bent down to hug her. It was just going to be a hug, but it ended up being a big hug that lasted for a while. Even though he knew he'd let her down a thousand times in his life, he never wondered if she loved him. Finally, he sat down next to her on the swing.

"Hi, Mom. What are you doing out here at this time of night?"

Her infinite, sweet patience was there in her voice, "Hi, Matt. I just couldn't sleep for some reason. Long time no see."

He was honest with her, "I know, and I'm sorry. I was living with Stacy and couldn't face you."

She just kept rocking as she said, "I know, honey. But you should know. I was disappointed in you living with her, but that didn't make me love you any less."

Feeling absolutely penitent, he said, "I know. Still, I couldn't face you."

"Did you say *was* living with Stacy? Are you not anymore?"

He shook his head in the dark. "Nope." Wondering how to put why he wasn't with her any more delicately, he finally just said right out, "I drove home tonight to try to find a way to get along better, and I accidentally busted her in bed with Justin."

There was a pause before his mom spoke, "Oh . . . Well, okay then." After another second she said, "You don't sound very upset about it."

Almost a little hesitantly, he admitted, "Honestly, I feel so relieved about it that I feel guilty. The truth is, I'm not even sure how she ended living there. I'd gotten so I didn't want to go to my apartment and Justin was a bad influence on me anyway. I'd come home with the idea to either find a way to make it work, which I really didn't want to do at all, or move out. They took all the stress out of deciding. Now, I just regret ever getting involved in the first place."

She looked over at him, but he couldn't see her face well in the dark. "I regret that too, Matt, but I always knew you'd figure it out. You're a good person, just a hard headed one from time to time."

He reached over and took her hand. "I don't deserve you, Mom. I'm sorry I disappoint you sometimes. Why couldn't you sleep?"

When she answered he could hear the tired smile in her voice, "Oh, I was just worrying and praying for my second child. I hadn't heard from him in a while."

"Honestly?"

"Honestly." After another few minutes she asked, "What are you going to do now?"

"Go back out to my project site and try to somehow find a miracle to pull it out. It's not going all that well. The guys who are supposed to be doing the field work have completely baled. They spend their days sleeping off the night before instead of stringing cable."

"Can't you put in a call to the boss?"

"One of them is the boss."

"Can you go over his head?"

"Not without admitting to the company that contracted for us to do this that it's not going well."

"Hmm. I'm sorry; I don't know what to tell you. How are you doing? Other than work and Stacy and Justin?"

"Good. Well, better. Work's a mess. And until tonight my personal life was dismal. But other than that I'm great."

"The desert must agree with you. You look good."

He chuckled. "It's pitch dark out here, Mom. How can you even tell how I look?"

"I saw you in the yard light as you went by. I think you look good. Now that you're single again, the girls are going to be much happier. Are there any girls in the desert?"

"The only thing I've seen out there that even comes close to being considered a girl is an Indian sheepherder." He didn't tell her she was an exquisitely beautiful sheepherder.

"How long until you're through with this one?"

"A couple of months, unless it goes completely south. In that case soon."

"Mmm. Are you going to come see your dad and me more now that you're done with Stacy?"

He chuckled and squeezed her hand. "Yes. I promise, but I'm still working like a hundred and ten hour weeks, so don't expect me too much."

"What are you doing tomorrow?"

"I haven't gotten that far yet. If Stacy is working then I had better go move out while I'm here in town. If not, I'll probably hang out for a while here if you don't mind and then head west."

"You can stay here as long as you want, you know that. And I'll go help you move if she's at work. Heck, I'll bring balloons and confetti!"

He laughed. "I could see you doing that, actually. What are you doing tomorrow?"

"The usual. Church in the morning, Sunday dinner at one or two, and a long, lazy nap after that while you guys clean up the mess. There's a standing invitation to all of those, in case you've forgotten while you've been AWOL. Since you're reinventing your life, do you want to come to church with us?"

"Actually, I would like to. I've kind of been missing it, but there's no way I can face the people there or even God until I have a little better handle on some things. I'm not really church going material right now."

She patted his hand that still held hers. "Matthew. You have it all backwards. Church isn't a place where perfect people get together to visit. It's a place where imperfect people meet to learn about the Savior and encourage each other to do better."

He'd never thought of it that way. "You may be right, but I still don't think I belong there yet. Maybe in a while. Maybe you could just pray for me while you're there."

In her sweet, mellow voice she reminded him, "I pray for you every single day, Matt. Several times a day."

"Really?"

"Of course."

"Thanks, Mom. I appreciate that."

****

It had been a truly good Sunday for a change. Stacy had been at work, so he and both of his parents actually went to pack up his stuff. His mom honestly did show up with balloons and confetti and he laughed harder than he had in forever. She was as entertaining as she had always been, and he hadn't realized how much he'd missed them.

He had already fulfilled his contract, so he was able to just tell his manager that he was leaving after he'd checked the apartment for damage and cleaning. Matt explained about Stacy still being there and the manager assured him she would either have to sign a rental contract and pay up or he would have the sheriff come and evict her. Matt tried to be empathetic, but he didn't feel the least bit sorry for her.

They packed up all his stuff and furniture, but when he got to the bed, he didn't even want it and said, "I think I'll just leave it. Let it haunt them."

His mother was more practical. "I can understand that, Matt, but at least give it to the homeless shelter or someone who needs it. It's a valuable bed. Don't reward her with it."

She was right, and they loaded it up too. He closed the door behind them without even a note and felt like he was making a new start.

They put all his stuff in storage and after doing the dishes like she'd joked, he loaded his Jeep, hugged her for a long minute, shook his dad's hand and hit the road again, more light hearted than he'd felt in months.

Jaclyn M. Hawkes

Chapter 7

The next morning, just before lunch time, he was hard pressed to keep up the light heartedness. He was alone again in the field. No surprise there, and he stood at the edge of a yawning ravine with steep rock sides that went straight down for more than thirty feet and then fifty feet or so ahead, it went straight back up the same way. There was no way he was going to get him and his equipment across that without turning into a very large bird.

The discouragement he'd been fighting for weeks threatened to overwhelm him. "Great. Just great." He stood there wanting to swear like a sailor. He looked up the little canyon and then down wondering which way looked more promising as far as finding a way down and back up that wasn't so steep. Neither direction gave him much hope of success.

He set down his gear and shrugged out of his pack, and went left down along the lip of the ravine. When he'd gone more than a quarter of a mile and it had only gotten worse, he turned and went back to scout the other direction. Another quarter mile's hike revealed nothing more than a small winding canyon with steep rock walls around every bend. He went back to his pack and stood and looked around.

This was it then. This was the end of it all. The hope of making a chunk of money and the loss of all the long hours he had put in here in the desert day after day by himself. Admitting defeat after trying so hard to pull this thing together without help made him want to be sick. He leaned down and dug into the side pocket of his pack to find his phone. There wasn't much left to do but call the helicopter and tell the pilot to come and get him for the last time. He found the phone and pulled it out and was scrolling down to find the number when he heard the far off sound of her whistle.

He looked up and turned around to see where the sound was coming from, but there was nothing. No sound, no dust, nothing, for more than a minute. Then he heard it again, closer, behind him and to the left. He set his pack back down and walked over to a point on the lip of the ravine that was higher than the rest and looked back toward where the sound had come from.

She was there, behind the herd, giving the dogs directions to guide the sheep that were strung out for hundreds of yards across the desert. The first of the herd began to spill over the ridge that was on his left, skirted the edge of the canyon below him and went on past him down the edge of the ravine. The sheep split around the point and passed by on both sides of him to continue in their trek to wherever it was she was taking them. He watched her come, wishing he had grabbed his camera out of his pack before climbing up here. The rugged country and the sheep with the dogs and the beautiful girl on the striking horse would have been fascinating images caught on film.

It took her more than half an hour after the first sheep had gone past him to reach the point where he stood watching. She had just about reached him when he realized he was hearing sheep bleat on the other side of the steep ravine. For a second he thought there must have been another herd on the other side that had wondered near, but then he heard her whistle and signal her dogs on the far side.

He'd been so focused on watching her that he hadn't even realized that somehow the sheep had found a way to cross the steep walled little canyon. He spun to look up to where the sheep were disappearing around the bend, but could see nothing. He turned back around toward her just in time to come face to face with a huge, white dog that was just now snarling at him and threatening to have him as a lunch appetizer. The hundred and sixty pound dog was slowly advancing and Matt looked around for an escape route or at least something to defend himself with. There was nothing and he was just starting to try and remember if he had ever heard of the best way to fend off an attacking dog the size of Cincinnati when he heard her call the great beast off.

"Zeus! No! Go on!" She whistled and did something with her hand to wave the dog off and he obeyed immediately, leaving Matt to breathe a sigh of relief. He wasn't typically afraid of dogs, but her Zeus was far bigger than any wolf he had ever seen in his life. And he'd seen a number of them in his travels.

He turned back to her at the sound of her voice as she said, "Sorry. I didn't realize he was so close. He gets a little protective of me."

Yeah, just a little. That was the understatement of the year. Up close, she was even prettier than she had been at a distance, which the other day he hadn't thought possible.

He was surprised when she spoke. She didn't sound anything like the other Native Americans he had seen while he'd been working out here. She didn't look anything like any he'd ever seen either. He tried not to stare at her when she walked her horse up to him, stopped several feet away and paused to look all around them. Almost all of her sheep had moved on down the canyon in front of them, and he wondered that she was stopping to talk to him. He would have thought a lone woman this far from anyone would be hesitant to approach a stranger very close. Then he noticed she had a rifle in the scabbard that hung from her saddle and a handgun in a holster clipped to her belt. For just a second he wondered if he was the one in trouble.

After noticing all the firepower, he looked up into her face, and he was surprised to see that she had startlingly blue eyes instead of the deep brown, almost black ones that most Indians had. Just now those eyes were taking him all in in a glance that seemed to sum him up in an instance as she said, "I'm sorry, I didn't realize your pack was back there, or I'd have sent them around it. I hope there wasn't anything too terribly fragile in it."

He looked away from her eyes to glance back at his pack. It had been directly in the path of about half of her sheep and definitely showed signs of having been trampled. "Uh, well actually." He looked back at her. It wasn't her fault he'd left it laying there. "It'll be okay. I shouldn't have left it laying there."

"Were you looking for something? I saw you walking up and down the wash."

He hadn't realized anyone was anywhere near when he'd been walking. Answering, he said, "Actually, I was looking for a way to cross this thing without repelling. Your herd of sheep feels like a gift from heaven just now. How did they get across?"

"There's a sheep bridge down there." She nodded to where the last of her sheep were disappearing around the bend. "There are several around here."

He'd never heard of a sheep bridge, but he figured if a sheep could cross it, so could he. "You have no idea how many problems you just solved for me. I'm working on a seismic crew here. I've seen you before back over to the east."

"You have a crew with you? I haven't seen anyone but you. And the helicopter. How many more of you are walking around out here?"

He wondered when she had seen him and the helicopter, but only said, "Actually, I'm usually the only one out here, but there are three other guys out here occasionally."

"What is it you're doing?"

"Seismic petroleum exploration, but what I do is completely environmentally friendly, I promise. Once I'm gone, there's nothing left behind to show I've been here."

She glanced over toward the disappearing herd. "That's good to know. Good luck with your project. It was nice to meet you." With that she turned her horse and loped off in the direction of her sheep, whistling to her dogs across the way as she went. He went to inspect the damage to his pack, wishing he'd at least gotten her name. Up close he was more amazed to find a woman like her in a place like this than ever. She hadn't sounded to him like a back country native.

On checking over his pack, he found that other than a number of little, stinky, green sheep droppings that had gotten inside it, it was relatively unscathed. One of his lunch sandwiches had a distinct little split hoof track in it, but the plastic baggie had remained intact, so he figured he'd just eat it anyway.

He picked up the rest of his gear and began to hike in the direction she and her sheep had gone and only a hundred yards or so beyond the point of the ravine he had scouted to, he found her sheep bridge. It was made of cable strung across with a board floor and sides fenced with wire. Looking at it, he'd have thought getting an animal to set foot on it would have been quite a trick, but apparently not. She'd even taken her horse across it without any problems.

He could see her in the distance among the sheep on the far hill, and looked around to see where her trailer was. It had been moved and was actually not far across the valley from the motel as the crow flies. Getting to it from a road would be another story. She was still a long way from civilization out here.

He found himself whistling as he worked for the balance of the afternoon. Her appearance had indeed been like a gift from some greater power. His project wasn't toasted after all, at least not for a few more days. Even Stacy trying to call him didn't squelch his good mood. He didn't answer his phone.

Back at the motel that night, the other crew members were in even worse shape than usual and Matt guessed that they had been dabbling in something stronger than beer this time. He finished his work in his own motel room and then went down to his Jeep and got his guitar out. He thought about taking it back to his room and decided against it. He knew how much he regretted being disturbed when he was trying to sleep, and he'd hate to do that to someone else.

Instead he climbed the small gravel rise that had been thrown up behind the motel when it had been built, and headed out into the rocky, brush covered flat beyond. When he thought he was far enough out to not bother anyone, he sat on a boulder and began to quietly play some old Jackson Brown stuff and occasionally sang along. Eventually he switched to playing some instrumental things he had written himself that just fit his mellow mood, and then played one or two more by John Denver before calling it a night. It had been too long since he'd taken the time to play like this.

The next morning, he was pleasantly surprised to find that all three of the others were actually going into the field with him that day. He had no idea what had spurred this, and none of the three looked like they felt very good, but he certainly wasn't going to complain. If they'd get back on board with him, the contract had every chance of being completed on time. They split up into sets of twos once off the chopper and Matt was mildly grateful to have gotten stuck with the least offensive of the three. They worked together well and got a surprising amount of work done in one day.

During the afternoon, he heard what sounded like a gunshot, and he wondered why someone would be shooting out there. When they met back up that evening to board the helicopter to fly back to the hotel, he found out what the shot had been. He was completely disgusted to learn that Hyatt and Greg had gotten close enough to the sheepherder woman to realize she was female and they had decided to "go have a little fun with an Indian squaw".

What they told him next helped him feel somewhat better. Apparently the two had started toward her and over the course of the afternoon had tried several times to get close to her, but she had changed directions and gotten too far away on her horse every time. Finally, she had apparently had enough of them and had gotten off her horse and gotten a dead rest on a rock and taken a shot at them. She'd hit the two quart Nalgene bottle Hyatt had strapped to the top of his back pack that was sitting beside him at the time and shattered it in their faces. Both of them were sporting cuts from the flying shards, and neither one of them had had enough water for the last of the afternoon and they weren't happy.

They were going on about what they were going to do when they finally did get their hands on her and Matt interrupted them with a thought. "If she could shoot well enough to shatter your water bottle, hadn't you better think twice about bothering her again? Next time she might shatter something more manly. Not only that, Native Americans are a sovereign nation. You don't want to be messing with them."

Hyatt sounded skeptical. "What does that mean?"

Wayne, the one who had been with Matt all day, pitched in, "It means they don't have to get permission from the American police to kill you, you dumb pineapple. Don't you go making these guys mad out here, Hyatt. You're liable to get us into a world of hurt. I don't want the whole tribe of them breathing down our necks, so leave the girl alone. And don't you read Louis L'Amour? The hero always shoots holes in the bad guy's canteens to warn them off before he has to finally kill them. Use half a brain and lay off."

He emphasized the last with several interesting expletives, and Matt hoped Hyatt got the message; although he shuddered to think what would happen if someone truly did get close to her. That dog of hers would eat them alive. At any rate, he was glad none of them had gotten close enough to her to see how beautiful she was. If they had, he didn't think their warnings would have stopped them.

He thought about what Wayne had said about the canteens. He didn't think the Indian nation thing worked quite the way he'd explained, but hey, Louis L'Amour would be proud!

Chapter 8

When the guys had shown up for work, he had hoped it meant they were going to get back on board to get the contract wrapped up, but it wasn't to be. They showed up for two days in a row, and then were back to hanging out partying all night. He knew for a fact that they were indeed messing around with drugs because they weren't even trying to hide it in their conversations around him. If he hadn't desperately hoped they would clue in and come back to work, he would have turned them in to the police himself.

The country he was working in was more rugged than ever and one evening when he couldn't even begin to plan out an attack route for the next day, he stood on a high point over looking a veritable maze of washes and canyons wishing that a beautiful sheepherder would miraculously appear. He had a thought. Maybe instead of her appearing, he could go to her. As he stood there, he decided he was going to go back to the sheepherder girl and ask for some help. He wasn't sure how he could get anywhere near her without becoming Zeus food, but he was going to try. After dinner that night, he grabbed a couple of folded maps and some brownies he had brought up from the cafe, and set out across the rocky flat toward her sheep camp more than a mile away.

At first he stumbled around in the dark, but his eyes soon grew accustomed and the half moon lit the trail enough that he crossed the flat with less trouble than he'd thought. He began to sweat a little as he got closer to her small fire. He was worried about that dog. It had already started to growl, low and deep in its throat.

He shouldn't have been worried about the dog; he should have been worried about her. He was still forty feet out in the brush when he heard that unmistakable cha chink of a shotgun as she jacked a shell into the chamber from wherever she stood somewhere out in the deepest dark away from the fire. The sound made him stop dead still in his tracks and put both hands out where she wouldn't be able to miss them. Talk about your Louis L'Amour! The thought of being at the point of a shotgun tightened his gut. The growling dog was coming closer and he hastened to call out to her, "Hello the camp. I'm friendly, I swear. It's Matt Maylon. I met you a couple days ago out by that sheep bridge."

"What do you want?"

"I was wondering if you could help me figure out how to get through the maze of these washes and ravines. Your sheep bridge the other day was a lifesaver. Have you got a minute? I brought you some brownies to sort of bribe you into talking to me."

"Who's with you?"

"I'm alone. You can see that. I would never bring those slime balls to your camp. Actually, I try not to spend one more minute than I have to with any of them. I don't hang around them unless we're working."

"Come on in to the fire, but watch yourself."

"I'm watching. I promise." He could still hear the dog snarling as it approached him, and he only let out a sigh of relief when she called the dog off just as it was within a few feet of him. As a guard dog he was the ultimate in effective.

Slowly, and with his hands held out, he advanced into the circle of her fire's light and stopped. He looked around, but she still wasn't anywhere to be seen, and he wondered if she still held a shotgun on him. Her camp was a cool set up complete with a small table and folding chair next to the fire, and what looked like a small porch swing that hung from the side of her trailer. Zeus was walking around him sniffing and he waited, wondering if he was going to get a chunk taken out of the side of one leg any second now. Somewhere out there in the dark he could hear her horse eating and the faint sounds of a large number of sheep.

He stood there looking around for what felt like several minutes before she stepped from the deepest shadows near the trailer. On foot, she was taller than he had thought, and as graceful as a cat, even in her jeans and simple knit shirt. He was relieved to notice that the barrel of the gun was pointed skyward at the moment. She kept her eyes on him and then seemed to have made a decision of some sort, because she leaned the shotgun against the side of the trailer and turned to light the little lantern that sat on the small table. As she lit it, he noticed she had a splint of some kind on her left hand and ring finger. When the lantern was glowing brightly, she turned to him and asked, "What is it you want to know?"

"I'm trying to find the best way through this rough stuff for my seismic work." What he really wanted to know was what in the heck a woman like her was doing in a situation like this? And what was the strange set up with the two garbage cans suspended on the pipe frame off to the side of her trailer?

Advancing to the table, he set the plastic wrapped brownies down and spread one of the maps out on its surface in the light of the lantern. She bent to look at the map and the light glistened off the hair she wore in a ponytail that hung part of the way down her back. He was flat out amazed when he caught the scent of apples or berries or he wasn't even sure what, when she leaned beside him. How could a woman who lived like this, look and even smell good?

He mentally shook himself and tried to focus on the map in front of them. She didn't look at the map very long, before she stood back up and went around to put another piece of wood onto her fire. She reached inside the trailer and picked up a zip sweatshirt, put it on and then sat down in the folding canvas chair between the fire and the table.

Disappointment wrestled with disbelief when she said, "I'm sorry. I don't know much about the country out in front of me. I've been told a little bit about where to go to take the sheep, but I'm not even sure where all the sheep bridges are. The guys who own the sheep just tell me what I need to know from time to time to keep them in feed and close enough to water. They would know what to tell you. Leave your phone number and when one of them is out this way, I'll have them call you."

He was a little skeptical and asked, "How often do you see them?"

"Every week or two."

He couldn't wait that long. "I was hoping to figure this out sooner than that. I'm not even sure where to head tomorrow."

"Where are you starting from? And where is it you need to end up?"

He pointed to a spot in the map. "From here to somehow eventually end up clear over here. The end destination is actually about four more maps this size in that general direction." He pointed. "But for right now, I just need to know how to get past this jumble." He pointed back to where he had started.

She stood up and leaned into the map again to study it. "There's a way through right here, but I'm not sure where the bridge is exactly. Joseph just said to get the sheep to this point, and they'll know where they're going. There are some old ewes in there that are incredibly seasoned. And then you can get through right here, and back around this way. There are bridges there somewhere. And then this way and then you have to go west right here. There's nothing right up through this way. He said you go along and then out of nowhere there's an impassable big wash. So when you plan either plan to go right down the wash or avoid it. Those are the only ways I'm aware of and honestly I've never been down there myself at all. I'm sorry I can't help more, but I will be taking my sheep through this whole area in the next while. You could follow them once they go through. Other than that, you'll have to ask someone who knows this area better."

She sat back down and he folded up the map and sat down on a nearby boulder. "How soon will you be taking them right where I was pointing?"

"Tomorrow or the day after."

He looked at the map again, trying to focus on it to figure out how long it would take him to get from place to place. The terrain had gotten rough enough that he probably wouldn't get around any sooner than she would. He looked up at her. "The men who were hassling you day before yesterday are supposed to be out here with me everyday, but they usually just hang around in the motel lounge and party. They didn't get close enough to see you, and the other guy and I tried to tell them to leave you alone, but it would be a bad thing if any of the three got very close to you. If they do decide to work, which is seriously doubtful, then I shouldn't follow you anywhere close, but if not then I'll try to get here by the time you take the sheep through or as near then as possible so that I can find the way. In the off chance that they see you, don't take chances. They aren't very . . . They're not . . . Uh . . . Just don't take chances with them. They are far from trustworthy. I'll just leave it at that."

"I figured that, although Zeus would take them apart. Still, I'd hate to actually have to shoot someone. How long is this project supposed to take?"

"It's supposed to be wrapped up in less than a month, but we're way behind schedule. I'm not even supposed to be out here at all. I'm the computer geek office guy who's supposed to be working back in Steamboat Springs, but when they stopped gathering data I came out to see what was going on and found them doing nothing." She looked over at him and glanced at him up and down before looking back at the map as he continued, "I've been trying to gather the data and then run it at night, but even working out here dark to dark I'm falling further and further behind."

"Where's your boss?"

"My incredibly industrious and professional boss is the jerk who was following you Tuesday. He thinks that what happens in the desert, stays in the desert. I have no idea what he's thinking about letting this all go, but I have nearly six months of my life invested, and I'd really like to get paid for it somehow."

"Do you think you're not going to get paid?"

"Honestly, I'm going to guess that Hyatt has already been paid for what I've done, but I have yet to see any of it. That's probably what's financing their parties. I'm supposed to get paid all at once when I'm done, but the deadline is breathing down my neck. If I don't meet it, the whole contract is off."

"Can you bypass your boss and renegotiate?"

"I hadn't thought about renegotiating. I was just worried that they'd completely yank the contract if they found out how far off schedule things are."

"They'll find out sooner or later. And somebody is expecting that their work is being done. They might be more open to working with you if you're honest with them. If you truly don't think it's going to fall into place, you'd be better off trying to salvage as much as you can."

He ran a hand through his hair. "You may be right. Anything would be better than nothing."

"The worst thing that could happen is they'll tell you no. That won't be any different than the status quo, so you have nothing to lose and possibly a lot to gain."

He looked up at her. "What do you mean? That I'll get paid for what I've done?"

"I mean that typically the guy who owns the contract makes far more than the people he hires to fill the contract. If your boss has violated the contract and it's now void, you may be able to pick it back up and you make the profit he would have made, plus all the money for the work you've done."

He looked at her wondering how what she had just said fit in with being a nomadic sheepherder. If she was that savvy about business, what was she doing out here? The more he found out about her, the more of an enigma she became. He glanced around at her camp. "Tell me. How does a sheepherder in the desert come up with something like that?"

She shrugged. "Maybe I have too much time to think out here."

He wondered out loud, "Does it ever get lonely?"

"Sometimes. It didn't for a long time. Usually there's just a peace that settles into your very bones."

He got up off the rock. "And I interrupted it. I'm sorry, I'll go. Thank you for your help."

In a mellow tone, she said, "Its okay. We were just winding down for the night anyway."

He looked up at the garbage can contraption as he went to leave. "What is it?"

"Isn't it obvious that that is a neato, high-tech shower?" She gave him a smile that made her face even prettier. "That's my only concessions to not being able to live without modern conveniences. I had to have a shower. It's not fancy, but it's heavenly after a day in the desert."

"I imagine it's a monster to fill with water."

She shrugged. "It's not too bad really. It's filled with a small ram-jet pump from the stream."

He turned back to look at her again. What kind of

woman knew what a ram-jet pump was? One he wanted to get to know better. He came right out and asked her, "If I visit you again sometime, are you going to pull a shotgun on me again?"

"Probably, but I'll put it down again when I figure out who it is. I'm wondering, if you find whatever it is that you're looking for with your project, will they drill for oil here?"

He used her same word. "Probably, but all I know much about is the geophysics of the process. I just tell them what I think is under the ground and they take it from there. See you around." After taking a few steps, he turned back around. "Hey, can I ask you one more thing? Do you know who Louis L'Amour is?"

"I'm a sheepherder. Of course I know who Louis L'Amour is."

As he walked back to the motel, he thought back over their conversation. Something didn't add up here. She was articulate and polished and business savvy. And she didn't have the slightest bit of an accent the way the rest of the Indians around here did. And a ram-jet pump? She had just gone from interesting to intriguing to flat out fascinating. He hoped he did see her as he found his way through.

Chapter 9

He did, in a manner of speaking. She actually saved his bacon. After talking to her that night, he had gone back to his room and pulled the whole area up on Google Earth, and she was right. In the area that from the map looked the most promising, there was a huge wash that would be impassable with the heavy packs of gear without a bridge. He looked at the other area that was more convoluted and was able to actually see what had to be another sheep bridge from the satellite images. What she had told him checked out so far and that coupled with his gut feeling that she was honest made him comfortable to go ahead and plan out his next few day's routes from their conversation.

Hyatt and the others were partying more than ever, so he was surprised again when on the third day after talking to her, they all showed up to meet the helicopter in the morning. They looked pretty trashed, but he certainly wasn't going to complain. He couldn't figure out what it was that made them all the sudden decide to work again, but he was okay with it big time. They were a pain in the hind end to work with, and he didn't want them anywhere near his sheepherder, but the fact that they were helping even a little gave his hope for the project a lift.

Everything went relatively well until just after lunch. They'd been in pairs again in the morning and then Wayne had wanted to go back to the others just a few hundred yards away to eat. Matt saw them break out a six pack of beer and he wondered if the afternoon was going to be as productive as the morning had been. He ate his own squashed peanut butter and jelly sandwiches and tried not to hear any more of their conversation than he had to. He got the impression that their sudden need to buckle down was due to the fact that they had been spending an inordinate amount of money on the local "ladies" and the illegal substances which they had so graciously supplied to them. They had decided they needed to get more serious about party funds.

They went through a six pack of cans and then Hyatt actually took out a long neck bottle. At this point Matt decided he was out of there and got up and began to gather up the gear to get back at it.

As he went to head out, he turned to them and said, "Just up ahead we need to veer right and head into that series of canyons and washes. There's a sheep trail that should be relatively plain. I'll see you around."

Hyatt jumped right up with his face red. "Now just a minute here, boy! I know I ain't been all that industrious of late, but I'm still in charge a this deal. I've let you call all the shots this morning, but ain't no way I'm letting you lead us on a wild goose chase through a maze of cliffs when we can set off right across the flat in the direction we need to go. We're going right straight across there to the left."

Matt had to remind himself to be patient and he wondered, not for the first time, how Hyatt had ever gotten far enough to be in a position of authority. "Hyatt, there's a huge wash out there that's impassable." He nodded at the broken country to the right. "It's longer, and it's going to be a pain to run lines and shoot, but it's the only way to get through."

Hyatt came rushing over to him, his face flushed from the alcohol and huffing like a mad bull. His voice rose about eighty decibels when he yelled, "I told you boy, you ain't telling me what I'm doing here. You understand me?" The other two had gotten up and come over grumbling under their breath and Hyatt turned to the others. "We're about sick and tired of old pretty boy goody two shoes, ain't we boys? Too good to live with us, or even eat with us, but now he wants to order us around, even when I'm the boss. I have half a mind to teach him a lesson or two right here and now!"

Until Hyatt smashed the bottom of his beer bottle against a rock, Matt had just thought he was blowing off steam from too much alcohol, but when Hyatt began to brandish the jagged bottle and then the other two grabbed Matt from behind, he began to realize that this could be serious. He struggled against the two who had both of his arms, watching Hyatt advance toward him with the broken bottle like a weapon. Hyatt was obviously not thinking too clearly, but that wouldn't matter a bit if he was able to do what it appeared he intended with the beer bottle in his hand.

Just as Matt was preparing to kick Hyatt just as hard as he could, restrained the way he was by the others, there was the sharp crack of a rifle and the bottle in Hyatt's hand exploded like a grenade. Hyatt screamed and pulled his hand into his body as the other two let go of Matt and ducked for cover. There were two more shots, right in a row and the Nalgene bottle sitting on a boulder beside one of their packs was blown to bits just before one of their beer cans sitting next to it went skittering off into the rocks with a tinny clink.

It took less than a second for Matt to figure out that she was hidden in the rocks at the mouth of the wash ahead. She probably hadn't saved just his bacon, she'd saved his whole dang pig, and he owed her big for it. He straightened his pack, picked up the coil of cable he'd had looped over his shoulder and headed for the wash without looking back. They could hike all over tarnation carrying their loads if they wanted to; he was getting out while the getting was good!

She was gone by the time he reached the mouth of the wash. He could see her ahead on the flashy horse and he saw where she'd left the three empty cartridges lined up on a rock almost as a warning. Grateful she'd been able to get away without any of them seeing her up close, he decided he'd have to find a way to repay her for this one.

The trail was easy to follow and he crossed two more sheep bridges that afternoon, before calling for the helicopter to pick him up at a little before dusk. He'd become relatively good friends with the pilot, Mac, through this project and when Matt asked about the others he had to grin when the pilot said, "I picked 'em up hours ago right smack dab out in the middle of that flat." He indicated the sage plain below them. "They were stranded high and dry by a big wash that cuts that thing right in two. And mad! They were mad as all get out! Picking at each other like you can't imagine. They'll probably kill each other tonight. You'll want to move right out, when you get back to the motel."

"Actually, I moved into my own room more than a week ago. They have some local ladies," He made a gesture to indicate quotation marks. "Who were making it uncomfortable to stay with them."

"I wondered how you were able to deal with them this far. I'd have wanted to murder them months ago."

"A lot of things have crossed my mind, but I hadn't gotten quite as far as murder. Although after today, maybe I should consider it."

Mac let go of one side of the controls to wave a hand. "Aah. They're not worth going to prison for. Their kind self destruct. Give 'em time and they'll take themselves out of your hair one way or another."

As they flew, Matt had been watching to see where she had moved her trailer. It was gone from near the motel, but was still relatively close to the highway, across another wide expanse of rocky sage flat. He wondered how she had been able to move it in that rough country. He could see her below, the stark blanket of her horse's rump standing out against its dark body as she rode among the sheep. The sheep dogs were bunching them again down the valley a ways from her camp, but the huge white one was like her horse's shadow. As threatening as Zeus had been toward him, it was still reassuring that she had protection like that.

A line had been crossed that day Matt wasn't sure what to do about. Working and living with slobs had been one thing, working or living with three men who were willing to do him physical injury was another. He decided to retrieve his own hand gun from under the seat of his Jeep and keep it in his pack for the foreseeable future.

To this point, he'd hoped they'd get back on track as far as helping, but after today, he decided they were more trouble than they were worth, and he was glad they were too busy in the lounge to hassle him as he went up the stairs to his room to shower and change. Rather than dealing with them and their women, he got into the jeep and drove the ten or so miles into the little town of LaHonda and ate in the Mexican diner there.

On a whim, he ordered a dinner of smothered enchiladas to go and on the way back pulled off the highway at the closest spot to her trailer. In his jeep, he could actually drive right up to her camp and he realized he was following the tracks that must have been how she got the trailer there in the first place.

When he got to her camp, at first he thought she wasn't around yet even though it was getting late, but then he noticed her saddle was sitting under the edge of the trailer, with her gun still in the scabbard. He put the enchiladas down on the table and was surprised to feel heat coming off the lantern. She had been here, but for some reason had left. The beat up truck was still hooked to the trailer, so he wondered where she could have gone. He could hear the sheep, but all was quiet and there wasn't a sign of a dog anywhere. As he looked around, he realized another vehicle was bouncing across the sage flat on the same track he had just come in on.

Deciding it must be her, he sat down in her folding chair to wait for her so he could thank her for saving his hide today. It wasn't quite full dark and he saw as the SUV neared, that it was two men in the vehicle and not the sheep fairy he had been expecting. He had no way of knowing if they were someone she was looking forward to or not, and without even thinking about it he reached across to her saddle and pulled the rifle out and put it across his knees. As the vehicle stopped the two got out and began walking toward him, looking all around them as they came. He heard one say quietly to the other, "It's not her."

The other one whispered back, "Maybe it's her boyfriend."

In the quiet of the evening he could hear their words perfectly. "Her and a sheepherder? I don't think so. She wouldn't be living with a guy out here anyway. She was too churchy, remember. I knew this whole sheepherder thing had to have been a hoax."

When they got near, Matt asked nonchalantly, "Can I help you two with something?"

The one who had been sure she was a hoax said, "Yes, actually. We were told this was a woman's camp. Is there a woman sheepherder that lives here?"

There was something about the two that had him replying, "I'm definitely not a woman. Sorry to disappoint you. Wish there was one around here though." He picked up the gun that sat across his knees and began to fiddle with the action. "Wouldn't a woman sheepherder be unusual? Doesn't seem like a very feminine lifestyle. Not but maybe one woman I know could hack it." He calmly pointed the gun out toward a small mound of dirt and pulled the trigger. At the explosive bang, both of them jumped and Matt said, "Dang rodents! Get into the trailer and really irritate a person. You know?"

The one quickly handed him a business card. "Well, if you ever do hear of a woman sheepherder, give us a call, huh? We'll make it worth your while."

Matt smiled. "Dude, you see any telephone poles out here? This is the end a the earth. Even if there was such a thing as a woman sheepherder, I couldn't call you, but this is a nice card. Shiny and all. Thanks." Both of them hastily turned back to their vehicle, leaving Matt to wonder why two slick guys with eastern accents and expensive clothes were looking for her.

They had driven away and the dust had completely settled before she appeared over the edge of the rim that fell away down into the creek bottom below. Zeus was at her heels, and though he didn't growl this time, he sniffed at Matt with raised hackles just to let him know that he didn't necessarily have to put up with him here. Matt indicated the Styrofoam container on the table. "I don't know if it's still hot, but I brought dinner."

She opened the carton and looked inside. "Thank you. It smells wonderful. I love Mexican." She sat down on the plastic bench of the little table and picked up the disposable fork he had brought. The only thing that gave her agitation away was the fact that the fork wasn't completely steady when she went to use it.

Matt nodded lazily at the highway. "Friends of yours?"

She was a little hesitant as she replied, "No. No, they weren't."

"Did you hear all of it?" She nodded. "Do you get many types like that out here looking for you?"

Finishing her bite, she shook her head. "They're the first."

"Yeah, well I'm just gonna guess they won't be the last." He put the safety back on on the rifle and returned it to the scabbard. "Don't forget that you're a bullet short now.

Thanks for today by the way. Louis L'Amour would have been proud."

She looked at him and nodded. "I guess after these two we're even."

"Not really." He looked at her steadily. "The guys I work with aren't anywhere near as dangerous as those two were."

She swallowed hard and looked away at the horizon for a minute or two, and absently fidgeted with the brace on her left hand. Finally, she changed the subject, "Are the guys you work with always like that?"

"No. Typically they're relatively harmless. Unless you're the wife who's home trying to make ends meet without the money that's being spent on other women and booze. Something else must have been bothering him today. Usually he's happy as a clam to have me do it all."

"How can you stand to live with them?"

"I don't live in the same room as them anymore. That ended the other day when I inadvertently walked into a game of strip poker with some rough local women in our room. Since then, it's just been a matter of avoiding them in the lounge or the coffee shop. After today, I'm not sure what to do about them. I'm generally pretty slow to rile, but today ticked me off."

"Why don't you just camp? Wouldn't that both keep you out of their scummy lifestyle and closer to your work as well?"

"I have to have electricity to run my laptop to process the data every night. And I'm like you. I've gotta have a shower after being out here in the dust and sand and heat all day."

She was quiet as she ate for a few minutes, and then she asked, "If you had electricity and a shower, would camping be an option?"

"Yes, probably, but I can't be rigging up a setup like you have. He waved at her "neato, high-tech" shower rig. "I'm working five in the morning 'til ten at night most nights, and I'm still hopelessly behind."

"What if you just camped close enough to me to share mine? Don't get the wrong idea, but it would be mutually beneficial. You could avoid dealing with the unsavories and I'd have one more set of eyes and ears nearby."

At first he thought she was joking, but she wasn't smiling. Then he wondered if she was hitting on him, but she wasn't flirting in the slightest. He didn't understand what was going on here. He shook his head. "You're forgetting that I need electricity to run my computer."

"I have a small solar power system on top of the trailer. Just for things like charging my phone. It produces far more than I need even after heating the shower water." He studied her for a minute in the lantern light. At length she said, "Never mind. It was just a thought."

"Whoa. Whoa. Just give me a minute. I didn't say no. I'm just a little caught off guard. You don't know anything about me. How do you dare to have me stay near you out here?"

She looked out across the sage flat to where the SUV had just disappeared. "I don't know. Intuition maybe. Instinct. I'm not sure. If you weren't trustworthy, you would have just sold me out when they offered you money." She hadn't come right out and admitted that she knew someone was looking for her, but it made a lot of things fall into place. What didn't compute was figuring out how much danger he was putting himself in if he actually did this and why that didn't even matter to him.

He hadn't figured out all the questions in his head, but he knew he was going to do it. The main reason was that even more importantly than the fact that she was beautiful and fascinating, she was afraid.

Before he'd even met her he'd respected the fact that she was gutty enough to do something no other woman he knew would dare do. Whatever had scared her must have been a big deal. So far, she hadn't frightened easily. Tonight she was good and scared to suggest he come camp nearby.

Casually, he said, "Camping would actually solve more things for me than you know. I'll have to go back to Steamboat to get some of my gear, but I think I could go get it tomorrow night and come back Wednesday with it. Will your trailer still be here Wednesday night? Or will you move it before that?"

"Zan will come and move it for me on Wednesday during the day while I'm with the sheep. It will just be another couple of miles up the road, but after these guys tonight I'll see if he can put it further down the hill more out of sight from the road. So if you don't see it right off, keep looking."

"I'll be able to find it from the helicopter. In the mean time, watch yourself." He got up to go.

"You too. Thanks for dinner. It was great to have real food for a change. Sometimes I don't cook like I should just for me."

"You're welcome. G'night."

Bouncing along back over the sage flat in his Jeep, he had to smile to himself when he realized he still didn't even know her name. He thought back to how discouraged he had been with the direction his life had been going a short nine days ago. He still had some huge obstacles to overcome both professionally and personally, but his life had just taken a very interesting twist and he looked forward to it immensely. He didn't look forward to dealing with Hyatt and the others at all, but then maybe he should do just what she had recommended the other day and see about renegotiating the contract.

It made sense. Everything she had said so far made sense. Somehow tonight he had come to know that she wasn't a Native American sheepherder by birth. He didn't know what she was other than beautiful, and it didn't even matter. He just knew he was a lot more hopeful about the future tonight than he'd been in a long time.

****

Taya sat at her little table finishing the dinner he had brought her and thinking about the strangers who had shown up and the plans she had just made. She had seen Matt several times by the time she came upon him on the edge of the ravine the other day, but she'd still been pleasantly surprised when she saw him up close. It had been forever since she had seen someone who was that masculine and that naturally attractive. He wasn't dressed up by any means. Jeans, hiking boots and a cotton button down he'd cut the sleeves off of, but standing there in the desert, with the Colorado sun turning his brown hair to gold where it was windblown, he had looked good. Really good.

Later that evening when she thought back to when she met him, she had passed off her assessment as the result of spending too much time with nothing but animals, but after seeing him tonight she had to admit to herself that he was more than attractive. Moreover, it wasn't just a looks thing, although he had way more than his fair share. His intelligence and quick thinking had been almost a miracle tonight when those men had shown up, and it was all wrapped up in a quiet confidence that left her knowing without anything being said, that he would handle whatever he had to, without making it a big deal. When he showed up in her camp it had only taken her a minute or two to discern that she was safe with him, and so far her gut had been right.

She had surprised even herself by suggesting he camp

near her, but she'd known at the time it was the right thing to suggest, and now after the fact, she still felt good about it. He'd told her her sheep were like a sign from heaven, but tonight that's about how she felt about him.

It had been two and a half months since John had hit her and scrambled her hand. The hand was still in the process of healing, but her life had settled into a comfortable rut of peace. Days without stress and nights without conflict. Seeing those two men in her camp tonight ended all that.

How had they found her? The only ones she had been in contact with were the police, the Talbots and the Bears. None of them would betray her willingly, so what had happened? And who here knew she was a woman sheepherder? She'd been to church, the grocery store and the post office. Oh, and the gas station. And she'd never told anyone what she did with her days. She had only met people out with the sheep a handful of times, but that must have been where she'd been discovered as a woman sheepherder. She was positive the Bears hadn't mentioned it to anyone.

It was after midnight back east or she would have called the police and Joshua right then. Zan picked up on the second ring. When she told him what had happened that night and asked if he would help her conceal her trailer better, at first he tried to insist that she had to leave and find another place to hide, but she simply insisted that the men weren't sure she was around and Zan finally gave up on trying to pressure her to leave. He ultimately agreed to come help her and arranged to be there to move it the next day actually.

Taya had mentioned that a geologist had been in her camp, but she didn't tell Zan about Matt camping near her. He'd find out eventually, but she could just about picture the two of them. Zan would try to intimidate Matt, but she knew without a doubt that Matt wouldn't intimidate easily so she decided to postpone that showdown as long as she could.

Zan was like a brother to her, but even brothers had to throw their weight around from time to time.

For these months she had been okay even when she'd had to go out after coyotes, but tonight she felt afraid for the first time and it made her mad in a way. She looked at the splint on her hand and tried to nurture the fragile sense of forgiveness she had for the things John had stolen from her like security and a strong, whole, pretty hand. Knowing Matt would soon be nearby nights helped to calm her fears, but she still knew she was in a lot of trouble.

Within the first two weeks after she had disappeared, the police had been able to video tape John accepting suspicious brief cases from people he should never have been accepting anything from clandestinely, and they had been able to ascertain that he was indeed taking pay-offs under the table in exchange for swaying legislation. They had a good case against him, but she was part of that case and the officer that first night had been right to assume there might be some truly nasty people who would try to keep her from testifying. The first trial for the assault charge was coming up in just three weeks time, but the other trial was still almost two months away. Tonight that felt like a long time to be able to stay invisible.

Jaclyn M. Hawkes

Chapter 10

Matt made it home to pick up his camping gear and spent another night talking to his mother in the porch swing. This morning as she tried to talk him into a third helping of a marvelous skillet breakfast his family had affectionately dubbed scrangled eggs, he thought about what the sheep princess had said about not cooking for herself, and asked his mom if he could take a plate of it with him. It couldn't hurt to soften her up with home cooked food.

By ten fifty that night, when he finally made it across the flat with his Jeep loaded down with gear, he was too tired to even care about dinner and was glad he had had the killer breakfast. It felt like it had been three full days since he had woken up that morning at his mom's. He'd stopped to fill his cooler with groceries, had words with Hyatt before even making it out of the motel lot and then put in a grueling day before calling for the chopper well after full dark. Once back at the motel he still had to load up as many coils of cable as he could fit into the Jeep so he wouldn't have to return to the storage area in the back parking lot of the motel any more often than necessary.

When he reached her camp he went a couple hundred feet further down the valley and threw out his sleeping gear without even setting up his tent. He went to sleep under the stars listening to her sheep and the barely discernable, mellow music of her radio.

Surprisingly, he was refreshed when he awoke as the sky in the east was just starting to lighten. He got up and started a fire in a ring of rocks and put the skillet breakfast in his little Dutch oven. While it heated, he organized his mess somewhat before stuffing peanut butter and jelly sandwiches into his pack. He called for the helicopter and gave him the GPS coordinates for the new jumping off points and then quickly set up his tent and stowed his gear inside.

He ate a couple of bagels smeared with cream cheese and washed them down with a quart of milk while he booted up his laptop to process as much of yesterdays data as he could before being picked up. In the crush of last night, he hadn't gotten any of it even inputted. When he could hear the chopper in the distance, he doused his fire and took the little Dutch oven back to her camp and left it on her table, and then headed out into the sage flat to lift off into a sky just turning yellow over the far horizon. It would be another long day trekking across the desert.

****

When Taya stepped out of her trailer that morning to find a wonderful hot breakfast sitting on her table, she put back the yogurt she'd been going to make do with and decided that this set up might be even better than she hoped. It had been months since she'd had a breakfast like this. She'd heard his Jeep last night as he pulled in and it had been a comforting sound as she sat at the table inside her trailer calculating the engineering on a new home back east. He'd said Wednesday night and he'd meant it. It had been almost eleven before he made it in, and he'd been gone this morning before six. That kind of a work ethic would kill a person.

She saw him at a distance every day that week at least a time or two, but except for Sunday, he was always gone by the time she was out of the trailer in the morning. That Sunday he must have slept in for once, and if the helicopter came, it was while she was gone for a few hours to church. He'd figured out how to use the shower by himself and the second morning she'd found his laptop plugged into the outdoor outlet she'd rigged up so she could work outside at night when she wanted to. That had surprised her, because she would have thought Zeus would come unglued with him that close to her, but apparently not.

They fell into an easy relationship where he showered at night whenever he finally made it in, and she showered in the morning before she headed out, like she always had, so her hair could air dry decently. Twice he had left her breakfast on her table in the morning and she had left him dinner the one night she made real food. Invariably at night, she saw the glow of his computer either at the table he had set up or inside his tent.

One night she was surprised to hear music through her screen door coming from his camp. At first she thought it was the radio, and then when she realized it was him playing a guitar, she had the most amazing reaction. She couldn't even begin to focus on her work and finally she shut her computer down and went out to sit on the little porch swing in the dark to listen, pushing with her foot occasionally to keep it gently rocking.

He played for the better part of an hour, singing along a time or two, and by the time he was done, Taya wasn't sure what had happened to her, but she didn't think she'd ever be the same. His music had been like a spell that wove around her—a misty potion that floated across the desert floor in the night to enchant her. That sweet, mellow guitar evoked a stronger feeling toward him than she had felt toward any man ever in her life. It almost scared her, except that every time she had been around him from that very first meeting on the canyon rim, his presence had been reassuring to her. Knowing he was there those couple hundred feet away was incredibly comforting.

She sat on the porch swing thinking long after he had quit playing and his camp had gone dark and quiet. The magical feeling of the night was so strong that finally she went in and got her pillow and comforter and brought it out to sleep on the swing, knowing that with the coming light of day the magic would be gone, but wishing it wouldn't be. She wished she could catch some of it and keep it in a jar in the window the way she'd kept treasures when she was little. She opened the swing out flat and lay looking up at the stars, thinking about nothing in particular and everything. Finally, she talked to God like he was right up there somewhere, looking down on her, having a pleasant conversation.

When she woke up on the swing in the half light of dawn, the magic was still there. The desert felt cool and crisp and the sage smelled like heaven's own secret spice. She pushed her hair out of her face and turned over on her stomach to watch the sun turn the few clouds on the eastern hills into pale fire. Zeus lay on the ground below her and she let one arm hang over the edge of the swing to rest gently on his curly, loyal head.

She was so happy this morning it was ridiculous, but it felt good. Matt must have had a guitar like the Pied Piper's flute or something to have had such an impact on her whole attitude. Thinking of Matt, she glanced in the direction of his camp, wondering if he was up yet. Probably up and long gone, knowing him. She closed her eyes again to think about his music last night one more time. There was something about it. She couldn't even explain it to herself, but it had definitely done something to her.

She was almost back to sleep when she heard a sound and sleepily opened her eyes to see him standing there next to her table looking at her. He even looked like a good dream this morning with his button down sans the sleeves showing off the sun browned muscles in his arms and shoulders. She blinked to see if he would disappear into her head again, but he was still there and she rubbed her eyes to clear them. His quiet good morning finally shook her out of her reverie and she lifted her head, startled that he really was there in front of her.

He put a paper plate covered by an inverted one, down on her table and put a nearby rock on top to keep them there and then turned to go out into the sage to catch the helicopter she realized she was hearing. She turned her head to watch him walk across the flat with the fluid motion of a mountain lion. Somehow that's what he reminded her of with his golden brown hair and muscles rippling under his skin when he picked up his gear. When he was gone and the sound of the chopper died away, she yawned and stretched and gave herself a lecture about the fact that she wasn't fifteen anymore and she should be able to actually say good morning without wondering what had happened to all the oxygen.

It wasn't until she got out of bed, that she noticed Zeus was happily gnawing on a bone at her feet. She should have known there was a reason he wasn't trying to take Matt apart any more. She picked up her bedding and took it inside after calling Zeus easily bought off. She was a little slow getting started that day and even once she was on Horse and underway, she kept catching herself daydreaming about his music last night and she'd feel adolescent again. He'd only been here eight days and she needed to get a handle on herself right now before he caught her staring. She spent the rest of the day giving herself a talking to about what an adult she was.

It was time to move the trailer again and she was glad the terrain was gentle enough that she could move it and handle the sheep too so she didn't need to call Zan in just now. There was no doubt about the lecture he would dole out about her being too trusting. She would have agreed that he had a point except for the prompting she had felt the night she'd recommended Matt camp near her. She'd followed her gut on this one and had obviously been right in doing so.

She moved the trailer a couple of miles down the little valley in the direction he was working, to where it couldn't be seen from the road, but Matt wouldn't have any trouble reaching it in his four wheel drive and she set it all back up before going back to get his stuff. She knew he would come in tired and she hoped he wouldn't care if she just pulled the tent pegs and put it in the back of his Jeep intact. They'd find out when he got back at any rate.

It was Saturday and she needed to go buy groceries and ship plans, but she was more than a little hesitant to be seen in civilization. She wanted to go to church tomorrow as well, which was also impossible to do without being seen. She thought about it all day while she watched over the sheep, and finally decided that even though it would be breaking the Sabbath, she would do all three tomorrow when she went in to church. She even decided she would go to a different town than she had been going to in case that was how they had figured out where she was.

She tried not to admit to herself that sooner or later whoever it was who was looking for her was going to figure out that she truly was the woman sheepherder and come back. She wasn't sure if it was John and he just wanted to demand the missing diamond back or if it was someone else who was going to try to find a way to make sure she couldn't testify against him. The one made her disgusted; the other scared her more than she wanted to admit. If she was honest with herself, it was probably both.

Matt came in early that afternoon and as she saw him drag in, she could tell he was tired to the bone. She had watched the helicopter drop bundle after bundle of whatever it was that Matt was stringing and recording, and Matt had crossed literally miles and miles of desert today with his heavy pack. She was glad she had brought over his gear and then made them a Dutch oven dinner before going back out with the sheep, and hoped he saw the note she'd left on his tent flap.

When she and Horse and Zeus came past his tent on the way in, she found him asleep in the camp chair near his table with one hiking boot off and one half way undone. She knew he hadn't even made it to the shower let alone to the Dutch oven. She almost decided to just let him sleep, but worried about him getting a stiff neck from sleeping with his head kinked in the chair.

She was sitting her horse there beside him wondering how best to wake him up when Zeus walked up to him and started to nose his hand. He woke up and started to pet the dog before he realized she was standing there watching him. When he looked up at her, she smiled at him and then accused him of ruining her guard dog.

He gave her a tired smile in return and said, "Hey, it was pure self preservation. For the first week I was here, he only didn't eat me because he knew you'd be mad at him. I had to do something to convince him I was on the same team. He still guards you; he just doesn't threaten to rip my limbs off anymore."

"You're neck is never going to forgive you if you don't get out of that chair. I made Dutch oven chicken for dinner if you decide you have the energy to eat tonight."

"Thanks. I'll take you up on that. The offer of something other than peanut butter is probably the only thing that could make me move right now. When are you eating?"

She shrugged. "Whenever you make it to my fire. I hope you didn't mind that I moved your stuff. I didn't get into anything, just moved it all in one piece, I promise."

"I'm just grateful you did it. I'm so tired tonight I think I'd have just stayed over there until tomorrow if you hadn't."

"You've put in a week. Have you heard from your boss lately?"

"Not a peep. I don't know whether to be thrilled or worried."

"Did you ever finalize what's going to happen to your contract?"

"I made an appointment to go talk to the man who hired my boss on Monday. Now I just have to find the energy to make it to Monday."

"A shower and food and sleep will help. See you in a while."

****

It was a few minutes before he realized that he was staring at her as she rode back to camp. It had been a busy week, but not too busy for him to have become even more fascinated with the sheep princess. He'd been okay those first couple of days, but then on Sunday, he'd slept in and only made it to the door of his tent as she came out of her trailer in an indigo blue dress and with her hair cascading down her back in shining waves and curls.

He hadn't been able to do anything but stare. Not even breathe. She looked like a different person altogether, and he'd sighed, wishing he was closer so he could have had an even better glimpse of her before she got into the beat up old truck and left. He realized later that she must have been headed off to church, and he remembered what one of the men who were looking for her the other night had said about her being too churchy to live with a boyfriend. The thought made him feel the guilt he'd been working on losing for the past couple of weeks now. He'd felt like he was doing better as far as repenting, but she obviously out classed him as a good person. Especially if she went to find a church from this remote place.

He'd rolled over onto his back, and tried to expel both the guilt and the fascination with her, but it was difficult on both counts. He had a lot to feel guilty about after Stacy, and the vision in the blue dress had left a deep mark. She was a beautiful girl, and seemed to get prettier every time he saw her, something he wouldn't necessarily have thought possible if he hadn't seen her with his own eyes.

And then this morning. Holy Cannoli! Coming upon her there on the swing asleep, she had looked like a beautiful sleeping angel. And when she'd opened those sleepy, blue eyes! Man! Maybe living this close to her was going to be harder than he'd come to assume it would be. He hadn't had a rational thought since.

He finished unlacing his boot and got his out shaving kit to go shower. Dutch oven chicken sounded divine right now, but the dust and sweat from the day needed to come off first. He stretched his back and shoulders as he stood up. He'd used muscles today that he hadn't even known he had. He certainly didn't need a fitness club out here to stay in shape. Today had been brutal.

The sun was setting in the west as he approached her camp, and the light was a clear saffron that brightened the sage into nearly lime green instead of its usual muted gray. The little valley spread out below them fairly glowed, and the peace of it seemed to smooth out all the wrinkles in his life in a way that was almost tangible. He just about wished that this project wasn't nearing completion. He could use a big dose of the serenity that permeated this place. Even with the grueling hours of hard work, his spirit was soaking in the stillness.

She was sitting in her little swing with one leg tucked underneath her and the other gently pushing off occasionally as she looked clear down the valley, lost somewhere far away in thought. She turned when she heard him and gave him a mellow smile. "How was the shower?"

"Great, thank you. I feel human again. Who came up with that rig anyway? It's pretty ingenious."

"Zan and I collaborated on it. It's been my lifeline some days. The heat here sometimes drains me, but the shower helps."

"Now, Zan is the man who owns the sheep? Or is that Joseph?"

"Joseph is Zan's father. So technically, they both own them, but mostly Joseph owns them and Zan usually handles other business for the Navajo Nation off the reservation. He's got a degree in some kind of business. Business law maybe. Something along those lines. I think Zan tends to pay far more attention to me than to the other sheepherders they employ. At first, he thought he had a thing for me, but now he just thinks he's my big brother supervisor slash baby sitter. He tends to over manage me, but his help has been invaluable. I think you'll like him, although he's not going to be very happy with me for having a stranger camping nearby."

She got up to put the Dutch oven on the table next to the dishes and utensils she had there. Pulling the folding chair over to the table, she said, "I think you'd better sit in the canvas chair. These plastic seats are not all that sturdy and I'd hate to have it collapse with you. I'll pray okay?" She did and began to dish the food up and then put the heavy cast iron pan back into the fire pit to get it out of the way. They each ate for a second and then she asked, "Did you say you've been eating a lot of peanut butter sandwiches?"

He grimaced. "Almost every day for awhile. I used to love it, but I'm well past that point after this summer. It works though. It's portable and doesn't spoil in the heat. I'm living proof that eating a lot of it won't kill a person, just their preference for it."

"I have it too sometimes. I have one sheep that follows me around trying to steal my sandwich if she's close enough to smell it. One time I let her eat a whole sandwich just to see what she would do. She got some stuck on the tip of her nose and it drove her crazy trying to lick it off that afternoon. It was very entertaining." She paused and said self consciously, "I have to get my entertainment where I can out here, you know."

"I can imagine, although the peace here more than makes up for the lack of entertainment."

"I think so, but then I'm strange enough to be a sheepherder. Even Zan and Joseph think I'm eccentric."

"Well, you have to admit that a woman sheepherder is a little unusual."

She was quiet for a minute and then said, "Maybe that was part of the allure for me."

He noticed she was fiddling with the splint on her hand again, and asked, "What happened to your hand?"

She shook her head and said with a sigh, "Something ugly happened to my hand. It's a long and not very interesting story. Let's don't talk about it. Tell me what it is that you're doing out there everyday."

"Technically, seismic petroleum exploration using geophysics. Now that is a long and not very interesting story."

"It sounds a bit more technical than sheep herding, huh? You said you don't typically do what you're doing out here. What is it you typically do?"

"Total computer geek stuff. I take the information we find out here and process it to standardize it and then interpret what it is that we're finding. I'm usually the office guy, not the field guy."

"Are you enjoying being the field guy on this one, or can you not wait to get back to your office?"

"At first, it was hot and tedious and the company was abysmal, but it's growing on me. I don't think I'll be very happy just in the computer lab ever again. And I'm finding that calling my own shots is much more satisfying than having a supervisor."

"You're one who can handle calling his own shots because of your self discipline. Not everyone can do that. Most people need to have a supervisor in order to get anything done."

"I guess being a sheepherder is the ultimate in unsupervised. You're alone all the time, aren't you?"

"Oh, heavens no. I have three dogs and a hundred and ninety-three sheep and Horse."

"A horse or just Horse?"

"Just Horse. I named her myself. It's kind of catchy, don't you think?"

"Positively poetic. Please tell me all the sheep aren't named Sheep."

She laughed. "No. Usually the only times I call the sheep names are when I am trying not to swear at them. There are a handful that stand out and have nicknames, but mostly they're a herd of sheep to me."

He finished eating and pushed his plate back. "Thank you for cooking. I know what you mean about not cooking just for one. And tonight I was too tired to even consider it. By morning I would have been starving. Can I help you clean up?"

"You know how the Dutch oven is to clean. And I'll burn the plates, so no. Go home and go to bed. Are you going anywhere to church tomorrow?"

"I hadn't planned on it. I have no idea even where there is one out here."

"I'm going to go, and you're welcome to come with if you'd like. I'm going to leave at about nine-forty-five or so."

"I'll think about it. If I'm awake by then that is. The helicopter doesn't fly on Sundays so I usually try to sleep in and rest up all in one day before the next week. Where do you have to go to find a church?"

"There are several around, but tomorrow I'm going to go to La Honda. That's about ten minutes from here."

"I should go with you, but the closest thing I have to dress clothes is a pair of chinos."

She waved a hand at him. "I can't imagine that God would mind if you wore a pair of Chinos to worship him. Especially out here. I'd guess He's just glad we show up."

"You have a point, but I'd hate to embarrass the sheep princess. Do I ever get to know what your name is?"

She looked at him surprised. "I've never told you my name? I'm sorry, I didn't even realize. It's Taya. Taya Kaye. And you are?"

"Matt Maylon. From Steamboat." He got up and threw his paper plate on the fire. "Well, thanks for dinner, Taya Kaye. It was great. See ya around." *Taya. It fit her perfectly. A little exotic, slightly mysterious, beautiful, but unpretentious.*

Jaclyn M. Hawkes

Chapter 11

Deep in the night he was awoken by the sound of coyotes yipping and howling out in the valley. He heard her trailer door shut and sat up in bed. He could hear her talking to her dogs and heard her whistle once and then there was nothing but the coyotes and the sounds of agitated sheep for several minutes.

The sound of the coyotes was abruptly cut short by the sound of a shot and then the short, crying whine of a dog and then silence. A minute later there were another two shots, one right after another, followed by another yelp and then nothing again. Slowly, the sheep began to settle down and from time to time he could hear her calm voice as she walked among them talking to them and the dogs. Her voice even calmed him and he fell back to sleep before he heard her come back in. In the morning, he felt guilty for not making sure she came back safely before drifting off.

He decided he was going to go to church with her after all, for a couple of reasons. One was that he knew he needed it in his life, especially right now, and the other was that he wanted to see her up close dressed up again. His glimpse of her from a distance last week had been enough to make him get out of bed even when he felt like he could have slept all day. Seeing her step out of her trailer this time in a tan suit dress and heels with her hair a shiny tumble of the deepest chocolate waves and curls, convinced him he'd made a good decision. Even as tired as he knew she had to be after spending hours with her herd in the night, she looked like a million bucks.

One thing she didn't look like was a nomadic sheepherder. More like a business executive maybe. Something still wasn't adding up with all of this, but he figured she'd either level with him eventually, or she wouldn't and he'd know it was none of his business. Either way, he was enjoying the view and the interesting company occasionally. It beat the heck out of dealing with Hyatt and the others and their "ladies".

She had gone back into her trailer and emerged with what looked like a huge canvas beach bag full of several cardboard tubes like the ones posters or architectural plans came in. She set the bag on the table and then he heard her grumble to herself and open the door of her trailer and set it back inside and close the door. She turned with a yogurt smoothie in one hand and a handbag that exactly matched her shoes in the other, and he had to grin to himself at the thought that somehow in that little trailer she had a stash of matching purses and shoes.

As she headed for the trailer hitch of the battered truck, he asked her if she would be offended if he drove. Somehow, there was just no way she could put that dress and that truck together. It was too incongruous. His four wheel drive Jeep was bad enough, but at least it was relatively new and unscathed in comparison.

When he asked, he startled her, and she looked up in surprise and then smiled at him. "Good morning. I thought you were going to pass. I'm glad you're going to go. You'll love it and I won't have to walk in alone. I hate that sometimes." She looked him over. "I thought you were whining about not having clothes. You look perfect. And yes, I'd love it if you'd drive. We have a much better chance of actually arriving at church if you drive than if we take Lancaster."

He laughed out loud. "Lancaster? The truck's name is Lancaster? Let me guess. You named it yourself and you think it's kind of catchy."

"No. Everything but Horse came already named. I'm not sure why the truck is Lancaster. Don't look over here, I'm going to try to climb up into your Jeep and it may not be a pretty sight. It's actually taller than Lancaster ever dreamed of being." He looked anyway, and she was wrong. It was an incredible sight. She busted him watching and laughing at her. "You weren't supposed to be looking, Matt. And don't laugh. You have no appreciation for what women do."

"Of course I do. Why else would I have watched? Pretty legs are one of the things I appreciate the very most. They're the real reason men drive four wheel drives. The view is absolutely worth the extra expense." He released the emergency brake and they headed out. "What do the sheep do when the sheep princess goes to town?"

"They'll be fine for a few hours during the day with just the dogs. Days I typically only have to make sure that they have food and are safe from things like the highway. Its nights that they might need someone to come save them usually. The dogs are probably smarter than I'll ever be as far as watching over them. As long as I'm not gone long they'll be fine."

"I heard the coyotes last night. I guess banker's hours and vacation and sick days aren't part of the deal with sheep, huh?"

"Only about as much as dairy cows from what I've heard, but the actual work is not all that demanding, so it's okay. I don't worry too much about office gossip or nepotism or being politically correct. And the dress code is great."

"Do you herd all year, or is there a season?"

"There's a season. I'll be done here by late October. Joseph will take them back down to the home ranch and feed them hay all winter."

"What does the sheep princess do in the off season?"

She was pensive for a minute and then said, "I don't know for sure yet. Maybe they'll need sheepherders in South

America. Or llama herders. Or are they alpacas? Maybe I'll go to the Pampas and herd alpacas. I could learn Spanish in two and a half months if I applied myself couldn't I?"

"Easily. Probably in just two. It's learning to handle the counterclockwise cyclones you'd have to work on."

"That's true. I was never any good with cyclones."

"Are you always this much of a smart Alec?"

"Mmm. Yeah, pretty much. Turn left when you reach the highway. Oh, but you know how to get to LaHonda, don't you?"

"That's where I got your enchilada dinner the other night."

"I didn't know there was Mexican food in LaHonda. It was very good. Thank you again. Did you cook everything else?"

"Everything but the first day's breakfast. I brought that to you from my mom. She's a much better cook than I will ever dream of being."

"It was very good. Does she live in Steamboat too?"

"Near Steamboat. What about you? Where are your parents?"

She hesitated and he looked over at her to see that her face was sad. "Actually, my parents and I don't keep in touch much these days. I assume they are living in Maryland." She changed the subject. "That's not a Colorado accent. Where did you grow up?"

"South Texas until I was fifteen. Now I have a half southern, half western accent."

"It's adorable. It exactly fits you. So, what kind of education do you have to have to do seismic petroleum exploration using geophysics?"

"That depends on what part of it you're doing. To do what I usually do, you need a degree in geophysics."

"That's like seventeen years more schooling than you need to herd sheep, which is why you probably make like seventeen times more money than a sheepherder."

He thought about that and then said, "But, you know. I don't think you can find a much better lifestyle in a way. As long as you don't mind the lonely part. There's a lot to be said for the way you live here."

"You're right. It's very nice most of the time."

"What kind of church are we headed to this morning? I guess I should have asked that sooner. We are talking Christian here aren't we?"

Taya laughed. "What, did you think I was Buddhist or something? Of course it's Christian."

"Just checking. I've never been to a Buddhist service. It might be interesting."

"It might. I went to a non-denominational one once that had a Hindu speaker. It was actually a bit strange, although I guess we should know a little about everything."

"That's true, but I always feel like I don't even know enough to truly understand Christianity, let alone studying something else."

"What did you grow up? What are your parents?"

"My dad is whatever my mother researches and tells him is good and she isn't necessarily any one thing. The couple of times that we moved, she kind of checked all the local churches out until she found a preacher she could agree with most of the time. I don't know that she's ever been a certain sect other than Christian. How did you grow up? What are your parents?"

"My parents think that organized religion is a waste of a perfectly good Sunday. They weren't very thrilled about me studying religion at all."

He could tell she wasn't happy when she talked about her parents, and he steered the conversation away from them again. "What's the elevation around here? How much snow do they get here in winter?"

"I have no idea what the elevation is here, and there's not much snow, but only because it's dry. It gets plenty cold enough to have snow."

"I wondered. The nights and mornings here are cooler than I expected, but then the days feel like they are over a hundred degrees."

"You're right on both counts. Sometimes the difference between the daytime and nighttime temperatures here is like fifty five degrees. It surprises me at times. I've learned to be ready for anything."

He thought about that, and about her, and decided that she probably was ready for anything. He turned the radio on low as they drove and they reached the little town within just a few more minutes. He was surprised when they turned into a church that seemed unduly large for such a small community. Not only that, but the parking lot was almost full.

When they got inside she seemed to know just where she was going even though he had gotten the impression that she hadn't been to this particular church before. They didn't go straight into the main chapel room at first, and even when they got to the room she was apparently going to go into, she hesitated outside the door for a second. She turned to him and whispered, "Let's stay out here for a second until the lesson has started so we won't have to tell anyone who we are."

Matt thought that was slightly paranoid until he heard the teacher inside ask if there were any visitors and a woman near the front stood and introduced her son-in-law. Matt looked at Taya who gave him a half hearted smile and then slipped in and took seats at the back. It was about a forty minute class on the part of the bible that included the woman caught in adultery and in some ways it made Matt want to squirm, but in other ways it was incredibly comforting to be reminded that the Savior was that forgiving.

After that class, they went into the main sanctuary of the church and sat right at the back again and Matt was surprised to find that there wasn't a preacher of sorts. Instead they had some kind of special ceremony in remembrance of the last supper and several different speakers that ranged in age from two teenagers to a soft spoken, gray haired, grandfather type.

They spoke on a variety of subjects that all seemed geared toward helping each other do a little better in their everyday lives and he thought about what his mother had said about church being a place where imperfect people got together to encourage each other. She had been right. That's just what this meeting felt like. As they began to sing the closing song, Taya leaned into him and whispered, "Let's go now."

He followed her out and they were all the way into the parking lot before the meeting officially ended, and she explained, "We needed to leave early because I didn't want to have to tell everyone who we are. And actually, we missed the first meeting where they separate the men and the women, because they truly would have tried to welcome us there. I hope you don't mind."

He shrugged. "Whatever is fine. Are they really all that nosy?"

"Not nosy. Friendly. I just don't care to be all that included right now. I hope I didn't offend you."

"Actually, no one had a coronary on seeing the rebel Matt Maylon show up in church and no one stood and called me to come down and confess my sins and come to repentance, so I thought it was great! Flying under the radar is fine with me."

She laughed. "I don't believe you're all that much of a rebel for a minute, Matt, so give it up. You could never convince me you're all that much of a sinner. You have too nice of a spirit about you. Do you have plans for Sunday dinner?"

"No, and I'm almost out of groceries so I have no idea what I even have. Do you have plans?"

"Yesterday, I had decided I'd break the Sabbath today and shop while I was in town and ship some things, but I forgot the post office isn't open on Sunday, so I have to come back tomorrow anyway, so I'm in the same boat. Maybe we could throw in together and make 'Whatchagot stew'."

"We could do that. It might be awful, but it would be both of our faults. You read Louis L'Amour and Patrick McMannis? Somehow, I can't picture that."

"His stuff came with the trailer."

"I guess that makes sense then. Did you feel stupid when you laughed when you were by yourself? That always makes me feel stupid when I read McMannis."

"Yes, but still it's not as bad as when I laugh when I'm with someone and they have no idea what's going on. I once read an article by Jeff Foxworthy in the doctor's office. I felt like an idiot."

He looked at her, surprised. "I can't truly picture you identifying with Jeff Foxworthy either."

She laughed. "Are you kidding me? Have you seen my shower? I could be in the 'You might be a redneck' hall of fame!"

Matt looked across the Jeep at her in her beautiful suit with matching purse and shoes and shook his head and laughed. *Redneck? Yeah right! Not in a million years.*

Their Whatchagot stew was actually surprisingly good and he had a great time making it on her little table beside her. She was one surprise after another and was a ton of fun to be with. He was almost disappointed to go back to his camp to nap and take care of his own things. His tent was too hot to nap in, so he took his bed and threw it in what little shade he could find and crashed until an ant woke him up crawling on his face in late afternoon. Later when he got his computer work done, he built a small fire and played his guitar for a while wishing he could have been with her again.

****

In the middle of the night, he heard her scream and sat straight up in bed, wondering if the two men from the other night had returned. His jeans were on and he was in search of his Tivas when he heard her outside his tent whispering as loud as she dared, "Matt. Matt."

He unzipped his tent and poked his head out. "What's wrong? What's going on?" She was wearing a pair of exercise pants and the matching tank top to it and a pair of hiking boots. Her hair was tousled and wild and she looked so good there in the moonlight that he almost forgot she was having a crisis.

"I'm so sorry to wake you up, but can you come help me for just a couple of minutes? There's a mouse in my trailer!"

She made it sound like she was dealing with a Bengal tiger and he looked hard at her to see if she was kidding. He didn't think she was and as he followed her to the offending rodent, he had to work to contain his smile. Was this the same woman who had gone out alone in the dark with a gun to protect her herd of sheep just last night? Apparently she didn't see the incongruity of the situation, because she was chattering about how a mouse had gotten into her trailer one other time and she had stayed outside for most of two days until she had been able to trap it. He looked at her and asked, "How did you empty the trap?"

"Oh, I didn't empty it. I just threw the whole thing as far out into the sage flat as I could. I know it was littering, but it's the only time I've done it I promise."

When they got to her trailer, she switched on her flashlight and began to quietly open the door with him standing right behind her. They leaned around the edge of the door and she shone the light inside and flitted it around on the floor for a second until it illuminated a small gray field mouse cowering in the corner.

As the light hit it, the mouse panicked and zipped across the floor of the trailer and out of the beam of the light. Taya screamed like she was being chased by an ax murderer and turned to flee and plowed face first into his chest. She almost knocked both of them flat, and Matt had to grab both of her arms to steady them. As soon as she had her balance, she dove around behind him and hid her head behind his shoulder. He was glad she couldn't see his face because there was no way he could have hidden his smile. It was all he could do not to laugh out loud. *What, did she think because she couldn't see it that she was safe from its large fangs?*

"Taya. Give me the light for a second and prop the door open, and then stand back, because it's going to come out fast." She handed him the light and then went and climbed up on the hood of her battered truck and pulled her legs up to hug them around the knees. She buried her head again and he chuckled as quietly as he could as he stepped into her little home on wheels.

He shone the light all around on the floor and couldn't see the mouse anywhere. He looked again and then heard a small sound and shone the light toward it and found the mouse crouched beside a mug sitting on the little table. He picked up one of the cardboard tubes he had seen her carrying the other day and went to brain the mouse with it, but it scooted across the table and jumped off and indeed went out the door of the trailer going ninety. Matt returned the tube to the stack where he had found it and shut off the light and went back out to tell her he had saved her from the man eating beast.

"You can come down now. It's gone and won't be coming back anytime soon. I think we scared the need to be anywhere in the county right out of him."

She looked all around the truck into the dark. "Are you sure?" Zeus, who had watched all of this with a bland expression stood below her next to the truck as if to tell her it was okay to trust him.

"I'm sure."

"How did it get in there in the first place?"

"I have no idea, but I don't think it will do it again. It was too traumatic." He didn't say that hearing her scream was what had traumatized the little creature, but he thought it. She was such a kick with this mouse that if he ever needed entertainment in the dead of night again he'd put one in himself, except she truly was afraid enough that he would never do something like that. Still, she'd been incredibly funny. He went over to the hood of her truck to give her a hand as she climbed down.

"Thank you, Matt. I'm so sorry I woke you up. You have no idea how much you just saved my life. I so owe you one. I know it's stupid to be afraid of something that little, but they're just so fast! They're horrible! Now, I'll probably have bad dreams for the rest of the night."

"You're welcome. Anytime." He reached up to help her down. "Try to focus on other thoughts and you'll be fine. 'Night."

He headed back to his camp, shaking his head. This girl was indeed entertaining.

****

Taya didn't end up having bad dreams after all. The mouse actually didn't cross her mind all that much. She was far too preoccupied with remembering how good Matt had looked in just his jeans in the moonlight. He did *not* look like any computer geek she had ever known!

Jaclyn M. Hawkes

Chapter 12

The next morning when he came back into camp just before noon to head in to his appointment about renegotiating the contract, he found a note and a box of Cracker Jacks on his table weighed down by a rock. It said, "Matt, thank you for saving me. Sorry again for waking you. I just wanted to wish you success at your appointment. Remember that being hard working, and honest, and easy to get along with are rare and valuable traits in the business world today. If I was a contract guy, I'd be thrilled to get you! I'll be praying for you today. Good Luck, Taya"

Her note and inference meant more to him than she could know, and he changed and got into the Jeep feeling much more confident than he'd been all morning. Thinking about it, she was right. He did have some things going for him that would be valuable to this guy. It wasn't everyone who would put their heart and soul into someone else's deal. If there was any way possible, he was going to talk this guy into extending the time frame so he could at least make something for the time he'd put in so far.

When he arrived at the office, he'd hardly gotten in the door when they got right down to business. The man who had given Hyatt the contract, Jim Horrocks, had no more than let him come in and sit down before he said, "Thank you for taking the time to come and meet with me. What is it you wanted to talk to me about?"

Matt put his cards right on the table and explained about Hyatt and being behind and ended with, "I'd like to see if you are open to working with me in order to both get your contract completed and see that I get paid. So far money has not been forthcoming from Hyatt."

Jim's answer took him by surprise. "This contract has been keeping me up nights. My company is expecting to have the results of your research in their hands within weeks and honestly I've been worried to death about what I was going to do about it. I've known from talking to Hyatt that he was dropping the ball, and I've quit sending any of the payments until I can get it back on track. I'm past the point of believing Hyatt is going to get with it, so I was thrilled when I talked to Mac, the pilot, the other day. I knew someone had been staying on task out there, because I was still receiving your data, but I didn't know much about you until Mac. Now, I know you're typically not the field guy, but I'm willing to more than make it worth your while if I could talk you into taking this contract over in its entirety."

Matt was confused at first. "What do you mean, take it over?"

"I mean that I'd be thrilled if you'd be willing to sign a new contract that you would take over instead of Hyatt and see this thing through to the end. I'd be willing to offer you the three-hundred-seventy-seven thousand dollar balance of the original contract, plus another ten percent to make up for the hassle of taking over someone else's mess and the critical time constraints. In addition, I'll provide all materials and pay for the helicopter and accommodations for you and whoever you end up hiring to help you."

Matt tried not to act overwhelmed. "What about Hyatt? He's already not very happy with me. Am I going to get sued over this?"

"No. Hyatt has fallen down on every single clause of his contract and it's legally null and void. And the equipment that's in the lot at the hotel is owned by my company. If there's anything left after their shenanigans. You'll have to go and take stock and get back with me about what you need. I'll do anything I can to help you, but I need to have this thing tied up and delivered by October fifteenth. I can cut the scope of it down to a certain extent, but that's the latest I can go."

"You don't even know me. Are you sure you're willing to offer me this?"

"I've talked to Mac at length. He assures me that you're hard working and honest and good to work with. I've met you now and feel good about it, and I know from the data you've already sent that you're smart and competent. Now I just need you to be willing to commit to an incredibly tight deadline."

He pulled a stack of papers out of a file folder he had on his desk. "I had these drawn up in the hopes I could talk you into taking over. Take as long as you like to look at them. If you'll excuse me for a minute, I need to step down the hall and have a quick meeting, but I'll be back within the half hour." He stood up and extended his hand to Matt. "I know this is a lot to ask, but I'm in a tight spot and will do all I can to expedite things as well as making it worth your while financially. I'll hope you'll consider this offer. If there are concerns about the contract, we'll discuss them when I come back. Excuse me."

It was a good thing there was no one there he had to talk to after Jim left, because Matt was stunned speechless. After the door shut behind the man, Matt sat there in shock. He'd come hoping to be able to talk him into giving him a break, but the man had offered him more than he'd ever dreamed of. He'd just been handed the opportunity to go from a hired scientist to a business man with a great contract ready for the taking. He took a deep breath and picked up the contract. Just about now he was incredibly grateful for Taya's prayers. He was out of his depth here, but he was going to jump right in.

He read over the contract three separate times looking for questionable fine print. Other than the looming deadline, there was nothing. This was a great deal. *If* he could finish in time. That was the kicker. If. But it was too good a chance not to try for.

As soon as Jim returned, he signed the paperwork and taking his copy, went back out to the Jeep. It took all of his self control to not throw his fist into the air. He owed Taya big time for encouraging him to make this appointment in the first place. Doing his laundry and grocery shopping were so anticlimactic that he almost decided to forget it and just go home to Taya, but he needed food and clean clothes, so he didn't. He even controlled himself and only bought his usual groceries except for the ingredients for his favorite Chinese stir-fry, before heading back out into the desert. He stopped at the hotel and took stock of the equipment stored there and was encouraged again to realize that most of what he would need was still there, intact.

When he made it to camp it was late afternoon, and she was nowhere to be seen so he went to work chopping vegetables and chicken. By the time she came in at dark, he had dinner ready and had been able to come to terms with the fact that his life had taken a huge turn in a good direction for the third time in three weeks. He was almost wondering what he had done to deserve it all.

She came past his camp table on Horse with Zeus and stopped nearby. "You look happy. How did it go?"

It was a good thing she was on the horse, because he probably would have hugged her. "I am happy. It went better than I ever dreamed. I signed a new contract that I own and you were right. The owner will make much more than the employee. I was so stoked that I was going to take you to a celebration dinner, but since I've just signed onto a contract that's going to kill me to finish in time, I decided to cook here instead so I can go straight back to work. Can I interest you in sesame chicken?"

"Are you kidding me? I could smell that a mile out in the sage. I'd arm wrestle you for some if I had to. Since we're celebrating, can we eat on real dishes and a table cloth?"

"Um, only if you have real dishes and a table cloth, because I don't."

"I do. And I'll do the dishes since you did all the food. Your place or mine?"

"You're the only one of the two of us who owns a sink, so let's eat at your house. It'll be done in about ten minutes."

Ten minutes later when he walked over carrying the pan, he was amazed to see that she had meant like real, real dishes. It looked like a real white linen table cloth and napkins and she had china plates with sterling silverware and stemware to drink out of. "Wow, you weren't kidding about real dishes. What kind of a sheepherder are you? Let me guess, you keep these in the same place as your matching shoes and purses."

She laughed and admitted, "Close. Sometimes I have to keep things in perspective with the dishes. I've only used them a few times and it's only been me and Zeus until now. It will be great to use them with another human being." She lit a candle on the table. "Do you like cranberry juice?"

"Anything that's cooler than eighty degrees is great as long as it isn't alcoholic." He filled their plates and then set the pan up on the hood of her truck so he wouldn't get soot on her fancy linens. As he sat in the canvas chair, she folded her arms and bowed her head and waited and he prayed over their dinner before they dug in.

She took one bite and made all of his time spent cooking and shopping worth it with her praise. "Oh, my gosh! This is the best Chinese food I've ever had in my life! Where did you learn to cook like this? It's marvelous!"

"It's good Taya, but the best in your life? You've been living in the desert too long is all."

She shook her head and finished another bite. "No. Honestly, this is incredible. Are you a chef or something on the side?"

He chuckled at her expression, "Nope, no chef. I just like to eat a lot, and in college I couldn't afford to eat out all the time, so I had to learn or starve. Plus, my mother was a big proponent of her children being self sufficient."

"I think I like your mother. She sounds like a good woman. You should thank her next time you see her for that."

"For being a good woman, or making me learn to cook?"

"Both. How do you get the chicken to be this tender?"

"It's a secret that can never be revealed, except on threat of death."

"I may come threaten you some night, when I'm making chicken. So, I want to hear all about your big appointment."

He knew she probably wasn't truly all that interested, but he was so stoked about it that he told her what had transpired that day. She ate and listened attentively and he told her about the contract and the money and the deadline. By the time they were through eating, he'd decided that between encouraging him, and then fueling his enthusiasm, she was the best thing that had ever happened to him since that good mother they had been speaking of. He'd never been around someone who helped him to feel this capable and confident. There was something about the way she talked to him that left him feeling like she believed he could do anything, and it made him believe it too.

She was very good for his ego, and when she reached across the table and squeezed his hand and said, "That is so awesome! I'm thrilled for you. You'll be great! He won't regret taking a chance on you. Maybe this contract will be a wonderful start of a whole new professional direction for you!" he knew she was being sincere. She truly was thrilled for him and it did wonders for his outlook on life. He knew it was going to require a grueling couple of months, but it had the potential of helping him to become financially set for the future and he looked forward to the challenge. He just wished he could hire her to hang around and fire him up forever.

Finally, they blew out the candle and she sent him back to his tent to get started on processing his data and she disappeared inside her trailer with her ridiculously elegant dishes. It had been a dinner he would never forget, that was for sure. He was coming to expect the unexpected from her every time. If he tried to tell someone about her who had never met her, they'd think he was making it all up. It certainly made for an interesting friendship.

The next day, he got back to camp just as it was getting dark and he was on his way to the shower when he realized another vehicle was headed their way through the brush. He glanced over at her camp just in time to see her disappear into the shadows on the edge of the valley rim behind her trailer with Zeus. The hair on the back of his neck stood up as he remembered the two men who had been looking for her that evening, and he detoured to her camp and sat down in her chair with the rifle again. This time it was a big, new pickup truck and only one tall dark haired man got out. He seemed to bristle when he saw Matt sitting there and stalked over toward him to demand, "Who are you? Where's Taya?"

Matt stood up just as she slipped back into her camp with the dog that seemed to not have any issues with this visitor. "I'm right here, Zan." She came toward the two of them as Matt looked over at this guy wondering who he was and why he thought he owned her. "Matt, this is Zan Bear. My friend I've been telling you about. Zan, this is Matt Maylon, my good friend and neighbor. He's camping nearby while he works on a seismic mapping project in this area. Is that the right thing to call it, Matt?"

Matt didn't look away from the tall man in the business clothes as he said, "Sure, that'll do. You know this guy? He's okay?"

Taya came and put a hand on both of their arms. "He's more than okay. I'm fine. Thanks for coming to check on me."

Matt was still staring at Zan. "Excuse me then." He picked up his shower bag from where he'd left it on her table and headed out of her camp to continue on to the shower. She'd said Zan wasn't going to be very happy to find him there, and she'd been right. Zan had tried to kill him with just his eyes.

Matt smiled to himself, wondering what the tall Indian man would have thought about their candlelight dinner last night. He couldn't imagine it would have pleased him. Taya thought this guy "used" to have a thing for her, but it had taken Matt about half a second to ascertain that it wasn't a thing of the past. Zan still had a major thing for her and had tried to stake out his territory in one pointed glare. It might have worked for some men, but to Matt it had been like a challenge. Only good manners and the knowledge that conflict would make her uncomfortable had gotten him to leave just then.

After showering, he stayed well out from her camp on the way back to his, and got out his laptop and went to work at his table. His camp had gotten closer to hers with every move until now he was only about one-hundred-fifty feet out behind her and their voices carried well in the still desert air. He could hear her trying to mollify Zan, and he could hear Zan not appearing to be very mollified. She told him flat out that she had asked Matt to come because she felt safer with him nearby.

108

When she finally convinced Zan that they were fine and that not only was Matt not a problem, but he wasn't going away if she had anything to do about it, Zan gave up and changed the subject. They were talking about Taya having to take a trip the next week and were making arrangements for someone else to come in for a couple of days to watch over the sheep.

Matt didn't think he had ever heard such a sad note in her voice and at one point she actually broke down and cried on Zan's shoulder before he left. Matt didn't understand what was going on, but he wished he did. He also had to stop and step back and examine the feelings he had felt when he had glanced up to see her in Zan's embrace. That simple hug had troubled him far more than finding Stacy in much more involved circumstances with Justin. It didn't make sense, but it was true and it made Matt have to think again about how he felt about Taya. They were just friends and neighbors weren't they? He had better watch himself or he'd find himself heart broken even if he finished the contract in good time.

That night he sat up late at his fire with his guitar. Taya with Zan had put him in an introspective mood and the guitar and the firelight and the night intensified it. For the first time, he was thinking long term professionally and it seemed to lead to thinking about the fact that he was almost twenty six and wondering if it wasn't time that he finally settled down and got serious about his future, and all that that entailed.

The only other time he'd thought about things like this was when he had found himself living with Stacy and had felt obligated to try to get her to agree to marry him. In retrospect, he was more grateful than ever that she had hesitated. None of the positive things that had happened to him lately would have come about if he'd been stuck with her, and he knew his widening plans for the future would never have happened with her lack of vision and foresight.

When he finally put the guitar in its case and stretched out on top of his sleeping bag, for the first time in a long, long time, he felt like he could pray. He had a lot to be grateful for and he finally felt like he was far enough from the questionable life he had been living to dare to face God.

Chapter 13

Taya was back on the swing with her comforter again, listening to Matt's enchanting music. He'd played a few times over the last couple of weeks, and it had been incredibly moving every time. Tonight even more so than usual and she wondered why. Part of it was talking to Zan about going back east to testify in the assault trial against John, and part of it was remembering the way Matt and Zan had acted when they'd met each other tonight. She'd known it was coming, but she honestly hadn't thought Zan would be *that* upset. Was he still having feelings for her? It would appear to be so, and while she loved Zan dearly, she knew their friendship would never be more than just friendship, and she hated the idea that she would hurt him.

He and Matt had looked like two political opponents at the beginning of a rather hostile debate. They were both strong men and she had been nervous for a minute. She would have to thank Matt when she saw him for leaving so discreetly. They had been interesting standing there though. Zan's tall dark good looks in his business clothes straight from his office, and Matt's even taller sun bronzed and bleached outdoorsman muscly good looks glaring back at each other. She made a mental note to start immediately calming the troubled waters between them. She needed them both to be firmly on her team together to face the coming weeks.

She wondered again if she should tell Matt exactly what had gone on in her life this spring. She trusted him enough now to let him know what her background was, but she was almost hesitant to have him think she was anything different than the girl who had become his friend. And was she putting him in danger here in this situation? There were times she thought not at all, but then there were times that she realized he would be right in the middle if trouble ever showed up again.

She let the magic of his music make her forget everything except that warmth she felt from the guitar and his mellow, sexy voice. She was too tired and happy to worry about anything else right now.

She woke up on the swing again and spent the day remembering his music of the night before. The memory of it preserved her sweet sense of all being right with the world, right up until she saw a car driving up to her camp late that afternoon. She went back down below the rim again until she realized it was a lone female who got out of the car and looked around. She didn't look like anyone John would have sent and Taya went back up the hill into camp again, with Zeus at her heels.

Taya approached the pretty blonde young woman wondering what was going on. She decided to let Zeus go ahead with his threatening posture until she found out what she wanted. "Did you need something?"

The blonde turned and looked at Taya with about the same look Zan had given Matt the night before. "I'm looking for a friend of mine. Matt Maylon. I was told he was camping somewhere near here. Do you happen to know where I could find him?"

For some reason, Taya didn't want to help this girl at all. She let Zeus continue to growl softly beside her as she answered, "Matt shows up here sometimes. Leave whatever it is you wanted to give him and I'll see he gets it when he drops in."

The scowl on the blonde's face deepened. "No, I wanted to see him. I know that's his Jeep. I'll just wait here until he comes back."

That idea rubbed Taya the wrong way. She was relatively sure Matt would have warned her that there would be a friend dropping by if he'd been aware of it, and somehow she didn't want this girl hanging out in her camp waiting for him. "No, you won't. If you want to talk to Matt, call him. I'm sure if he wants to see you he'll agree to meet you." Without any visible signal, Zeus cranked up his low growl to a snarl and the girl backed up and got into her car and headed away. Taya knew she wouldn't stay gone, but at least she didn't have to feel obligated to entertain her.

When the helicopter came in to drop him off at dusk that evening, Taya was feeling sufficiently penitent to walk over to his camp and be honest about how she had turned his friend out on her ear. She apologized for doing so and then went back to her camp and was in the middle of eating Chinese leftovers she had kept some of the other night, when the car showed up again. She recognized it and was sitting comfortably on her swing with Zeus at her feet when the blonde got out of her car. Zeus began to growl again and Taya just let him and said, "Matt's in the shower. He'll be out in a minute."

The blonde looked shocked and then outraged and then scared of Zeus. "I'll just wait in the car thanks."

You do that. Taya thought to herself, and then felt guilty again, both for being inhospitable and for letting the girl think they were on closer terms than they were. She didn't want her to think she and Matt were doing anything that was the slightest bit inappropriate here, but she wasn't terribly thrilled to have a pretty girl show up to see Matt either.

Matt came out of the shower and headed for his camp, but then pulled up sharply when he saw the little car in front of her trailer. He must have recognized it, because he turned back around to her camp. He met Taya's eyes for a second as she nodded. "You have company." It was some consolation that he definitely didn't look very happy about it.

He walked over to the car and opened the driver's side door. "Stacy. What are you doing here? How did you find me?"

There was a hint of a whine when she replied, "I've tried to call you like a hundred times, and couldn't get hold of you. So finally, I called your work and they gave me your boss's home phone number and his wife told me the motel she thought you were staying in. You weren't there, and your boss didn't know where you were so he told me to try the helicopter pilot. He's the one that told me to try by the sheep camp. How are you anyway?"

"I'm good, Stacy. Did it ever occur to you that I didn't answer your calls for a reason?" Matt glanced up at Taya still lazily swinging with her plate of left overs. "Come on over to my camp, so we can let her eat her dinner." He turned and headed toward his tent and the blonde gave Taya one more crusty and followed him. Taya could hear them as well as she knew he had been able to hear her and Zan the night before. "Stacy, I didn't answer your calls because I didn't particularly want to talk to you. Why are you here?"

"Look, Matt. I know what you saw was bad." Matt made a sound of utter disgust. "I was a fool, and I realize now. I've come to beg your forgiveness and tell you that I'll do anything for one more chance with you. Honest. I love you, Matt, and I can't even face living without you. These last few weeks have been too miserable to even say." She took a couple of steps toward him and he backed up.

"Stacy, I'm sorry to be abrupt, but I'm much happier, and I have no intention whatsoever of doing anything with you again. It was miserable long before that night, and after that . . . There's just no way. Go back to Justin and be happy.

You're far more suited to him than me. You guys are perfect for each other."

"No. We're not. You're perfect for me. I realize that now. I'm sorry that I had to find out the hard way. Please don't be so mean. I've driven all this way to be with you."

"I'm not trying to be mean, Stacy, but it's over. I had driven all that way to see you too. Remember? But even then it was over. We wouldn't be together now even if I hadn't busted you. We're not even friends anymore. We have nothing in common. We never did, it just took me awhile to figure that out."

"Of course we do, Matt. We had so much fun together."

"Go home, Stacy. There's no point in having this conversation." He went to turn away and she stomped her foot in anger and swore at him. At that he turned right back around and asked her, "You've been drinking this afternoon, haven't you?"

"If it's over, what do you care if I drink? Yes. I've had a couple. With your boss while I was waiting for you to come home. So what! It's not a big deal. You don't care anyway, remember?"

"Stace, we've been over this before. It is a big deal if you get behind the wheel when you've been drinking. Give me your keys."

"Oh, now you want me to stay with you. Fine, here are my keys. Now, can we talk about getting back together?"

"We're never going to get back together, Stacy. Wait here."

Matt came back across to Taya, looking extremely apologetic. "Taya, can I ask you a huge favor? She's been drinking. I'm going to take her back to the motel to get rid of her. Would you come and pick me up in my Jeep? Sorry about this."

"Sure. Just tell me when."

"Right now. Let's just get it over with. I have a ton of work to do tonight. I shouldn't have been playing my guitar last night."

Stacy wasn't very happy when she understood what the plan was, but she didn't have much choice. Taya could hear her swearing at him as he climbed in and moved the seat back. She drove the fifteen minutes to the motel, wondering what had happened between the two of them and enjoying the fact that his Jeep smelled like he had smelled the other night when she had stood behind him during the mouse incident. It was aftershave and sagebrush and something else that was him.

In the parking lot of the motel Stacy was still half pleading with him and half defiant and Matt was practically ordering her to get a room and sleep it off. Finally, he got into the Jeep in spite of her attitude and Taya pulled out of the parking lot, leaving Stacy behind them swearing. Taya felt bad for him for ever having had to deal with her, and because she knew he was embarrassed right now. As she reached for the radio, she said, "If it's any consolation, my last relationship makes her look saintly."

"Is that possible?"

"Oh, yeah."

"That's hard to believe as level headed as you are."

"You live and learn, I guess." She left it at that and turned the radio on. Back at camp they both worked late.

Matt had placed an ad in the local paper for some help to string his lines across the desert, but after more than a week, he had gotten no response and decided to place one in the larger county paper. In the mean time, Taya suggested she see if there were any of the Indian youth who would be willing to come and help him out. She had been able to find two young men who were seventeen or eighteen who could help him between hay cuttings and they would come to camp early in the morning to catch the helicopter with him.

Sunday morning he went to church with her again and they had a good conversation about it in the car on the way home, but other than that, they hardly saw each other either all week.

Matt had thrown himself into his new contract with a passion and was gone in the dark and didn't get home until after dark again. Taya had left him dinner four nights and he had left her some brownies he'd bought when he went to pick up the gear from the motel before it disappeared. By the time she dropped by his campfire late one night to tell him she was flying out the next day for a few days, they had only waved to each other for days.

Jaclyn M. Hawkes

Chapter 14

Zan came by to pick her up and she was glad he had talked her into letting him come with her back to Maryland because from the start, the trip was intimidating. She had FBI protection enroute and while she was there, and while the serious men and women in dark suits were reassuring, she also felt like she was a prisoner. She did her best to remain stoic during the trial, and was okay seeing John again, but seeing her parents there broke her heart into pieces. The only way she even made it through was to not look at them.

She stayed until they were sure they no longer needed her testimony and then they flew her back out without her even waiting to see what the verdict was and she was fine with that. She had done the best she could to see that justice was done and had to let it go emotionally and give the whole thing over to the system. She was convinced John was only going to keep trying to have everything thrown out on technicalities or appeal everything over and over anyway.

She and Zan had an incredibly involved travel plan both ways and by the time he dropped her back off at her trailer four days after she had left, she was tired to the bone. It was after ten o'clock at night, but she went over to Matt's tent to talk to him anyway.

She must have looked just how she felt, because he got right up and walked over to her, studied her for a moment and the leaned to hug her. After a second, he pulled back to look at her. "You okay?"

She nodded. "I'm okay now. It's way nice to be home."

He pulled her back into his arms. "You ever gonna tell me where you had to go so mysteriously?"

She sighed and decided to be honest. "I had to go testify against my ex-fiancé' in an assault trial."

He looked at her warily for a second. "Who did he assault?"

She did her best to sound matter-of-fact. "Me."

Quietly, he said, "I'm sorry. You weren't kidding when you said he made Stacy look good. Was there anyone there when it happened?"

It took her a second to answer, "My parents were there."

"So at least they stopped him and you had witnesses then."

She shook her head sadly. "No. They walked out and left me bleeding on his office floor and refused to give any testimony at all." He pulled back to look at her shocked and she said, "They *really* liked my fiancé'." She was afraid she was going to cry and pulled out of his arms. "I'm tired. I'm going to go home and go to bed. Where is that other herder camped?"

Matt nodded to the back of the trailer, and then stopped her. "Are you sure you have to go to bed right now? Is there any way you could just sit with me and talk to me for a minute?"

"Do we have to talk? Could you play your guitar?"

"Sure."

"Can you bring it over to my swing?"

"Sure. I'll be right there. Go put on some sweats or something that will make you relax."

A few minutes later, he sat next to her and played and she did her best not to let him see the tears that overflowed her tired eyes from time to time and slid down her cheeks.

Finally, he stopped playing, turned to her and put an arm around her and pulled her into a hug and held her. When she finally pulled back and wiped her face on her sleeve, he let her go and went back to his guitar. Crying had helped and she leaned back in the swing with a sigh. He turned to her. "Feel better?"

"Much, thanks. Sorry for being such a baby."

"It's okay. Can I ask you a question?" She nodded. "Are you sad about the fiancé' or your parents?"

"Definitely not the fiancé'. Why?"

He shook his head. "I just wondered." He went back to playing again and she took a deep breath and closed her eyes. She had needed this. He was the perfect therapy for a sad heart.

****

The next day was Sunday and this time when he showed up for church with her he was in a beautiful suit. She looked up at him and smiled. "Dang, Matt, you clean up nice!"

"Thanks. I always felt a little like the ugly stepsister when you looked so good, so I stopped home and picked up some more clothes. You look nice this morning. Are you any happier?"

"Yes, thanks to you. Thank you for not letting me go to bed sad."

"You're welcome. I only have one sister and my mom, but that was enough to figure out that sometimes crying does help. I'll never understand it, but I've seen it work. Was he convicted at the trial? I never got around to asking."

She shook her head. "I don't even know. I didn't stay around to find out. I've tried so hard to forgive and forget that night that I had to just do what I felt was right and then give the rest of it over to God."

He looked at her in surprise for a second and then seemed to understand that and changed the subject. "What town are we going to today?"

"Let's go south. How about Halloran? We haven't been there before."

"Did you ever tell me why we can't just go to one place?"

"No, I never did. But I should. You should have the chance to decide if you want to get clear away from me or not. It's kind of a long story. You know the fiancé' I wasn't sad about last night? Well, he's sort of a congressman. When he was arrested for assault, it just happened to be at the political fundraiser I was supposed to be attending with him that night. It was quite well publicized."

Matt turned to stare at her. "That was you?" She nodded. "Back east somewhere, right?"

"Maryland. Smack in the center of D.C. Anyway, when the police came to his office where I was at the time, they took some things as evidence that had my blood on them that ended up making him be indicted for several other things. Corruption kinds of things with some nasty people. I didn't realize what was going on at the time, but I had seen some things that helped the police come up with more incriminating evidence.

"Long story short. There are some people who stand to lose a great deal of money if he isn't re-elected. Keeping me from testifying would help that re-election bid. The two men who came to my camp that first night are connected to John Channing. Somehow they've found out approximately where I am, but they're not sure. Just the fact that no one would believe I'm here is the main thing that's keeping them away. That's why the different churches. We still don't know how they thought of western Colorado, but I'm trying not to be too obviously in any one place. I actually, probably ought to be in the witness protection program, but it seemed like a better idea to me to simply fall completely off the earth into a sheep camp."

She paused and gave an almost inaudible sigh. "Incidentally. one of the other people who were indicted was my father. He's a lobbyist back there. I'm not sure what the connection between him and John is, but it's much stronger than my parents' connection to me. That's the part in all of this that is so hurtful. They walked out that night and left me lying on his office floor bleeding and headed for emergency surgery to put my hand back together."

He winced and she continued, "Zan's family has been wonderful to me. His sister is my best friend from high school and college. They've helped me disappear as much as possible. But sooner or later they'll find me and I'll have to find another place to hide. I'm telling you all of this because I could be putting you in danger too. You can go back to the motel if you need to. I'll understand."

As she wound down, he turned and looked at her again. "That's the ugly thing that happened to your hand."

She sighed. "Yeah. That's the ugly thing that happened. All over the fact that I wouldn't go to his fundraiser in a strapless dress without a jacket."

He was shocked. "You're kidding."

"Well, something else had to be bothering him too. I'd never seen him so much as raise his voice, let alone hit someone like that. But when I refused to take off the jacket it pretty well ticked him off."

"Pretty well. What did he do to your hand? Can I ask?"

"The hand being mangled was because I was wearing this obscene eight carat diamond solitaire that got caught in my beaded gown and I landed on it wrong. It broke the diamond right off the ring and it never has been found by anyone willing to admit it. It disappeared that night. That's another reason John wants to find me. He thinks I walked with the diamond I tried to talk him out of in the first place."

"How did a girl as honest and good as you get involved with someone like John Channing?"

She paused for a minute. "I don't know, truthfully. I had no idea what was going on until right at the end. A week or two before all of this happened I had mentioned to my mother that I was thinking of breaking off the engagement and going on a mission. She totally freaked. But even then I was questioning if being a congressman's wife was what I truly wanted. Now I know it's not, but there in the thick of things it didn't seem like that bad of an idea. I knew I wasn't in love with him, but at the time I thought that would be okay."

He looked over at her in surprise. "Why would you consent to marry someone you weren't in love with? That doesn't seem like you either."

"Well, I'm twenty-four years old and have never felt all that strongly about anyone. Sometimes I wonder if I'm just not wired to fall in love. Wouldn't I have done it by now if I was?"

He looked horrified. "Taya! You'd be better off staying single than marrying someone you weren't head over heels with. What were you thinking?"

"I know that now. If you want to know the truth, at the time I was thinking I wanted a family even if I was never going to do the head over heels thing. Staying single is one thing. Never being a mother is another."

He looked across the car at her like she'd lost her mind, and shook his head. "And you were going to have this not in love family in metro D.C.? You never cease to surprise me. You've done it again."

"Lay off, Matt, or I'll hassle you about having a girlfriend who's all of two inches deep. I have the right to my own mistakes. I was honestly always trying to make good decisions. I just failed a lot. It makes for wisdom, okay? By the time I'm ninety two I'll have this life thing down pat.

Until then, you're on your own as far as cornering good judgment. I'll be the first to admit to being a failure. I'm learning. Slowly. At least he hit me before we were married and had kids. That's the good thing in all of this."

"There is that. When is the next trial?"

"Supposedly in October, unless his attorneys can pull something. I was still in surgery that night when they started to whine about technicalities."

"How long do you have to wear the brace?"

"Another month or two. Then more physical therapy."

"Does it still hurt?"

"The hand injury or being left laying on the floor bleeding?"

"Being left will probably always hurt. I was asking about the hand."

"Only when I'm overly tired or if I've done too much with it. I used to be able to keyboard about three times faster than I can now."

"What does a sheepherder need to keyboard fast for?"

"Um, well, since I'm being all confessional here this morning. I'm a structural engineer. That's what I do on the laptop while you're doing your stuff."

This time he stared at her long enough that she pointed back toward the road. "Uh, Matt."

"You've been engineering nights while I work? Holy Cannoli girl! Why do you hide things like that? Although it only took me about thirty seconds to figure out you weren't an Indian sheepherder."

She tried to defend herself. "At first I didn't know you. I didn't want to reveal enough about me to make anyone start to wonder why I'm here. It's hard enough trying to pull off being a female sheepherder."

Drily, he said, "Female isn't that hard to swallow. Gorgeous and articulate and polished are what's hard to buy. But you should be fine, as long as you stick to sheep. If no one sees you, no one will be intrigued."

She rolled her eyes. "I think you're being a tad heavy on the blarney, but that's the reason for moving around to different churches and sneaking in late and out early."

"Okay, I understand that now. What I don't understand is what a woman who once thought she wanted to go on a mission is doing not trying to convert me."

"What do you mean?"

"Well, this is the fourth week in a row I've gone to church with you. Last week, I finally figured out that you're the church some people call the Mormons. With those famous teenage boy missionaries on bicycles. Why is no one pouncing on me?"

She couldn't help but laugh. "You want pouncing? Sorry, I'm not much of a pouncing kind of a girl. You should have mentioned that to Stacy. She seemed to want to pounce. Speaking of Stacy, what exactly did you see that ended that relationship so soundly? I was honest with you about everything."

"Oh, my story isn't nearly as juicy as a corrupt and violent congressman. I just caught her in bed with my best friend."

This time it was Taya's turn to be shocked. "You're kidding! Your best friend? Oh! That's awful! I'm so sorry!"

"Ahh. I'm like you. I'm just incredibly thankful that I clued in before too long. About both of them. Walking away from the two of them was the best thing that has happened to me in years. I feel like my life is headed in a much better direction than it was five weeks ago. You've been a very good influence on me. Thanks."

"How have I been an influence on you? You're the one who just said I've been a lousy missionary."

"No, you've been a great missionary for me. Just not a pushy one. Which would never work anyway. I'm too rebellious. You've been a good influence. It's just that I have so far to go still."

"Ah. There's the church on the left. If you think you're rebellious, you have never seen what the headstrong daughter of a lobbyist can pull when she wants to. I'm not even going to admit to some of the stuff I did. I just hope I never have a child like me! Come on. We're even later than I wanted to be. Hey, maybe you'll be in luck and someone will pounce on you!"

They only went to Sunday school and Sacrament meeting again. Taya was hesitant to take him into a Gospel Essentials class for fear of drawing attention. Poor Matt had to try to muddle through a class that got off on a tangent about which original apostle was related to who and who was going to take care of Jesus' mother Mary. It was less than spiritual epiphany material to say the least. At least Sacrament meeting went better. The theme for the day was the importance of temple marriage and Taya found herself with the giggles when Matt turned and gave her a pointed look in the middle of one of the talks. He wasn't even sure what temple marriage was, but he was giving her the look anyway.

On the way home she still had the giggles in the car and teased him about being the pouncer instead of the pouncee. Once back in camp, they cooked another version of Whatchagot stew and ate together again before he headed back to his tent to rest up for the coming grueling week.

Jaclyn M. Hawkes

Chapter 15

Monday and Tuesday, he was up and gone before the sun was up and then didn't come back with his two helpers until well after dark. Taya had begun to just make him dinner as sort of her contribution to the success of his venture. Tuesday night when he dragged into camp he didn't look so good and she was a little concerned about him when he ate quietly and then went to his tent and didn't even come back over to shower.

She didn't see any lights on in his camp that night like she usually did, and the next morning the helicopter touched down as usual but then didn't take right back off. She opened the door of her trailer in the first light of day to see the two Indian helpers approaching with another man. Matt was nowhere to be seen. When they approached her and asked her where he was, she really started to worry. They all trooped over to his camp and the first thing she saw were his legs hanging out of his tent with his boots on, only face down.

She leaned down and started to wake him up, but he didn't respond to her speaking to him. She got louder and finally climbed right into his tent to find out what was going on. Once she was inside, she could practically smell his fever. It was that sick smell that she only recognized from the few times she had been really, really ill. He didn't wake up even when she'd climbed right in with him and when she finally shouted at him, he only groaned and turned on his side in his sleep. She put a hand on his head and it was so searingly hot that she gasped. She climbed back out and told the others

Matt was extremely ill and asked if they thought they knew what they were doing enough to go without him today, while she took him in to the doctor.

They left on the chopper and she ran to her trailer and got her first aid box and ran back. Once inside his tent again, she took his temperature with the scan thermometer and was horrified when it read one-hundred-six point three. She started waking him up again and had to almost hit him to get him to open his eyes. Pushing her box back out the door, she said, "Come on, Matt. We have to get you out and into the shower right now!"

She had to keep after him for a few minutes until he finally dragged himself up. She picked up the shaving kit he usually carried to the shower and dug in his bag for a pair of sweat pants, and his Tivas and followed him out of his tent. He almost staggered through the brush, and she took his hand and led him back to the trailer and pushed a glass of orange juice and two Tylenol into his hand and ordered him to take them. Then she sent him to the shower, but worried he'd be able to handle standing up in it and ran back to grab her chair.

Back at the shower she stood right in front of him and talked to him to see if he was with it enough to know he needed to shower to take down the fever. He did, but only just barely. Leaning down, she helped him untie his boots and then left him to help himself, while she went to dig out the phone book and find a doctor who would see him right away.

After ten phone calls, she got an appointment and went and met him coming out of the shower in his sweat pants and sandals. He was headed back to his tent and she gently steered him back over to the trailer and had him sit in the swing. She took his temperature again and was glad to see it was down to just over one-hundred-five already. She took his other things back to his tent and dug out a t-shirt. As nice as his physique was shirtless, she figured he'd better wear a shirt in to the doctor's office.

She ran out to the sheep and signaled the dogs to start the herd down into the valley for the morning and then went back and got Matt into the passenger side of his Jeep. Getting in the other side, she dug out of camp, heading for the road and trying to talk him into drinking a yogurt smoothie as they drove. He got most of it down before going back to being half unconscious against the window.

Seeing him like this scared her. She didn't ever remember being around someone whose fever was so high that they were mostly out of it. She finally pulled into the clinic parking lot and then had to work to rouse him again. She put an arm around him and literally dragged him into the waiting room where the woman at the front desk took one look at him and immediately took him back to an exam room.

He collapsed on the bed and was out again within seconds and Taya stood beside him to ensure he didn't accidentally roll off in his lethargy. When the nurse came back and took his temperature it was still over a hundred and five in spite of the fact that she had had the A.C. on in the Jeep as high as it would go the whole way over. The nurse called for the doctor and then began to sponge him off with a mixture of water and isopropyl alcohol. She asked Taya if he had taken anything to knock the fever down, and when she mentioned the Tylenol, they gave him some Ibuprofen soft gels too.

When the doctor finally came in, Taya wanted to scream when he regretfully said that this particular bad flu that was going around was viral and he couldn't do much more than treat the symptoms and encourage fluids. They told Taya to keep alternating with the two medicines every two hours and to get him back into the shower and sponge him off with the alcohol mixture if it spiked and wouldn't come back down. Worst case scenario, she could take him to the emergency room and see if they could get it down.

Taya loaded him back into the Jeep in absolute frustration. How could a person be this sick, and medical professionals send him away again? As she drove, she phoned Zan, told him what was going on and asked him to come and give him a blessing. She could tell he wasn't happy about her request in the least, but he agreed to come and bring someone else with him.

Actually, by the time she got Matt back to camp, the Ibuprofen had begun to help and the fever came down to one-hundred-three point five. It was still horribly high, but not nearly as scary to her as it had been. With the drop in temperature, Matt became more lucid and she explained what the doctor had said and what she needed to do for him.

She stressed that the doctor had cautioned her that Matt had to take the Ibuprofen with food and she talked him into eating some more. She put a sheet on her little swing and laid him on it where she could check him easier. Climbing in and out of his tent wasn't an option and it would be roasting hot in there all day anyway. She rigged up another sheet over the top of the swing to keep the sun off and then went to check on the sheep while she waited for Zan.

She had to hand it to Zan. He had come when she asked, even though she knew he wasn't thrilled in the least to be sharing her with Matt. He had brought another elder who worked in his office with him and Matt was actually awake enough to know somewhat what was going on as they administered to him. He went back to sleep immediately and she offered Zan and his friend a sandwich which they both declined before they left. Matt's fever dropped right down three degrees and stayed there for more than two hours while she moved the sheep again, but it spiked back up over one-hundred-four and she prayed for faith to help the blessing bring it back down. She got out her rubbing alcohol and made the mixture they had recommended and then stripped his shirt back off. She sat on the swing with him and sponged off his chest, trying to help bring that scary heat under control.

All day long, she switched off between tending to him and tending the sheep right around camp. She gave him the two medicines religiously and cajoled him into eating from time to time. The helicopter touched down at sunset again, and the pilot came in to check on him and planned to leave without him again in the morning.

By nightfall, when she had gotten the sheep somewhat bedded down, she was too tired to even eat dinner. She set an alarm to wake her every two hours and kept up her vigil all night, sponging off his chest again at ten after three when his fever went back up to one-hundred-five again. At twenty after five it was over one-hundred-six and she dragged him back to the shower to see if that would help to bring it down. It appeared to and she sat back on the swing to continue sponging off his chest and arms from time to time between doses.

When she heard the helicopter again, she was too tired to even check her watch and felt like she had sandpaper in her eyes. It felt like it had been a lot longer than twenty four hours that she had been fighting this eternal raging fever. She woke Matt gently and gave him the medicine and sweet talked him into eating most of a banana before dosing off. She took the sheep into a new section of the valley and went back to her vigil of sponging and tending to him. That day went by in a blur of sheep and fever and rubbing him with the alcohol and twice she got him to get back in the shower. By dark that evening, she had become a zombie who tended him and the sheep automatically. Bedding the sheep down, she sat in the swing with his head on her lap, wiping his brow occasionally.

She woke up sometime in the middle of the night and realized she had missed one of the doses of medicine and had let his fever rage clear up again. She felt terrible about it as she forced him to wake up and eat and dragged him into the shower. It was a good thing he was an amiable man as out of it as he was with her keeping after him.

When he came back out of the shower, they sat together on the swing leaning on each other. By this time she thought she was about as with it as he was.

Somehow they made it through that night and the next day, doing the same exhausting and frightening dance of shuffling sheep and medicine and food between trying to cool his burning body and snatching a rest between. The night was completely unintelligible. Where sheep and fever and exhaustion began and ended was anyone's guess.

The next morning, she actually felt more rested. Maybe her body was growing accustomed to bits and pieces of sleep between his frightening fevers. She dosed him and moved the sheep and came back to the swing to take up her round of sponging off his chest and arms. The brisk morning temperature seemed to help her. At least she felt better. She'd brought her pillow and propped it behind her back as she rolled him onto her lap again.

By now she was beginning to be able to feel about how high his fever was just with her hand, and even though it was still in the hundred-three range, it was about as low as she'd been able to get it. She sponged off his chest one more time and then his head and leaned hers back against the pillow to close her eyes. She prayed silently one more time for him and accidentally fell asleep in the middle of it.

Waking, she wasn't sure how long she had been asleep, but her sheep had gotten completely out of control and when she glanced up again, she could see them on almost every side of camp. She absently felt Matt's head and was surprised that it didn't feel as hot as it had. When she touched his forehead, he opened his eyes and looked at her and she thought his eyes looked clearer than they had in more than four days and said, "Welcome back. How are you feeling?"

He groaned and stretched and laid his head back down on her lap. "Pretty much like I've been through the fires of hell and back. Thanks for watching over me. I'm sorry I've been such a pain."

She smiled a tired smile. "You have been a pain, but there wasn't much you could do about it. Are you hungry? It's time you had more medicine."

"Not hungry, just achy. Your sheep have completely run amok."

"I know. They've probably eaten your tent by now, but your fever's down some so it's all okay." She brushed the hair back from his brow. "You scared me. I've never been around a fever that high. I never knew if I was keeping it down enough or not. I'm sorry that I've nagged at you for four days."

"Four days! You're kidding! I've been like this for four days?"

She smiled and ran her hand over his forehead again. "No, you've been semi comatose with a fever that has threatened to spontaneously combust for four days. It was nothing like this."

"I'm sorry. I haven't even realized what you've been going through. No wonder your sheep have gone everywhere."

"It's okay." She put a hand on his cheek and leaned back and closed her eyes. "It's all okay. We made it through."

After resting there for a few minutes, she pushed him off her lap and got up to go bring him some more medicine and another banana and a glass of milk. "Sorry, I haven't had much time to cook. Are you up to hanging out by yourself for a while, so I can go after the sheep?"

"Yes, but do I have to move?"

"Nope, you don't have to do anything. Just don't let your fever go so high again, deal?"

"Deal." He closed his eyes and she headed out to find her dogs. It took most of an hour to get the sheep bunched and started down the valley. The feed was eaten down to the dirt and she sighed, knowing she was going to have to move the trailer before dark tonight. She left the dogs to take over and went back into camp and ate a banana of her own on the way to the shower.

Primitive as it was, it felt like the fountain of youth, and she emerged feeling like a new woman who had strength enough to pack up camp and take it down the road after all. This time she put her trailer almost right down in the stream bottom. Talking to Matt about John had made her rethink what kind of danger they were in here and she was practically hidden in the trees, even from the helicopter. It was a pain to get there, but at dusk when she settled the sheep for the night, it smelled like heaven. Matt had gone back to sleep on the swing after eating and taking another dose of Ibuprofen, and Taya felt like he was going to be okay. She went in and lay down on her own bed planning to actually really sleep without the worry. Stretching out on her cool sheets had never felt so good!

Getting up at midnight wasn't such a struggle after real rest and she didn't mind it tonight. Matt was sleeping peacefully, and she debated waking him until she felt his forehead. His fever was still probably a hundred and two. She sat on the edge of the swing and rubbed his back until he came awake and she quietly handed him his medicine with a tall glass of milk. He took it with a sigh and a mellow thank you, before throwing the pills back and draining the glass. He closed his eyes again and she smoothed the hair back from his brow with a gentle hand. She probably should put a cool cloth there. They were out of rubbing alcohol and most of everything else and she would have to go to the grocery store tomorrow.

Going inside, she dampened a wash cloth with plain water and used it to wipe his head and shoulders and chest. He was out of the woods now, hopefully. What an exhausting and scary few days. It had been awful to see a man this strong be so incredibly sick. Tucking his sheet back around him, she gently kissed his forehead and went back to bed where she even dreamed about his chest and shoulders.

Twice more in the night she got up with him. Caring for him these few days was now as natural to her as caring for her sheep.

That next morning she got up, dosed Matt again and went out to move the sheep. When she came back in, she gathered up her laundry and her purse and then went and gathered up Matt's laundry bag as well. She loaded it all into her truck and bounced over the sage brush into town to grocery shop and run errands.

When she arrived back at the trailer, two and a half hours later, Matt was gone off the swing. As she unloaded groceries and put away clothes, she saw him come out of the shower. He was moving slow, but he was up and moving and she sighed with relief to see him that much better. She had made lunch and was back out with her sheep before she realized she had just done all of her errands in town on the Sabbath. She said a quick sorry prayer and hoped God would understand that in the insanity of the last few days, she had completely lost track of what day it was.

Jaclyn M. Hawkes

Chapter 16

Zan dropped by that afternoon just to visit. He'd had to call her from the highway to figure out where to look for the trailer, which was encouraging. He climbed out of his truck and walked over and sat next to her on her swing looking at her all the while, and when he was settled, he said, "You look awful, Taya. What happened? Are you sick too?" His blatant honesty made her laugh harder than she had laughed in months and he looked sheepish. "Sorry. I guess that was kind of rude. But seriously, are you okay?"

"I'm fine. Just tired. Matt's fever has been hellacious. I don't think it came down below like a hundred and two or three for most of four days. Trying to watch the sheep and give him medicine every two hours and fit in a little sleep was a trick. But at least I know you'll always be honest with me." She laughed at him again.

"If I was honest, I'd tell you that I think you shouldn't be living here with him like this. You don't even know him, and now look. You've spent nearly a week of your life caring for some guy who has a work project near you."

"Yes and you know what, Zan? If you had been here, you'd have done the same thing. I know you, Zan. You're too Christian to let someone suffer when you know you could be helping them when they need it, so quit lecturing. And thank you for coming when we needed you. I know he isn't necessarily your favorite guy, but you came anyway. I'm sure the Savior was proud of you."

"Now you're making me feel guilty for not liking him when I don't even know him."

"It isn't like you, but I knew it was coming anyway."

He looked at her with eyes so dark it was hard to read them and said, "Only because you know I'm in love with you and don't want to share."

"Alexander Bear! Don't even pull that on me! You and I both know you're not truly in love with me, so don't joke like that. It isn't very funny."

"I'm not joking, Taya, even though I long ago gave up any hope of you ever falling in love with me back. But that still doesn't mean I like sharing. Especially not with a non-member. Have you stopped to consider that he doesn't hold the priesthood? You could never ask him for a blessing when you needed it."

"Zan, he's my neighbor and has become a very good friend, but that's all. And priesthood or no, he's a great human being. He's helped me a lot out here when he didn't need to. I was honest with him the other day about the mess I'm in and said I'd understand if he wanted to move further away from me, and he didn't even blink. I know he's not a member, but God loves him anyway. He's been going to church with me for weeks now, and somehow or another, it's all going to be okay. I've felt that from the start, so calm down. You do have to share me with him, but I'm not in love with him either. At any rate, be happy for me that he's here and watches over me. Can't you?"

"Yeah, I can, Taya. But I don't think you know your own mind. You're different about him than about anyone else since I've known you. You're not a very trusting person anymore, but you trusted him to move almost right in with you from the start. And when you talk about him or to him, your voice is different than I've ever heard it. You'd better step back and really look at yourself, or your going to end up married to a non-member yet, and you don't have much track record there. You learned the hard way about John. Don't put yourself back into that same situation with this guy."

She turned in the swing to look at him and couldn't help the smile, and it made him start in again. "Don't look at me like that, Taya. I know what I'm talking about. I've known you for a long time. You never felt as strongly about John as you do about Matt, even though you were engaged. Somehow, he's gotten you to trust him in a way that doesn't seem wise. How do you know you're even safe here with him when you've only known him this long?"

"I don't know, Zan. He's been here for over a month now, but I knew I could trust him within minutes of meeting him. Don't ask me how, but I was right. He's always treated me well and has even come to my rescue when he didn't truly want to a couple of times. If you had met him under any other circumstances, you would really like him, so lighten up."

"All right, but don't you marry a non-member. You need the blessing of having a man as strong as you are in your life. Don't settle."

"Okay, I won't settle. I promise. Can we talk about something else? How is your work going?"

"Fine. As fine as being employed by a bunch of bureaucrats can be. Sometimes I think the Navajo Nation has as much red tape as the U.S. government."

"Listen to the whining going on here this afternoon! My, oh, my, we're negative! Hey, and I've tried to talk you into being self employed about a million times. So don't complain to me about someone's red tape. You could be calling all the shots yourself."

"I'm beginning to think you're actually right about that one. I'm sorry I'm so negative. I'll do better. I think it's just that I'm jealous of your neighbor that has me in a bad mood."

"That's silly, there's nothing to be jealous of, and don't be in a bad mood. You're too happy a guy for that kind of thing. Let me enjoy the little time I get to see you without being an old grump. How old are you now anyway. Twenty-six? Twenty-seven? How come you're giving me flack about marrying the wrong guy and you're not even so much as full out shopping when you're an old guy? You gotta get out there and find your princess charming."

"I'm only twenty-six, thanks."

"That's way, way older than my youthful twenty-four by the way. What happened to that beautiful girl you were so serious with at BYU when I got here? She was adorable."

"Let's don't talk about this either. The reason I came is to tell you John's case was finally thrown out on a technicality. You never asked, but you probably ought to know. You're still as much at risk as ever."

She looked up at him quietly, but didn't comment, and he asked, "How is the hand these days?"

"Uh, let's don't." She changed the subject. "How am I doing as far as the sheep and feed for the rest of the season? Am I doing okay?"

"The feed's fine. Why can't I ask you about your hand?"

"It depresses the heck out of me to even think about it. I may just wear the brace forever; it's so ugly and weird shaped now. What do you think I should do when I'm done here at the end of next month? I'm starting to worry about what my plan is next."

He reached over and took off the brace and looked at her hand. "It's not ugly and weird shaped. Once you get used to using it all the way again it will loosen up. Give it time. It was pretty hammered."

He paused and then said, "That's right. You don't even know where you're going to go, do you? There's life after sheep, I promise."

He didn't mention the witness protection program and she chose not to either as she continued to half joke, "I told Matt maybe South America. Or maybe a cruise ship or some island in the Caribbean for the winter. What do you think?"

"Oh, come off it, Taya. You're not going to South America or the Crib. You're going to stay here where we can know you're safe and well cared for. Just get a house in some little town where John wouldn't expect you to go, and ski all winter. You can engineer at night and actually go to the same ward several weeks in a row. It'll be whole new religious experience to have your bishop know who you are. By then, maybe this whole trial thing will be over and so will the election. You'll be safe and you can settle down and marry a rich tourist. An LDS one."

"Nah. No tourists. They have those stupid, flowered shirts. They're so tacky at weddings. If I stay, will you ski with me sometimes?"

"You're just trying to make sure my heart stays shredded indefinitely, aren't you? Sure, I'll ski with you. Heck, maybe I'll quit my job and we'll both be ski bums."

She laughed and nudged him. "You could never pass yourself off as a ski bum. Your fancy watch would give you away. Plus you love your job for all your whining, and you know the Navajo Nation needs all the sharp, sober help they can get. No offense."

"You're a smart Alec. But it's very entertaining. I gotta get going. Is there anything else you need from me right now?"

"Just for you to come by occasionally and tell me I look awful. It keeps me humble and makes me laugh. Tell your family I love them. And would you hurry and find a wife, so you'll quit hassling me?"

"Sure, I'll get right on that." He got up to go. "Take care, Taya. Call if you need something."

"You're my number one speed dial. Thanks, Zan. See ya."

Jaclyn M. Hawkes

Chapter 17

Matt dragged himself off her swing and back to his tent after a shower. He found that not only had she moved all of his gear, but she had done his wash as well. When Zan drove up a couple of hours later, Matt was glad he wasn't still a zombie on her swing. He wasn't up to a battle of wills with Zan right now.

Getting out his lap top, he tried to figure out where he was in his data processing. The last night's numbers he had, had never been run. He couldn't remember much about that evening, he'd just known that making it home that day had taken everything he had. He couldn't ever remember being this sick before in his life.

His mind traveled back over the last while with her. Taya had unselfishly cared for him non-stop for days. He couldn't remember much except bits and pieces and the fact that she had always been there, always helping, always gentle and patient, even when she had to have been dead tired. He'd been just awake enough to understand that she kissed him as she went back to bed last night, and it had done something warm to his heart.

He could hear her over there talking quietly with Zan. From time to time he could hear what they were saying even when he was trying to focus on his work. Taya had told Zan that she knew he wasn't really in love with her, but even Matt knew that wasn't true. One look at him was all it took. At least the guy wasn't insisting she try to care for him back. That was decent of him.

Zan obviously didn't want Matt with her, but she wasn't letting him push her around a bit about it, which was good because Matt would have stepped in and said something that Zan probably wouldn't like much. Matt could understand that Zan didn't want to share, because he didn't either. Only the fact that she obviously liked Zan, and that he was apparently good to watch over her made Matt feel somewhat better about having him over there on her swing. He'd come in the last few weeks to feel some ownership here that he probably shouldn't.

He didn't know how to feel when he heard her say he was just a neighbor and a friend. It was true at any rate, but he'd never felt the way he felt about her toward any other neighbor.

Then he truly didn't know how to feel when Zan had insinuated that Matt meant more to Taya than her fiancé' had. He had come here simply to expedite his project, although if he was honest he probably would never have come clear out here if she hadn't fascinated him so from the very first. Their friendship had come easy from the get go, even though, honestly, most days and nights they had little or nothing to do with each other. The way she had cared for him the last few days had taken that friendship to a whole new level. Something had happened there in the dead of nights when she had served him so diligently. She had earned a place in his emotions that no one had ever owned before. It was almost a little frightening that she had come to mean as much to him as she did, as fast as she had.

He'd also heard Zan's argument about him being a non-member of her church. Once again, Matt had to agree that Zan did have a point. Had Taya been his daughter, he would have wanted her to have a husband who was strong enough in her own faith that she could lean on him spiritually when she needed to. Zan coming to give him that blessing had been incredibly thought provoking.

Matt wasn't sure yet what he thought about her church, but he certainly knew that if he ever got to the point where he believed it was Christ's own church the way Taya did, that he wanted to be the one she called when she needed that kind of help. He'd been too hammered to feel anything but grateful for the help Zan had rendered even to someone he didn't want here. Much as he didn't want to, he had to respect Zan.

When it was all said and done, Matt was relieved when Zan finally got up and climbed into his shiny truck and left. Not only did Matt not want to share, but he felt like heck and wanted to go back over to her swing and go back to sleep. He wondered where Taya had gone off to when he did just exactly that.

Long after dark, he felt her cool hand on his brow again and rolled over to take the medicine she was offering him. She was a saint, she truly was. A saint who smelled like some kind of berries and the stream after dark. He went back to sleep with the feel of her putting a cool cloth on his head and neck, and wishing she'd give him that gentle kiss again. It had been really nice.

Finally, the next morning, he woke up feeling like he could face the world again. He rolled off her swing in the half light of pre-dawn and went back to his tent to get ready to go to work. He actually cooked a substantial breakfast because he was ravenous. He made some for Taya too and left it on her little table under another plate. He'd have to find a way to make things up to her.

He touched base with Mac in the chopper and then was gratified to see the two young men who had been helping him show up right on time. Hopefully, the last few days hadn't set him too far back on his contract.

When the helpers showed him what they had accomplished in his absence, he was thrilled. They had made a couple of small mistakes, but for the most part, they were working out fabulously. He wished he had about four more just like them.

With that thought, he checked his phone messages as they hiked over the desert and was surprised that there were so many. Stacy hadn't given up, even when he had been so blunt with her. There were another eleven messages from her since the day he had dumped her off at the motel. His mom had called to check on him a couple of times and there were four calls from people responding to his ad.

While he walked along, he deleted the ones from Stacy, called his mom to talk for a few minutes and then made appointments to meet with the potential employees the next day in town. When he told his mom how sick he'd been, she had been worried. When he told her a neighbor girl had taken care of him, she hadn't sounded sure whether she should be relieved or even more worried. He laughed as he hung up, knowing he was just about due for a visit from his mother. It would be just like her to show up here to check on him, now that she knew there was another female on the horizon.

It was an incredible relief to know his mother would wholeheartedly approve of the girl this time. He had no doubts that she would adore Taya. She was good and kind and sweet and beautiful. All it would take to sway his mother was to tell her that Taya had been dragging him to church with her every week. He wondered for a time what his mother would think of the fact that he'd been attending a Mormon church, and then decided he couldn't worry about that. He'd figured out that this had to be between him and his Father in Heaven, and though he respected his mother's and Taya's judgment, this one had to be all up to him in the end.

They got a lot done that day, but he was still ridiculously tired by the time he got back to camp that night. He was still running a fever, and though his temperature was high, he felt chilled to the bone and put sweats and a sweatshirt on to wear to bed.

He was just about to crawl into his tent when Taya appeared in his camp with a plate of dinner for him. "I know this is going to sound silly, but come sleep in my swing again so I can check on you for one more night. I'll worry about you all night over here and I know I'd wake you up trying to climb in there again to feel your forehead."

He chuckled as he took the plate and followed her back to her trailer. "Okay, Mother. But really, I'm fine. Just slightly out of shape from the last few days. Today took it out of me. Thanks for dinner, by the way."

"You're welcome. Think of it as my contribution to the success of your project. How is it going as far as your deadline?"

"Barring anymore unforeseens, I'm gonna be fine. I have appointments to meet with more potential helpers tomorrow. It's going to be a long, long month and a half, but it will be well worth it."

"Have you heard anymore from your old boss at all?"

"Not a peep. I keep hoping he's sobered up and gone home to his wife, but I honestly doubt that."

Taya was disgusted. "He has a wife? Oh, that poor woman. How would you ever put up with something like that?"

Matt shook his head. "Not for long, I can tell you that. If she has half a brain, she'll send him packing before she ends up with AIDS or something."

"Not to mention the fact that he's spending her grocery money on beer and scummy women."

"But then if she had half a brain, she wouldn't have married him in the first place."

At this Taya got introspective. "Although, maybe she was like me. Maybe she just didn't know what all she was getting into until it was too late. Women can be incredibly foolish sometimes."

He put a hand on her shoulder. "I don't think that is necessarily reserved just for women, Taya. Men have their share of being brain dead. It's probably even worse with men because our thinking gets clouded by things like bathing suits."

As they neared her trailer she laughed. "At least you're honest. Night, Matt. I'll check on you late."

It was actually earlier than she thought it would be. The dogs went off about eleven-forty and then she heard coyotes and headed out with her thirty thirty. Here in the creek bottom there were a million places for a coyote to hide. As she went out the door, she touched him gently on the forehead and was relieved to find it wasn't any hotter than it should have been.

It was a dark night and she was having trouble seeing in the deep shadows under the trees and knew she'd lost a sheep before she ever caught sight of the offending pack of wild dogs. She was able to get two of them with the first two fast shots and the rest of them took off into the night.

She found the downed sheep and had to shoot it too and came back into camp after moving the three bodies out from the herd to haul off in the morning. She hated it when she lost one of her little herd. It made her feel like such a failure.

She checked on Matt again and then got Horse out and saddled her to spend the balance of the hours of darkness doing slow circles around and among the sheep. She fully expected the coyotes back again before dawn. There was too much cover for them here and it had been too easy the first time. Zeus knew there was a problem as well and stayed out in the midst of the sheep the whole time, which had become completely unlike him.

She was right, and the pack returned in that darkest hour just before dawn. Zeus must have been right there because as soon as she heard the coyotes she heard him growl and tear into them and then she heard the coyotes run off whining and bawling. By the time Taya got there they were long gone and the rest of the night passed uneventfully.

When it was full light, she came in and found Matt had left her a hot breakfast. She was tired enough that it felt like a bigger deal than it was. Zeus came in with a deep cut from his run in in the night and it took her a while to clean it up and patch him back up with bandages. She fed all three dogs and hobbled Horse nearby and gratefully got into the warm water of the shower before collapsing on her little swing. She had changed the sheet that had been covering it, but she could still smell Matt's aftershave as she fell into the sleep of exhaustion. He smelled really nice.

That afternoon she didn't feel that great and by late that night, she had begun praying that she wasn't getting Matt's virus. She had been so careful to keep things clean and sterilize dishes that as she went out among the sheep that night again, she had just about talked herself into believing it was just a summer cold coming on. The desert night air revived her nicely and at dawn she went back in and to bed on the swing, thanking her lucky stars she hadn't gotten it.

It had been a nice theory, and she believed in both the power of prayer, and the power of positive thinking, but it didn't work. She could feel the heat coming up in her and wondered how in the world a fever could make you this cold. She took some Ibuprofen, forced down some lunch and committed that she was not going to slow down Matt's project.

She opened the windows of the trailer and went to go sleep inside thinking that if he didn't see her, he would be able to go off to work not knowing, but in the end it was simply too hot even chilled and she went back out onto the swing. Somewhere along there the fever took hold and she wrapped her comforter around her like a cocoon and tried to fight off the chills with sheer will to no avail.

By mid afternoon she felt awful, and she wasn't aware of much at all by the time he came in. She could hear him like he was a long way away, but not a lot penetrated far into her hazy mind.

Chapter 18

After another full day of first interviewing three people, and hiring one, and then heading back out to work, Matt came back to camp at dark dead tired again. He was surprised that just a few days of being down could make him tire this easily. When he came in, camp was quieter than usual and it took him a second to realize it was the absence of bedded sheep that he wasn't hearing. Taya usually had them in and settled by this time at dusk and he wondered if she had had more trouble with predators today.

He dumped off his pack at his tent and gathered up his gear to shower and headed for her neato rig. The hot water on his tired muscles felt wonderful, and on the way back he was speculating about whether she had had time to even think about making dinner with her coyote troubles and if it would be something he could eat in front of his laptop when he almost walked into Horse in his reverie.

It finally clicked that Taya wasn't out on her horse somewhere with her sheep, and he looked around him to see what was really going on. He could see the white shapes of her herd in more than three different directions and instantly he knew something was definitely wrong.

He called her name out as he tossed his shower stuff back inside his tent and caught up Horse. He headed for her trailer to get her saddle so he could go look for her, and was just slinging it onto Horse's back when he realized Taya was right there beside him on her swing, wrapped up in her big blanket. Even that was weird. It was still eighty degrees out here. He had gotten clear to the swing and started talking to her when it finally dawned on him that she had gotten it. It hit him like an ugly and incriminating lightning bolt. She had been his angel of mercy and he had in turn made her sick with the virus from the devil himself.

Sitting on the swing beside her, he gathered her into his arms and pulled her right up onto his lap. The heat rolled off of her like a furnace and he reached up to feel her scorching forehead and was floored at how hot it was. He knew now what she had meant when she said his fever had scared her. That high of a fever was more than scary. That was the kind of thing that caused brain damage, wasn't it?

Gently, he pulled her out of the quilt and tossed it aside, talking to her as he did so, "Oh, Taya, honey. I'm so sorry. I had no idea." Guiltily, he wondered how long she had been like this. She had seemed okay when he had come in last night, but he hadn't even talked to her, just waved on his way back from the shower. And this morning she had still been out with her herd when he'd left on the helicopter. He tried to think back to how long it had taken for him to be this gone with the fever and realized it was all too hazy. He'd felt so lousy he couldn't truly recall.

He got up and set her down and went into her trailer to find something to bathe her face with, then dug around until he found the plastic tool box that held her medicines. He had no idea if she had taken anything, but he was desperate and gave her both Tylenol and Ibuprofen at the same time. Seeing the scan thermometer, he ran it over her head and felt like throwing up when he understood that it was reading one-hundred-seven degrees.

She needed to go straight into the shower like she had forced him when he'd been so miserable, but he had just drained it before he had realized the shape she was in. It occurred to him to take her to the nearby stream, but first he had to do something with her sheep. The coyotes would have a heyday with them spread all over the county.

Not sure what he was going to do about them, he got on Horse and went in search of her dogs. In the dark the only way he found them was by listening for them as they moved among the sheep. Mimicking what he had heard and seen her do, he whistled and gestured and was absolutely amazed when miraculously the dogs began to bunch the sheep and take them back toward her camp. There was no hope of helping her and guarding them from coyotes at the same time unless they were practically in her fire pit, so that's where he decided to take them and sent the dogs straight back toward her trailer with their charges.

He hurried Horse ahead and jumped down to zip his tent securely closed and gather up his lap top and paperwork. This he took back and set inside her trailer and then mounted Horse once more and went back out to the dogs. It took them forever, but finally Matt thought the herd was gathered enough to head back to Taya. Sheep settling down around him for the night as he rehobbled Horse made him hope he could possibly get through this night without a disaster.

He went back to her and scooped her up off the swing and carried her right to the stream with the cloth from her trailer in his hand. On the bank, he sat down within arms reach of the water and began to gently bath her face and neck and arms with the cool water. He was totally out of his league here and he knew it. He thought about taking her to the hospital, but was afraid they would tell him the same thing the doctor had told her about him and send them home.

He prayed for both inspiration about how to help her and just for her, and almost immediately he thought about calling Zan to come and give her a blessing like he had given him that afternoon. Even though he was calling in the competition to do something he couldn't do himself, he didn't hesitate for a minute. He picked her up and took her back to the swing and went in search of her phone. He finally located it in the fold of the quilt he had thrown aside and found that she had been serious about Zan being her number one speed dial.

Zan didn't pick up at first and Matt was just about to give up in frustration when Zan finally answered, "Hey, pretty girl."

Matt cleared his throat. "Sorry to disappoint you, Zan, but it's Matt. Taya's neighbor in the tent. I'm sorry to bother you. I'm sure you're busy, but I got in from working out in the desert tonight to find Taya in the swing with a fever of a hundred and seven and her sheep in four counties. I've given her some medicine and done the best I could to bring in the sheep, but she needs you to come and give her a blessing. Is that a possibility?"

There was a slight pause and then Zan replied, "Sure, absolutely. Is her trailer still where it was Sunday?"

"Same place, now it just has sheep surrounding it. There have been coyotes around for the last couple of nights so I had the dogs bring them right into camp."

"Okay, I'll be there as soon as I can find some help. Take care of her."

"I'm trying. Thanks, Zan. See ya." Matt closed her phone, grateful Zan would put Taya's well being before his personal dislike of Matt.

For the next hour, Matt rocked her in the swing as he bathed her with a bowl of water. Slowly, her fever came down to one hundred six, but then it seemed to stall, and Matt had absolutely no idea what to do next. Finally at his wit's end he called his mom and told her what was going on and asked her. She recommended he use rubbing alcohol instead of just plain water and even to set her right into the stream water if he had to. As he thanked her and hung up she told him she would be praying for them and he knew she truly would and it helped. He could use a higher power just about now.

He set Taya down and went back into her trailer to look for rubbing alcohol. He hadn't figured out yet where a light was in there so he was using just a flashlight and it took a minute this time.

Back in the swing, the alcohol smelled familiar and he remembered that Taya must have been using it on him this last week while she had been battling the same virus. Now he had a little better idea just what she had been through and he was more grateful than ever. He pulled her long hair back and pushed the sleeves of her t-shirt up and almost splashed the rubbing alcohol on her trying to bring the fire of the fever down even a hair. He didn't think he was winning the battle in the slightest and was amazed at how glad he was to see Zan arrive.

He pulled up and slammed out of the truck followed by another older man from the passenger side. There were no lights lit in camp at all and Matt spoke to them from the swing in the dark.

When they came up, Matt realized the other man must be Joseph. He was the exact image of Zan, only older and much less confrontational. Joseph came straight to her and made a sound deep in his throat when he felt the heat of her skin. "Good heavens! I've never seen a fever like that! How long has she been like this?"

"I don't know. I found her about two hours ago like this when I got off the helicopter. She was still out with the sheep when I left. For two nights, she's been dealing with coyotes, and sleeping days. I've given her all the medicine I dare. When you're through, I'll take her right down into the stream."

The two men placed their hands on her head and gave her a blessing that helped Matt as much as he knew it would help her. Some of that awful feeling of helplessness dissipated with their amens.

Zan immediately went out to check on the sheep and Joseph came with Matt to take her down to the stream bank again. This time instead of wetting a cloth, he set her right into the water, clothes and all and let her sweats and t-shirt become soaked through. After two or three minutes, he picked her back up and took her up to the trailer and put her back on his lap on the swing. He went back to bathing her face with the alcohol and within just a few minutes her fever had come down to just over a hundred-four. Matt breathed a huge sigh of relief when he read the scanner. A hundred-four felt like miles from a hundred-seven.

Joseph went inside her trailer and turned on the light and began digging around, and shortly Matt smelled something cooking. In the mix of things he'd forgotten he was ravenous when he came in. Presently Joseph came back out and pulled up her camp chair and sat there beside them. He began to small talk and then soon got around to asking Matt several pertinent questions about himself and where he was from and his background. Matt had never been more subtly or thoroughly questioned by any father in his life. It was clear that Joseph felt some responsibility for Taya and her physical and emotional well being.

Finally, apparently satisfied that Matt had no intention of harming her, Joseph switched gears and asked Matt why he had called and asked them to come and administer to her.

Matt wasn't sure how to answer that for a few seconds and finally settled for, "I knew she needed a higher power than anything I could come up with. And I knew a blessing was what she would want right now, why?"

Joseph replied, "I just wondered. Zan doesn't think you're LDS. But you must be."

"I'm sorry. I'm not even sure what being LDS means."

"Then you must not be, and Zan was right. Sometimes we call members of the Church of Jesus Christ of Latter Day Saints, LDS. I just meant that you were a member of the church. Some people refer to us as Mormons."

"No, I'm not a member. Although I've been going with her for a few weeks. You're a member too then."

"Yes. It's my greatest treasure. And so are you taking the discussions?"

"I'm sorry, I'm afraid I don't know what that means either."

Joseph was surprised. "You've been going to church for a few weeks and no one has pounced on you about taking the missionary discussions? That's unusual. Did you tell anyone you weren't a member?"

Matt continued to bath her face and arms as he smiled at the use of the word pounce and answered, "Actually, Taya's been trying to fly under the radar. We've been going in late and then leaving early, before anyone can ask us anything."

"I see." Joseph went back into the trailer and stirred whatever it was he was cooking and came back to the door. "Do you happen to know if she has any chili powder?"

"I'm afraid I'm not answering anything right here tonight. I'm sorry, except for chasing a mouse out for her one night; I've never been inside except trying to find her phone and medicines earlier."

"Actually, you answered that exactly right, young man. Now tell me, what is it you're doing out here in the desert?"

Matt smiled at the serene old Indian, and explained what he was doing. When he finished, Joseph said, "I can tell you where there's oil out here. Not that I want them to drill, but it's over south up under that big bluff there."

Again Matt smiled at him. "Maybe you'd be willing to come out and help me sometime. It would be good to have your wisdom around."

"I'll give you some wisdom, Matt. Hang onto that girl on your lap for all you're worth and try not to let Zan and his possessiveness faze you. Oh, and don't tell either one of them I said that."

Matt chuckled right out loud. "Zan does seem disgusted that I'm here at all. Taya handles him though. She doesn't take his guff and then smoothes over his rough feathers without him realizing she's doing it."

Joseph nodded. "She's a born politician, that one. Don't tell her I said that either. How much longer are you going to be working out here?"

"I have to have this thing completely buttoned up by October fifteenth or I lose it all. It's going to take everything I have to make that deadline and then some. Why do you ask?"

"Well, Zan doesn't want you here, but if you weren't, we would have already talked her into going somewhere else. We probably should even with you. She's not safe now that they've figured out she's somewhere around here. And if they find her, they might do anything. Zan and I will stay tonight, and we'll bring in another herder until she's better. But if you can't be with her while she's this ill, let us know so we can make sure she's never left where she can't get away."

Wanting to reassure him, Matt said, "Joseph, my project is up against a hard deadline, but she sat with me night and day while I went through this same thing last week. I'm not going to leave her where someone could come in and hurt her while she's completely out of it."

"Good. See to it you don't. If you have to go somewhere, let us know and we'll come spell you. Do you like chili?"

"I love it."

"Even hot?"

"Especially hot."

"I'll bring you some."

Matt was eating bites of chili between bathing her face. The rubbing alcohol reeked, but he didn't care. It was bringing her fever down and that was all that mattered. Zan came back and Matt asked him to go across and bring back his other chair from near his tent, which he did. The three of them sat eating chili and listening to the sheep.

Eventually Joseph built a fire and then went inside her trailer and apparently went to bed while Zan went out to check on the sheep again. Matt pulled her closer into his arms and tried to untangle her hair and pull it out of her face. He wished he'd brought a pillow, and reached down to pick up her quilt and stuff it behind him to lean against. He took out his phone and set the alarm to go off when it had been four hours, and then leaned his head back and closed his eyes.

Matt didn't know when Zan came in, but when his alarm went off, he saw him crashed on a sleeping bag beside the trailer. Matt tried not to wake either of the men up as he tried to wake Taya, but she was so out of it that he practically had to shout and shake her to get her to respond. He gave her another dose of Ibuprofen and insisted she drink a full glass of milk. She was like an obedient zombie and he wondered if he had been as easy to get to obey as she was. Probably not. She still acted cold, even this feverish and she snuggled right up against him before she went back to sleep. He was chilled because of her wet clothes and it made him feel guilty that her fever actually felt good against him.

This time he set the alarm for only two hours and got up and gave her Tylenol for this round and then continued to bath her face again with the alcohol. Her fever was over one-hundred-three and to him that was still far too hot but he wasn't sure what else to do about it. When it went back up to one-hundred-four, he picked her up and grabbed a towel and took her to the shower. It took a few minutes to revive her enough that she understood what he wanted, but she finally seemed to. He left her and went to grab the chair she had put in for him and came back to hand it to her, but she was already in and out. She seemed to understand that she needed to cool off and had stood under the shower fully clothed.

He wrapped the towel around her wet clothes and led her back to the swing. This time he laid it out flat and let her lie down on it and covered her loosely with the quilt. He stayed with her until she was back to sleep and then went back to his tent for another hour and fifteen minutes until the alarm went off again.

After another round of Ibuprofen she seemed to be doing better. The fever was down to one-oh-two and she was more with it this time when he roused her to take the medicine. She actually looked right at him and thanked him. She patted his cheek with a gentle hand and told him to go back to bed, that she would be fine. He didn't doubt that. She was the toughest woman he'd ever known. Only his mother came even close to comparing with her. The sun was going to be coming up before the alarm went off again and he sat back on the swing and gathered her onto his lap again to hold her until it did. It seemed to help her. She snuggled up against him and went right back to sleep.

The sun in his face didn't even wake him and when the alarm went off at six-thirty Matt wanted to keep on sleeping. He got up and gave her some more medicine and made sure his three helpers headed out on the chopper. Hopefully the two who had been here helping would continue to progress with the new guy like they had. He had them plan to work without him for at least the next couple of days. Zan and Joseph had the sheep under control, so Matt took her temperature again and went back to bed for another hour and some.

At eight thirty her temperature had gone up again and Matt woke her and helped her get to the shower. She took a change of clothes this time and a gear bag that must have contained her toiletries, because when she emerged ten minutes later, her hair smelled like fruit again. She was still incredibly sick and collapsed onto her swing in a limp heap with her old clothes and toiletries beside her. Matt took her things and got a hair brush and elastic out and put the rest of them just inside her trailer door and then sat on the swing beside her to help her comb her long dark hair out before it dried in a tangle. Once it was relatively snarl free, he had her sit up just long enough to pull it into a rough braid that he caught with the elastic, and then let her lay back down.

The shower and the medicine helped and by the time Zan and Joseph pulled out at nine-forty-five she was only at one-hundred-two point three again. Matt brought his sleeping bag and pad over to the trailer and tossed it out on the ground in the sliver of shade from the sheet that was still draped over her swing and stretched out to wait until her next dose at ten-thirty. He'd only been at this for just over twelve hours and already he was tired. She'd taken care of him alone for more than four days, and she had had her sheep to care for on top of everything else.

It was no wonder Zan had teased her about looking awful. He felt guilty knowing that her taking such good care of him was probably what had made her get it as well. At least he knew what to expect and could work to make her as comfortable as possible.

When his alarm went off, he got up and got her medicine and tried to get her to eat something. She didn't really want anything and finally he just began to poke a banana in and she automatically kept taking bites. The fever was creeping back up and he sat with her again to bathe her face and neck and arms with the nasty smelling alcohol mixture. Once it was somewhat lower, he gathered her up onto his lap again and began to gently, but firmly rub her low back. He assumed her whole body was aching the way his had and when she smiled tiredly and thanked him, he knew he'd been right.

The fever had made his head pound and his body ache all over and he had alternated between freezing and roasting, so he assumed she was the same and rubbed her head where it lay on his lap that afternoon. Then, he turned her over and rubbed her back again and then pulled her back up into his arms when she was cold. He napped between doses when she did and toward evening he got up and made real food for her.

Another herder showed up to take over for her for a few days and Matt was glad to not have to worry about her sheep the whole time. He got her to eat better with her medicine and then he thought she had gone right back to sleep until she opened her cloudy blue eyes and asked him if he would play for her for a little while. He went back to his camp and got his guitar and came to sit in a camp chair beside her with it. He began to play and he could almost see her relax with the music. The guitar even seemed to help her body fight the fever and it stayed at under one-oh-two until her next dose.

Either his alarm didn't go off, or he slept through it and missed a dose late in the night. When he awoke she was searingly hot again. The thermometer showed over one-hundred-six, and Matt felt terrible. He carried her to the shower and actually had to help her to stand there under the water. He just let it soak her clothes again and then took her back to the swing and spent the rest of the night working to get the fever back down. It felt like a task that couldn't be accomplished no matter what he did, until finally just as the sun began to brighten the sky in the east it eased.

The helicopter picked his guys up clear up by the highway, and Matt had no idea where the Indian with the sheep had gone. He gave her another dose of medicine and gratefully stretched out on his bag to get as much sleep as he could before she needed him again. Several times as he napped he reached up to touch her hand and make sure her fever hadn't shot back up, and when the alarm went off, he got up and gave her some Tylenol and it hardly even woke her up. He decided to let her sleep until the next dose before making her eat something, and went back to sleep himself.

He was back in the swing with her that afternoon, bathing her face and rubbing her back to try to help with the ache he knew she was fighting. As he rubbed her she sighed and leaned right into him and a few minutes later he knew she had gone to sleep again. He pulled her up into his arms and gently rocked the swing from time to time.

In a way, he hated the fact that she was so terribly sick and miserable, and in a way, he loved the fact that he could hold her and help her feel better. Holding her like this was a wake up call for him. He'd known she was fascinating from the first, but he'd thought it was just the intrigue of this whole situation. He didn't truly think he would come to like her even as beautiful as she was. But he hadn't figured on how that one little kiss when he was so sick would make him feel. It had only been a gentle, almost motherly kiss like she would have given a sick baby, but it had felt wonderful to be cared for that way.

And holding her now on his lap was incredibly nice. Right now she wasn't the sharp, brave, competent friend she'd been. She was just a sick, helpless, sweet girl who needed him to be there to take care of her, and it made him feel like a white knight. A knight who had just been taken care of by the damsel of course, but holding her and helping her felt so right.

Getting to know her had been like peeling back the layers on a flower. She was so much more than she appeared on the surface, but then at that she was refreshingly simple. He knew from her background that she must have been used to a life of relative luxury, but she dealt with the primitive life here like she was born to it and she never complained no matter how inconvenient things got. And now when she was so sick, she was still sweet and patient and grateful.

He had never known a woman who was this beautiful to be unselfish and hard working. Actually, he had never known a woman this beautiful at all. She was exquisite physically, and the more he got to know her the more he realized she was that way to the core. There was nothing superficial or fake about her. How in the world had her congressman not recognized how precious she was and guarded her rather than harming her?

Matt knew he wasn't worthy of her, but the last two days had made his feelings for her very clear, and he was going to do everything he could to somehow get to where he was worthy of her. It might take him years, but maybe she would be patient enough to wait for him. At least he was going to give it his best shot. He did recognize how precious she was and he was going hang on to her just like Joseph had suggested, if she'd let him.

Zeus came up to them and sniffed at her for about the thousandth time. Matt leaned to pet his curly, white head. "Did you finally figure out that we're on the same team here, buddy? I want to watch over her too, ya know." Zeus wagged his tail and flopped down in front of the swing. He seemed to know she was gravely ill. Matt cuddled her to him again. He was going to have to work his tail off when she was on her feet to make headway on his contract, but he wouldn't have traded being able to hold her for anything.

Three times over the next couple of days when he was at his wits end, she asked him to play for her and it helped her to rest easier. Something in the music strengthened her body or her will or he wasn't even sure what. He just knew his music was helping her to fight this thing.

Zan and Joseph came back to check on her again and then Zan called her phone everyday to see how she was.

Chapter 19

On the fifth day the fever didn't show any signs of letting up and Matt wondered again if he should take her in to the doctor. She looked like a ghost of her usual self. She was so pale and had lost weight and he felt like a total failure as a care giver as he carried her back to the shower when the fever spiked again.

He had just about decided to run her in to town to see someone when he got a call on his cell phone. He looked down at it almost in a stupor he was so tired. It was his mother's cell number and he answered it gladly. Her voice was exactly what he needed to hear right now. He was even more grateful for such a wonderful mom when he understood that she was calling from just down the road at the motel and wanted directions to his camp. He told her how to get there and was basically given a new lease on life when she pulled over the hill in her dusty Trailblazer.

The sun felt like it started to shine brighter as she got out and walked over to him. She'd called him a couple of times that week, so she knew what he'd been up against to a certain extent, but she was still dismayed when she felt the heat of Taya's head. "Poor girl. Has she been this bad the whole time?"

"This bad or worse. Hi, Mom." He hugged her. "I've never been as glad to see someone as I am to see you right now. I'm just wondering if I should take her in to a doctor. She hauled me in and they told her it was viral and that there was nothing they could do except try to keep the fever down.

Jaclyn M. Hawkes

I've been giving her the medicines every two hours like they said, and it does bring it down some, but I'm so worried about her. My fever broke on the fourth day, but we're going on the fifth here with no change."

Taya opened her eyes at the sound of his voice and looked up at him and around blankly. Matt tried to introduce his mom to her, but she was still pretty out of it. He turned back to his mom. "And, Mom, I'd like you to meet Taya Kaye. You can't tell it right now, but she's the most beautiful and nicest girl I've ever met in my life. You're going to love her. If we can get her better that is. At this point I'm pretty much a failure at that."

Taya opened her eyes again and said tiredly, "You've been wonderful, Matt. I'm fine. It's not like you to be negative."

She closed her eyes again, and Matt looked up at his mom with a grin. "See what I mean?"

Sue Maylon raised her eyebrows. "Yes, I believe I do." She rolled up her sleeves. "I brought real food. What else can I do to help you?"

"Honestly, just let me sleep for more than two hours at a shot and I'll be a new man."

"All right, I'm good with that. Uh, but am I safe or is that dog going to eat me if I touch her?"

Matt looked over at Zeus. "That's a good question. Come, Zeus." The dog obediently padded over to him and Matt petted his head and then stood up and hugged his mom. Zeus came over and sniffed at her. When she leaned down to pet him, he wagged his tail Matt said, "He likes you. It took me days to be able to make friends with him. Days and several steak bones. He's actually wonderful. He watches over her like a canine secret service agent. He makes me feel a lot better knowing he's around. Remind me when I get up to tell you what's going on with her."

He nodded at Taya. "But in the mean time just know that if you see anyone coming get me up immediately. She needs Ibuprofen and enough food that it won't make her sick at four o'clock. In the mean time. Make your self at home. It's a little rough right now, but it's peaceful."

Matt rolled off the swing to stretch out on his sleeping bag that he'd never moved from beside the trailer and was asleep within less than a minute.

****

Sue leaned and felt Taya's forehead again, and then seeing the scan thermometer there she took her temperature. One-hundred-three point five. She shook her head. This was a nasty virus. Matt looked terrible and he looked great compared to this poor girl, although even sick she was amazingly pretty. Sue didn't think she'd ever heard Matt talk about a girl the way he just had.

She went around camp straightening and picking up. She ventured into Taya's trailer and straightened it too and washed the dishes that had piled up, after adding a few drops of bleach she found to the wash water to hopefully stop the spread of the bug. She looked around the trailer as she worked. From the outside it just looked like a sheepherder's trailer. Inside it looked like a miniature office. There was a laptop and a cell phone on the table and an oversized printer on the top bunk with rolls and rolls of paper and what looked like house plans piled nearby with a stack of card board mailing tubes.

Matt hadn't said much about this girl, but this was not what Sue had expected. For some reason, she had been expecting a Native American girl who was maybe a bit socially backward. Even deathly ill this girl wasn't a bit backward. Sue sighed, hoping he hadn't gone from living with one girl to living with another, but even she would have to admit that the beauty lying out there with the raging fever would be hard to resist.

****

Taya knew that whoever was trying to wake her wasn't Matt and it made her almost afraid for a moment until she was able to wake up enough to realize that no, it wasn't Matt, but it had to be his mother. She looked amazingly like him, just older and female. Her voice and her touch were gentle as she encouraged Taya to wake up and take some more medicine. Taya took it gratefully and then pulled herself to sit upright and eat the plate of food she was handed. It was some kind of casserole and it was hot and homemade and she thought she had gone to heaven.

She knew his mom was watching her but she honestly didn't have the energy to visit right now. Silently, she worked her way through the whole plate before she decided she was going to get up and shower. Matt had made her get wet to try to cool her down several times in the last few days, but now she just wanted to wash her hair and brush her teeth.

Matt's mom took her plate and she struggled to her feet and pulled herself into the trailer to find some clean clothes and her shower bag. Back outside, she felt like she had had too much to drink as she walked to the shower for the first time without help in days. She tripped over a branch of a sage brush and almost went down on her face, and decided she'd better take it easier.

The shower felt wonderful, but she must have been moving slow because she almost ran out of water before she had her hair rinsed all the way. Clean felt better and she wended her way back to the swing wondering if she was finally maybe going to kick this thing. She sat in the swing and combed her hair out and French braided it wet.

Matt had been so good to help her with it while she felt so awful. He must have known it was uncomfortable to have it tangled around her when she was laying there. He had been so sweet to her the whole time. She set her brush aside and lay back down and dangled one arm over the side of the swing to rest on his shoulder as he slept there below her. The days had all run together in the muddle of her fever and dreams, but he had been there for her the whole time, through it all. Even in the deepest feverish stupors she had known he was there with her.

He was incredibly reassuring. He always had been. She didn't think she wanted him to go away at the end of this summer.

****

Sue had been over to straighten up Matt's tent and she checked out their shower set up. She had no idea how it worked, but Taya had gone into it a mess and came out looking clean. Walking back over to the trailer, she saw the two of them laying there with Taya's hand on Matt's shoulder. She prayed for him everyday and part of that prayer was that he would find the right girl. It would be interesting to hear what Matt was going to tell her about Taya when he got up.

She let him sleep until eight o'clock, and then woke him because she worried he wouldn't sleep that night if he didn't get up. He made such a big deal of her cooking that she wished she had brought more of something else for the next day. These two must have had a rough couple of weeks. He sat up and leaned back against the swing as he ate and finally he began to tell her about what Taya had been through and was still dealing with. He ended with, "Hopefully, when the trial's through in October and the election is over in November, she'll be safe again and will be able to have her life back. Although, I'm going to try to talk her into staying out here somewhere if I can."

Sue didn't want to offend him, but she felt like she needed to voice her concerns. "Matt, honey. You didn't jump out of the frying pan with Stacy and into the fire with this girl, did you?"

He looked at her. "What do you mean, Mom?" She saw what she was asking dawn on him. "Oh, heavens no, Mother. Taya would never live like that. I'm sure the only reason she even let me come here was because she was afraid and knew she could trust me. She's a nice girl, Mom. She's been taking me to church with her for weeks now."

Sue perked right up at this and he continued, "You're probably not going to be very happy to know that I've been going to a Mormon church with her. But it's helped me, and I've grown to love it. She's been wonderful for me. She has a way of encouraging me that I don't think she even realizes she does, but she makes me feel like I'm capable of anything. I've never been around another girl or even another person, other than you maybe, who makes me such a better person just by being with them. She does that for me. I wish I deserved to be with her. I'd be around her forever if I could."

"Why would you not deserve to be with her?"

"She knows about Stacy. In fact, she met Stacy one day, but I haven't told her yet that I was living with her. She's a much better person than that."

"Aren't Mormons Christian? Doesn't she believe in forgiveness and God's grace?"

"Yes, they're Christian. And I'm sure they believe in forgiveness and grace, but she's still a much better person than me."

Taya groaned behind his head and opened her eyes and said, "Oh, Matt, for heaven's sake. You're being ridiculous." She closed her eyes again and rolled over, but a few seconds later she rolled back and draped one arm down on his neck. He looked a bit startled and Sue smiled as she ate her dinner.

****

Matt tried to get his mom to go back to the hotel and get a room saying that the conditions here were too rough for her. Sue just put her hands on her hips and said, "Matthew

Maylon, I have lived in hunting camps from here to Africa with your father over the years. Why in the world would you think I couldn't handle a sheep camp?"

She got in the back of her SUV and pulled a sleeping bag out and Matt insisted, "Then at least go in and sleep on her bed, Mom. She'll be horrified when she gets better if she finds out you slept out in a tent or on the ground. Take her sheets off first so you don't get this and then crash on her bed."

"I'll take you up on that. She probably wouldn't mind if you slept on the other one instead of there on the ground."

"I'll be fine here where I can keep an eye on her. Plus it would be a pain to move her big printer."

"What's the printer for, dare I ask?"

"She's a structural engineer and works on plans at night and she has to print one or two copies out so she can stamp them before she ships them back to her partner."

"A beauty queen structural engineer who was engaged to a senator and is now a nomadic sheepherder?"

"Congressman, not senator."

"Oh, my mistake. That's not my point. Where in the world did you find this girl?"

He smiled, remembering. "The beautiful sheep princess found me. One day out there in the desert, I had just come to the last dead end that my discouragement could handle and had decided to give up and go home and take a huge loss, and out of the sagebrush came this beautiful girl and a herd of sheep and a dog that wanted to have me for lunch. She showed me how to get across the canyon I was stuck at and she's pretty much showed me how to move forward with my whole life since then.

"She's the one who talked me into going to renegotiate the contract. She helped me find some guys to work with, and honestly, she's probably the impetus that had me going home to either patch it up with Stacy or get away from her.

And I hadn't even met her at that time. I'd only seen her across the desert."

"Where is her family?"

"Her parents still live in D.C., but she doesn't have anything to do with them. They were there the night her fiancé hurt her and left her laying on the floor bleeding while they went with the fiancé to his fundraiser dinner."

"That's awful!"

Sadly, he nodded in agreement. "It is. It still makes her cry every time. And even sadder is the fact that they don't realize what a price they paid when they did that to her. She's an extraordinary person, and they didn't even realize it."

Sue looked at him. "You truly like this girl."

Guiltily, he admitted, "I do. A lot. I wish I deserved her."

"Matt, you keep acting like you're this terrible person who is hopelessly lost. Don't you realize that when you talk like that you're insinuating that the Savior's atonement is trivial?" He looked at her as he thought about that. "Matt, everyone makes mistakes. Even that beautiful girl over there has made mistakes. Jesus knew we'd screw up sometimes. That's why He gave his very life. To help us right the wrongs and move on. It's not some trivial little thing that can only handle minimal sins. The atonement is for everyone and every problem if we'll just honestly try to change our ways."

She smiled and pointed a motherly index finger at him. "It even applies to you, hon. No matter what terrible, awful, very bad things you seem to think you've done. Repent and make it right and get it over with and move on. You have your whole life ahead of you, leave the heavy baggage behind and go out there and reach your potential. You're a very good man, Matt Maylon. Don't let some stupid girl with fake nails and bleached hair trip you up. Admit you made a mistake and get past it to the great future that's ahead of you.

"You and I both know what you're capable of, Matt. It sounds like maybe even she does too." She nodded at Taya. "Don't let the garbage that goes on in this world make you lose sight of your goals and dreams. Stuff does happen. Go around it, go over it, tunnel under it, go right through it if you have to, but get past it and move on. There's greatness waiting on the other side."

She smiled and lightened up. "Now, enough from your mother. I'm going to bed. Wake me if you need me."

"G'night, Mom. Thank you. I love you."

Matt still sat leaning against the swing with his legs stretched out in front of him, thinking about what his mother had just said to him. He was startled again when Taya rolled over and put her arm around his neck, and mumbled, "You have an incredibly wise mother." Then she went back to sleep.

****

He knew when she leaned her head over the edge of the swing at dawn the next morning to look down at him with clear, blue eyes, that they had made it. He reached up to feel her head and let out a long sigh. "Hey, Taya, long time no see."

"Thank you for helping me get through. How many days has it been?"

"Today's the sixth."

"Did I ruin your project?"

"No, you didn't ruin my project. How do you feel?"

"Like I've been through the fires of hell and back. But I also feel like I've been well taken care of. Thank you."

"You're very welcome. It was only honorable. You did the same for me."

She rolled over on her back. "I dreamed that your mother came, and she gave you this most amazing little talking to. I wish I could remember what she said exactly so I could write it down. It was incredible."

Just then Sue walked out of the trailer door and Taya jumped and turned to look at her and then back at Matt with wide eyes. He sat up and smiled at her and said, "I did write it down. I'll give you a copy some time. You were a little out of it the first time I introduced you. Taya, I'd like you to meet my mom, Sue Maylon. Mom, you remember Taya from yesterday."

Taya sat up slowly and extended her hand. "I thought I dreamed you. It's nice to meet you."

"And it's nice to meet you again. I think you'll remember this time. You look better. How do you feel?"

"Fine, thank you."

Matt looked up at Taya, shook his head, smiled and said, "You'll learn never to lie to my mother. She knows every time. You might as well be honest."

Taya turned back to his mom looking slightly embarrassed and said, "Okay, maybe not fine, but better. Much better, thank you."

"Would you like something to eat?"

"Actually, yes. I'm honestly hungry for once."

"Do you want to sit at the table? Or should I just give it to you there in the swing?"

"Let's sit at the table." She pulled herself to a sitting position and put a hand to her head and sighed, "Ah, I'm light headed."

Matt got up and moved his bedding out of the way and gave her a hand with a smile. "Are you telling me that this fever made you an airhead?"

She gave a tired laugh. "I think maybe it has." He seated her at the little table and she said, "Thanks."

Sue came out with the pan of scrangled eggs and a hot pad to set it on, and Taya exclaimed, "Oh, I remember these eggs. Mrs. Maylon this is the best breakfast I've ever eaten in my life."

She smiled, but said, "You haven't even had a bite yet. How do you know?"

"Matt shared some with me that you sent before."

"Well, I'm glad you enjoyed it. Shall I pray?"

"Yes, please." Sue asked a simple blessing on the food and added a request for Taya to continue feeling better.

When she was through and was dishing up the food, Matt asked her, "What are your plans, Mom? How long can we keep you?"

"I'll stay through the day today and then probably head home this evening. Why?"

"I just wondered. Would you think I was rude if I went to work today? I was behind before either one of us got sick."

"No, of course not. I knew you needed some help, that's why I came out in the first place. You head out and I'll stay here and watch over Taya for you."

Taya volunteered, "You're welcome to stay, but today I think I'm with it enough to take my own medicine and watch myself if I need to. You can go help Matt if you want."

Matt shook his head. "No, Taya. You need her and she's not going out in the heat to carry a heavy pack anyway." He raised his hand at his mom. "I'm not saying you couldn't handle it, Mom. I'm just saying I'm not going to let you. Stay and visit and feed her. I'm afraid I didn't do so hot and she's lost weight on my watch that she couldn't really spare."

Taya looked at him, questioning, "Are you saying I'm too skinny?"

Matt looked at them both and then grinned and said, "I'm not even gonna touch that one. I've buried myself already. Just be as healthy as you can today, okay? I'll see you this afternoon. I'll come in early."

A few minutes later when he came back dressed to go with his pack, he kissed his mom and wished he could lean down and kiss Taya too. "Keep that fever down. Deal?" He grabbed her hand as he went past.

"Deal."

Jaclyn M. Hawkes

Chapter 20

When he was gone, Taya went to the shower again and hoped that she washed away the last of the fever. She felt immensely better. Now she was just achy and drained. She left her dirty clothes in a pile at her feet and sat back down on her swing to tackle her hair. She wished Matt could have been here to help her. Having him do her hair had been the ultimate act of service.

Something had happened to their relationship over the last week or two of this flu. They had pulled together so hard out of necessity that they were now tight friends. Those hours of serving and being served had bonded them somehow. Before the fevers they hadn't touched each other, now that touch was absolutely natural. She missed him ridiculously today.

Sue spent a while in the trailer working and Taya just stayed on the swing. When she was through combing her hair out and had it braided, she laid back down again. She just wanted to rest for a minute before she got up and found out what had happened to her whole herd of sheep and checked to see how behind she was in her engineering. Joshua was probably going to want to murder her. She hadn't done much in most of two weeks.

When she felt Sue gently waking her to give her some more Tylenol she was surprised. She hadn't intended to go to sleep. Her fever was back some and she took the medicine gratefully and lay back down. It was so nice to be mothered like this. It had been a long time since her mom had done things like this for her. She tried unsuccessfully not to cry as she went back to sleep. Twice more that afternoon Sue roused her to give her medicine and something to eat. The second time she tried to stay awake to talk to her because she didn't want her to think she was being rude, but she was struggling and Sue acknowledged it and encouraged her to go back to sleep.

It was Matt who woke her in the early evening to be dosed and have something to eat. He sat down on the swing with her and automatically pulled her up onto his lap and began to rub her low back where it ached so badly. She wished he would have told her he'd ached like this. She could have rubbed his aches out too if she'd known. His mom came out and sat in the chair with them and talked to him while he rubbed her. After a minute or two Taya just lay against his chest and went back to sleep and he had to wake her up again to hand her a plate of dinner. She didn't even make it through a third of it before she fell asleep almost into her mashed potatoes.

Hours later it seemed, she woke up and found that his mother had left and asked him if he would tell Taya goodbye for her. She was on Matt's lap on the swing in the darkness slowly rocking occasionally. It was the most peaceful feeling she had ever known and she didn't want to move once she was awake. She put a hand on his arm and asked, "Tell me about the rest of your family."

With his soft, mellow, South Texas drawl, he mused, "My family. My dad is a career hunting guide who started in Colorado, went to Africa for a year or two before they had kids and then Texas for seventeen years, and then back to where he and Mom grew up near Steamboat Springs. They live on a hunting preserve that you have to go through a series of locked gates to get into and out of, that backs up onto the national forest. They're seriously secluded most of the time except in the fall when there are hunters staying there.

"Both sets of my grandparents live nearby and about a thousand cousins and aunts and uncles. Family parties are a little crazy.

"I have an older brother, Peter, who farms near there. He's married and has two kids. And I have a younger brother and sister who are twins. Andrew and Elizabeth. Drew is still single and is a deputy county sheriff and lives in one of the cabins on my parents' compound, and Elizabeth is married to a surgeon and lives in Steamboat with her two kids. They're all nice, respectable people and we're close compared to some families. I was the rebel of the bunch unfortunately. I had one friend who I let talk me into a few stupid stunts that probably aged my mom more than all the rest of the kids put together."

In a sleepy voice, she said, "Peter, Matthew, Andrew and Elizabeth. They sound like nice Christian names."

"My parents are nice, Christian people. Now I just wish I was still a nice, Christian son."

"Matt, look back at the last week of your life. You've been like the Christian poster boy haven't you? I wish you'd lay off with the negative self talk. That's just what Satan wants you to tell yourself, but it's the opposite of what Jesus wants you to tell yourself."

He sighed. "There are some things you don't know about me, Taya. I've made some incredibly stupid decisions in my life. I told you Stacy was my girlfriend, but I didn't tell you I'd been living with her when I found her in bed with Justin. It wasn't like we were having a torrid affair. But she was living there."

She turned in his arms to look at him. "So you completely fell off the wagon. No one's perfect, Matt. Just don't lay there and wallow. Get back on. Leave it behind like your mom recommended and move on. I've only known you a few weeks, but even in that short time, I've come to know you're a good man. You're honest and hardworking and kind. And you have a wonderful spirit about you."

Her voice softened, "God is disappointed with us when we make poor choices, but He doesn't love us any less. He's just patiently waiting for us to figure things out and come back to Him. So you blew it with Stacy. Which is a big deal. Physical intimacy is supposed to be sacred, and only between a husband and wife. It's a vital part of marriage, but destructive outside of it, which I'm sure you figured out. In God's eyes sexual sins are extremely serious because they defile the power God has given us to create life. But they can be overcome through Christ's atonement. That's the key."

She reached and put a gentle hand on his arm. "Repent and leave that baggage behind and get on to the greatness that your mom mentioned is waiting. That's why God gave us his Son. To find our way back. If you were a bad person who was constantly screwing up and had no interest in doing what's right that would be one thing. But you're a wonderful person, so don't sell yourself short. Just make it right and get past it."

"That's easy for you to say, Taya. But you don't know how hard it is to face God again when you know you've blown it big time."

She groaned and rolled back into his arms and buried her face in his neck. "Oh, Matt. I only wish that were true. I was a hard headed, rebellious politician's daughter growing up in Washington, D.C. I wasn't even introduced to the church until I was seventeen. I'm not going to tell you all the mistakes I made because I've honestly done my best to leave them behind and try to do what I know is right, but please don't put me on some kind of pedestal because I don't belong there. I have way more than my fair share of mistakes in the past.

"And I'm sure I'll mess up a lot more before I end up, but I truly know that you can put stuff behind you and be as white as snow again like it talks about in the scriptures. And it's the best feeling. Don't put it off. Carrying around baggage is like putting rocks in your backpack. It makes the journey hard and it's pointless. Taking care of the rocks is the best feeling in the world. Just get it over with and commit to doing better from here on out. I have a great book about repentance and forgiveness. I'll lend it to you if you'd like."

Answering in his mellow Texas accent, he said, "I'll take you up on that. You make it all sound so easy. It doesn't feel like it's going to be easy."

Her voice was gentle when she continued, "It's not easy, Matt. But God is a loving Father. He wants the best for us and He knows what's in our hearts. He wants us to be happy and reach our potential. We can't do either one with unresolved problems weighing us down. But just the feeling of being on track and knowing that you're working in the right direction for the eternities is wonderful. Do it sooner than later. You'll be glad you did. You'll be happier."

He rubbed a hand down her achy back, and asked quietly, "I don't know, Taya. Does it get any happier than this?"

After a second, she let out a long breath against his neck. "It can't get a whole lot better can it?"

At length, he went on quietly, "As hard as I'm working to finish this contract, I've been incredibly content here with you and your sheep."

She looked up at him in the moonlight and wondered what she was going to do about the way she was beginning to feel about him. He looked back down at her and she knew he must have been thinking the same thing about her because he glanced at her mouth and then said softly with his gentle southern drawl, "Taya, we have a problem. I keep having the urge to kiss you tonight."

She didn't say anything, just looked at him. How did you answer something like that? Especially when she truly wanted him to. A few minutes later, she quietly asked, "Is that a good problem or bad?"

He smiled his mellow smile. "I don't know."

Still in a soft, sleepy voice, she went on, "Kissing me would probably really change our friendship, wouldn't it?"

"Probably."

"Mmm. But, it might be nice."

He smiled again and nodded in agreement. "Definitely."

"But it might not be very wise. We still need to be able to live out here alone comfortably."

"We do."

She paused and then quietly admitted, "But I would really like to you to."

He gently rubbed down her back again. "You might regret that later when you don't have a fever that muddles your brain."

"That's true, but I might also regret not doing it."

After another pause, he said, "Yeah, I guess there's that."

She was so tired. She snuggled down into his arms more and yawned. "I'm going to finish thinking later, when I'm not so perfectly comfortable. Okay?"

He leaned his cheek on her hair and whispered, "Okay."

Some time later, when she woke up again, she laid there in his arms for several minutes before she whispered, "What did you ever decide about kissing me?"

He gently smoothed back her hair. "Uh, that I'd better not run the risk of missing it and regretting it for the rest of forever."

Still snuggled against him, finally, she simply said, "Oh."

"Why do you ask?"

She hid her face against his chest. "Just wondered."

He gave a low, quiet chuckle and began to stroke the

little bone behind her ear with his thumb. "Give me two more minutes of holding you like this and I'll go back to my tent."

"Three minutes."

She could hear him smile in the dark. "Three it is."

It was more like eight before he gently pushed her off his lap so he could get up to go. She reached for his hand and he pulled her up to stand beside him. As she looked up at him in the moonlight, he put both arms around her to hug her to him. She hugged him back and didn't want to let go.

Finally, he leaned down and gently kissed the pink scar above her eyebrow. He pulled back and they looked at each other for a few seconds and then he kissed her one lingering tender kiss on the mouth. "Good night, Taya. Sleep well. Don't forget to take some more Tylenol before you lay back down."

When he was gone, she stood there in the dark for a few minutes before going to get her medicine. She put her fingertips to her lips and then gently touched the scar he had kissed. She had never felt so valuable in her life. It was weird to think of it that way, but that's how he made her feel. That one little kiss had told her more than he could have in an hour. Not only did she never have to be afraid of him, but she knew he would protect her from anything that would harm her if he could.

She took the medicine and lay back down to look up at the stars. When he started to play his guitar, she smiled into the darkness. How did he know that that would be the perfect ending to this night? He played a mellow Allen Jackson song that had been written about the nine eleven attacks. The lyrics were something about just being a singer of simple songs, and ended with how the greatest thing we could learn from the Savior was love. It was perfect for this night.

Matt was the antithesis of the power hungry, flashy politician. He truly was a singer of simple songs. That fit him just the way his long faded jeans and shirts with the sleeves cut out fit him. His quiet, gentle confidence completely negated any need for loud or ostentatious displays of power. He was strong enough to be gentle and no one on earth would question whether he was powerful. It emanated from him like an aura, but was so understated that it didn't draw attention. Laying on his chest tonight had been the purest taste of heaven.

Chapter 21

He was up and gone with the dawn again and Taya began to pick up the pieces of her life. She spent the morning getting ready to move the trailer, figuring out a grocery list and gathering up her laundry and linens. She went and gathered up Matt's laundry bag and sleeping bag and pillow too. She was going to do her best to not let this virus affect anyone else if she could help it.

She called Zan and found out where her sheep were and had him make arrangements to have the other herder bring them toward where she would move the trailer to that afternoon. He talked her into letting the other herder stay on until the next morning so she could have the night to rest up. She was still drained and took a short nap and then went into town and did wash and shopped and sent a shipment off to Joshua via the FBI. By five o'clock that afternoon, she had camp set back up and real food cooking and was tired and looking forward to seeing Matt before she went down to bed. He had been on her mind nonstop all day.

She'd been back and forth between thinking how nice it was to like someone this much and worrying about the fact that he wasn't a member of the church. Zan had tried to warn her, but she truly hadn't thought she would end up feeling like this about Matt. Zan had been right, too, about the fact that her feelings were stronger for him than any other guys she had liked over the years.

In a way it was encouraging in that for the first time in her life, she honestly wondered if she could be falling in love, but then she had to wonder why she'd finally fallen for someone who didn't even share her faith. She'd start to give herself the why did you do this stupid thing talk and then she'd pull herself up short with the reminder that she had honestly felt like this was what she was supposed to be doing. Both the sheep herding and asking Matt to camp near her. With that in mind, she decided she had better figure out what the Lord had in mind for her as far as Matt was concerned before she let herself like him any more than she already did.

When he came back to camp at dark, tired and dirty but as attractive as ever, she began to understand that controlling her feelings might be more of a trick than she had bargained for.

She had eaten and had set him aside a plate and was working on her laptop on the outside table when he came through on his way out of the shower. She'd wondered all day if it would be uncomfortable when she finally saw him after kissing him last night, but she should have realized their friendship would stay as easy as it had always been. He came up to her and very first thing put a gentle hand to her forehead to check on the fever. "Hey, you. How have you felt today?"

She stood up and turned to him and felt more comfortable than ever when he stood close enough to her that she could smell his shampoo. "Good, thanks. I'm still tired, but I got a lot done. How did you do? Have you got enough help, or do you still need more guys?"

He put an arm around her and kneaded the muscles at the top of her shoulder. "I think I'm good. I'm going to go over things more in depth tonight and take stock. Did Zan help you move, or did you do all of this yourself?"

"I did it myself, but I still have no sheep so I had all day. I put some clean clothes just inside your tent and put some bread and milk and eggs in your cooler. And brought you some more water. I hope you don't mind. I washed your sleeping bag and pillow. I'm hoping to have the virus stop here."

He hugged her with one arm. "That was good thinking. I know I'm busy, but you don't need to do my stuff. Especially not when you're sick, but thank you."

"It's the least I could do since I put your project so far behind schedule, Matt. Plus it only takes a second longer than just doing mine. You're not allergic to any certain detergent or anything are you?"

He shook his head. "Not a thing. When are the sheep coming home?"

"Tomorrow morning." She hesitated, a little embarrassed. "I really missed them today. How silly is that?"

"I don't think it's silly." He smiled. "I think it's cute. I'll bet Zeus is going crazy trying to figure out how to guard you and the sheep at the same time when you're in two different places."

"If in doubt he chooses me. It's very endearing."

His eyes met hers. "He's just incredibly wise. He knows you are infinitely more valuable than sheep. I'm glad you have him, especially now that he's finally decided to completely trust me. Somehow I think he understood you were sick and that I was trying to help you."

She glanced away for a moment. "I'm sure he did. That's a good thing. If he hadn't, that could have been a problem."

"He's smart enough that he may have figured out how to help you all by himself."

She was quiet for a second and then looked back up and softly said, "I thought about what would have happened to me if you hadn't been here. I'm so grateful for you."

Meeting her eyes again, he agreed, "It would have been awful without each other, wouldn't it?" At length he finally looked away and asked, "Is this for me?" He indicated the plate.

"Yes. It's probably gotten cold. Sorry. Maybe we need to add a microwave to our shower set up."

"No." He shook his head. "I'd rather eat cold food than be that high tech out here. It keeps us simple. I don't think there's any such thing as a microwave in the desert."

"I don't know." She grinned and mused, "Jeff Foxworthy would probably love one attached to one of the garbage cans."

He laughed. "You're a nut! Thanks for dinner." He paused looking down at her and glanced at her mouth again. "I should never have kissed you last night. I thought about it all day. I'll never get anything done now for thinking about you."

She smiled shyly. "You can't take it back."

His voice was husky when he softly said, "Trying might be fun though." He brushed a thumb across her lower lip, and then leaned in to kiss her again gently. "I wondered if it was as nice as it seemed last night. It absolutely was. G'night, Taya."

"Good night, Matt."

As she read her scriptures that night in bed, she worried again about him not being a member. In the middle of worrying she sat straight up in bed and realized that part of that was her fault. She'd invited him to church, and she'd been a good example, but she'd never once offered him a Book of Mormon or encouraged him to meet with the missionaries. In fact, she had actually kept them away to keep her identity a secret.

It was important that John or any of his associates not find her, but wasn't Matt learning the gospel more important? She made a mental note right then to give him the little copy of the Book of Mormon she kept in her purse and see if he would be interested in meeting with the missionaries. She wondered how he would react to that.

She shouldn't have worried. He dealt with her offer of the book the next night with the same easy going grace that he had handled everything else so far. "Sure I'll read it. And I'll meet with the missionaries. Hadn't we better wait until the trial and the election are over before I do though? Meeting with the missionaries won't be very inconspicuous."

She looked up at him in wonder. "Maybe meeting with the missionaries is more important than being inconspicuous."

He shook his head. "Not if it means possibly putting you in danger, Taya. I'll make you a deal. I promise I'll check into the church eventually, but for right now the priority has to be keeping you safe."

"Maybe the missionaries could come here and we'd still be inconspicuous."

He was surprised. "They'd come clear out here to teach me?"

She looked at him quietly. "The worth of a soul is great, Matt, especially one as solid as yours."

Smiling, he said, "You know. I guy could really get used to hearing you tell him he's okay. Thanks. You've been good for me. I have to do better because you expect it of me."

She shook her head. "I've never known you to do anything but your best. It has nothing to do with me."

He cupped her cheek with his hand. "It must have something to do with you. I never felt bullet proof until you."

"Well, you should have. You were bulletproof long before you knew me. I think you must have come wired that way."

"If I came that way I wasn't aware of it until you."

"Well, then I'm glad I could be the messenger."

She went to turn away, but he put an arm around the waist. "You're the most appealing messenger I've ever known."

That made her smile. "Thank you, kind sir. I don't think I've ever been anyone's appealing messenger before. It's kind of fun!"

"I'll bet you've been more people's messenger of building them up than you know. I think you don't even realize that you're helping. It's just your personality."

She looked right at him. "You make it sound like I'm always saying nice things. I'm not insincere about it. I wouldn't say something untrue just to butter you up. There are times that I'm brutally honest, too."

His brown eyes met hers. "That's what makes the good stuff so nice. Because I believe you truly mean it."

"You have a lot of gifts." She was only being honest with him. "You should be grateful. Not everyone gets it all like you."

He grinned. "See what I mean?"

Finally, she asked, "Are you ever going to kiss me? Or what?"

He laughed. "Is that where this is going?"

"Either that or you're a terrible tease, being this close and just tempting me."

Smiling a lazy smile, he admitted, "I don't think I've been anyone's terrible tease before. It's kind of fun."

"I'll bet you've been that more than you know, too. You probably drove the girls crazy in college."

He shook his head. "Nope. I'm shy and I'm a computer geek. Remember?"

This time she was the one who laughed. "Oh, yeah, sure. A shy, computer geek. Who do you think you're trying to kid, Matt?"

He let go of her waist to hold up both hands. "Hey, I'm being honest. I'm the guy who was always afraid of girls."

She smiled, but she doubted him, "I'm sorry, but I don't believe you. No one who looks like you do could have possibly been afraid of girls."

"They terrified me. The only reason you don't is because my competition out here is three dogs, a horse, and some sheep."

She nudged him with her elbow. "They're nice dogs. And Horse is sweet. So the sheep aren't all that dynamic, but they're pretty easy to get along with typically. They've mellowed me unbelievably."

"Did you use to be unmellow?"

"No, but I used to be more impatient. The peace here does something to me."

He looked at her for a minute. "Peace looks good on you, Taya."

It took her a second to answer, "Thanks. It feels good." She looked down. "The things I want out of life have changed since last spring. Living here has a lot to do with that. The centrifugal force that used to make me wonder if I was going to go winging off from the crazy pace back in the city is nonexistent. I doubt I'll ever want to live like that again. It was fun for awhile, but doesn't appeal to me at all anymore."

"When that happens does it mean we're grown up now or that we're just getting boring?"

She looked back up and smiled. "I don't think boring would ever describe you. There's too much undercurrent to you. It's like still waters on the surface that run deep."

"Is that good or bad?"

"What I know so far is great. Except for the teasing part. I'm still waiting for you to kiss me."

He smiled and shrugged. "Personally, I think teasing is underrated."

"Oh, really? Then if all you're going to do is torture me, I'm going in to work." She pushed on his chest.

He chuckled at her as he pulled her into his arms and began to plant little teasing kisses on her face and neck and finally zeroed in on her mouth. The teasing stuff died away for a few minutes while he concentrated there. Finally, he lifted his head. "Better?"

"Mmm. Much. But I'm not done. Come back."

He laughed at her softly again. "Okay, one more kiss before we die."

She laughed. "You're a John Wayne fan too?"

"Shh. I'm busy."

Chapter 22

The herder brought her sheep back and they all settled into a comfortable routine again. The only thing that was different was that now they could admit they liked each other. Most nights, she made dinner and they would talk for a few minutes before he went to work on his computer and she went to hers. That few minutes in his arms was easily the highlight of her day. Time spent with him felt right and good and she was no longer lonely the way she had been before he came. Sundays they went to church and spent the afternoon relaxing. Taya arranged for the missionaries to come to their camp on Sunday afternoons so they had that now too.

They were well into September and the evenings and mornings had gotten brisk, although the days were still hotter than was comfortable. They continued to slowly migrate down the valley and eventually came to another rugged area broken by washes and ravines. It slowed down Matt's crew and Taya had to move the sheep more often to find feed.

One day a flash flood came down one of the big washes unexpectedly. It wasn't raining where they were and she hadn't even noticed it was raining further up in the hills until she heard the roar of the water raging toward them. The sheep were all up on the bench, but Taya thought Matt and his crew were down in the wash and she raced Horse down the rim trying to warn him. The water roared past her before she made it to where he was and she was absolutely sick with worry until she rounded a bend and found him and his crew on a ledge high up on the wall of the wash waiting for the water to recede.

She stopped Horse on the rim and tried to catch her breath, unbelievably grateful to see the tall man in the muddy jeans across there. Their eyes met and held and that night the hug lasted a long, long time.

The next day the rain hit where they were with a vengeance. Taya wore her rain gear the entire day and on returning to camp in the late afternoon, discovered the lashing winds had collapsed his tent and his belongings were totally soaked through. She brought his computer and camera and guitar inside the trailer and tried to dry them out and then took his bedding and clothes into town to the laundromat so he'd at least have something to wear and somewhere to sleep when he got in that night.

He spent that night in the other bunk in the trailer for once and then the next day they rigged up a waterproof fly for her swing and moved him outside for the duration of the storm that lasted three more days. By the time it was over they were down to almost no power and tepid shower water and for once were ridiculously thankful for the desert sunshine.

Stacy showed up one afternoon in camp again. Taya wasn't feeling great at all that day and was much less than thrilled to see her. When Stacy got out of her car Taya just let Zeus growl at her and then she did too, "You have a lot of guts showing up here after sleeping with his best friend in his own house. You ought to be ashamed of yourself. It's no wonder he doesn't want to see you anymore."

Stacy was somewhat taken aback and then asked, "It's not really any of your business, is it?"

In no mood to deal with her, Taya answered. "No, you're right. It isn't. So maybe you should take it out of my camp. You can wait in your car until he gets back."

Stacy meekly climbed back into her car and Taya finished making dinner and then crashed on her swing with Zeus at her feet. Matt came in at dark, hungry and tired and dirty and Taya felt sorry for him for having to get rid of Stacy again. At least this time she hadn't been drinking. Once Stacy had driven off in a huff, he came over to her camp and sat on the swing with her and pulled her up onto his lap. "Are you sick again? Don't breathe on me."

She shook her head tiredly. "No. I'm just not feeling so hot, but I'm sure it's not contagious this time. I'm afraid I took it out on Stacy. I owe you another apology. I told her just what I thought about her cheating on you."

He smiled. "It's okay. It's not like she didn't deserve it. I can't believe she came back here. I haven't taken one call since that night. She should have gotten the hint. I'm sorry she bothered you. I'll tell the helicopter pilot not to tell her where I am anymore."

Taya felt a little sheepish. "She didn't truly bother me. I actually think I was being a bit territorial. I didn't know I had it in me. I really wasn't very hospitable. *Really.*"

He laughed. "Gosh. I almost wish I'd been here to see that. I'll bet you were cute while you were being territorial."

Raising her eyebrows, she admitted, "I'm not sure cute is the word. Are you hungry? I made some lovely gourmet sloppy Joes and potato chips."

"I'll eat in a minute. What can I do to help you feel better?"

"You're doing it. Just give me five minutes of your time before you have to go to work and I'll be fine. How was your day?"

"Good. We're actually going to make this deadline. I almost can't believe it."

"Believe it. You've worked you tail off for it, and you deserve it. You make a very good looking business man." She touched his mouth with one finger. "Did you know that small business is the life blood of this country? Without small business our economy would collapse. A lot of people have lost sight of that I'm afraid."

He kissed her finger and then said, "How come if you're such a proponent of free enterprise, you work for someone else instead of yourself?"

She snuggled against him. "Actually, I own forty-nine percent of the company I work for. I helped put up the capital for them to start it. I chose structural engineering because I could do it from home easiest. I probably should have been a mechanical engineer instead. But honestly, I don't want to work forever. I want to quit and be a mom eventually. I know that's breaking the whole feminist sisterhood thing, but that's what I want."

He looked out at the desert in the dark. "I'm relatively positive you're safe from the feminists here. They haven't made it all the way to sheep yet. I could see you as a mom. You'll be great."

For a second she was thoughtful. "Sometimes I worry about that. I don't think I had all that great of a role model. I need to do better than my mother did with me. She was gone a lot. And oversight wasn't her strong point."

He hugged her. "You are gonna be a great mom! You're whole personality will be perfect. Plus you have all the church's guidance. You'll be just fine."

"I wish I was as confident as you about that. I read a lot of books, but sometimes the 'experts' are a bit wacko to me."

He smiled as he said, "I think that's part of the technical definition of being an expert. How did your day go?'

"Okay. I came in earlier than usual. But with the days getting shorter I'm getting more done at night. And I haven't had much trouble with coyotes lately, thank goodness. I thought I would have now that we're getting closer to the mountains.'"

He leaned his cheek against her hair. "Did you ever decide what you're going to do when you're through with the sheep here? Aren't you going to be done within a couple or three weeks?"

It took her a while to answer. "I still don't know for sure. It's hard to know what to do until I know how this trial is going to go in a couple of weeks. I got calls today from both the police and my partner. The man who's running against John Channing has been trying to get hold of me. He wants me to come out for a fundraiser event on the eighteenth of October. It's just a day before the trial, so it might be dangerous, but I feel like it's important enough to try not to let John be re-elected that I should go."

"Have you prayed about it?"

She turned to stare at him. "Yes. Why?"

"What did you think you should do?"

"Go."

"Then you should go. We'll have to hire you some serious security."

She searched his eyes. "You're not going to try to talk me out of it?"

Shaking his head, he said, "Taya, you're the sharpest lady I've ever known. And who am I to try to sway you from what you think you should be doing when you've prayed about it?"

She hesitated and then asked, "Will you go with me? Your contract will be done by then, won't it?"

"To D.C. or to the fundraiser?"

"Both. I'll bet you look hot in a tux."

He smiled in the dark. "I don't know about that, but sure I'll go with you. Maybe we should take my brother Drew with. It couldn't hurt to have another cop along just in case. He's not a big city cop, but he's good at what he does."

"Would you ask him if he can take the time and I'll see about getting invitations for extra security. Tell Drew I'll pay him for his time. The FBI guys will hate it. They think I'm their turf. And we'll need to get clothes. I wonder where I can buy an evening gown around here."

Matt laughed. "Good luck with that one. There's not an evening gown within a hundred miles of this place. Maybe two." He paused. "Did you ever end up wearing your dress from the last one anywhere? Or was it ruined when you were hurt?"

She looked puzzled for a minute. "I didn't wear it anywhere. And honestly, I don't know if it was ruined. They gave it back to me in one of those hospital belongings bags and I haven't even gotten it out since. I think it's somewhere inside the trailer in the back of a cupboard. That's an idea. I'll have to check it out." She got up to go into the trailer and start digging around in storage compartments.

She found the blue hospital bag and brought it back out to the swing. She pulled the dress out and then reached back in for the jacket and jewelry and held the jacket up and tried to look at it in the dark. "I'll have to look at in the day time and see if it's ruined or not. I think I'm smaller than I was then. I wonder if it will still fit."

He reached over and clasped the necklace around her neck. "I'm going to get to see a side of you I've never seen. This is going to be fun."

"Well, sometimes the parties are boring, but the clothes are great! We can pretend that it's just you and me at the ball and maybe it will be better than it usually is. But it will be for a good cause. I think I'll even very publicly donate a chunk to this guy's campaign fund."

"Is this a vendetta or are you doing it for the good of the land?"

She gently shook her head. "No, actually I've forgiven John for hurting me, and in all honesty, I'm totally grateful to him for keeping me from making the huge mistake of marrying him. I just don't want any more corrupt politicians. And he truly is corrupt. I know that now."

Matt stroked the little bone behind her ear. "Good. Grudges aren't like you."

"No. They're not." She was quiet and then admitted sadly, "But I am still having such a hard time dealing with my parents leaving me that night. I'm still heartbroken. You'd think it would be easier to forgive someone in your family, but it hasn't been. They killed me when they walked out that night."

Gently, he said, "It has to have been hard. I don't even know what to tell you except that they just don't understand the big picture. Maybe someday they will."

"Maybe. Thank you. Thanks for agreeing to go and for listening to me and even for hugging me when I'm ornery and don't feel good. I'll be better tomorrow. I'll reheat the sloppy Joe filling for you."

She went to stand up but he pulled her back into his arms. "I'll reheat the sloppy Joes. Can I have two more minutes? I'm not ready to leave you yet."

"Three minutes."

He smiled as he bent to kiss her. "Okay, three."

Jaclyn M. Hawkes

Chapter 23

It was sometime in the very middle of the night and she was instantly wide awake. It wasn't that she thought one of John's people was around. She almost wished it was. The problem was there was another mouse in her trailer and this time she was pretty sure it was in her bed. It was all she could do not to let out a blood curdling scream.

She made a flying leap out of her bed and was out the door of her trailer bare foot and in her pajamas tiptoeing through the brush to Matt's tent doing her best not to step in a cactus on the way. She tried to whisper just loud enough to wake him, "Matt. Matt."

She could hear him move inside his tent and he answered back sleepily, "What?" He zipped down his tent door. "What's wrong?"

"Um. I'm so sorry to bother you. I know you're tired. Please forgive me."

"Taya. What? You're not saying anything. Have you got a prowler or another mouse?"

She looked down, embarrassed. "Another mouse. I'm sorry. I tried to be brave, but it's in my bed this time!"

He sighed. "Give me a sec. Let me put some shoes on."

A minute later he climbed out of his tent in jeans and his Tivas and took her hand to take her back to her trailer. It took him a moment to realize she was barefoot. "Taya! Barefoot in cactus? What are you thinking? Here. Get on. I'll give you a piggy back."

"No. I'm okay. Just go slow enough that I can see. I didn't dare to stop for shoes. I know! I know! They're more afraid of me than I am of them. Technically that isn't true, but it should be. I know I'm a marshmallow, but I can't help it. I can't even breathe when I know one is there!"

He squeezed her hand. "It's okay, Tay. No one says our issues have to make sense. We just need someone to help us with them. I'll save you from mice whenever you need saving. That's what friends do."

"Have I ever told you how glad I am that you came to camp by me?"

He grinned at her in the dark. "No. Maybe you'd better."

She hugged his arm. "I am so, so glad that you came to . . . Aahh! Cactus! Ow! Aahh!"

Reaching for her arm, he tried to stop her hopping. "Here. Quit jumping around one legged and get on and I'll take you to your chair."

"I'm too heavy. I'll kill you."

"You're fine. Taya, stop! You're gonna step in another one. Just get on. Taya, be careful, you're going to end up with both feet toasted. Taya! Stop hopping and listen to me! Just get on."

When she finally climbed on his back, he said, "You're a lunatic sometimes. You know that?"

"I know." She was truly apologetic. "I'm sorry. Thank you. Set me down here. Okay, now give me just a second to pull the thorns out so I can climb up on the truck."

He tried not to laugh. "Sweetie, you're gonna be fine right there. A mouse can't jump like twenty feet."

"Are you sure? They're so fast! How can you be sure when they're that fast?"

"I promise a mouse isn't going to jump from the door clear to your chair. Do you have a flashlight anywhere?"

"Just inside the door on the counter. I think it was in my bed with me, so look there." He disappeared inside the trailer and she could hear him moving around inside for a minute while she stared at the door. Suddenly, the mouse jumped out doing about a hundred and twenty and it ran straight at her! She screamed and tried to stand up on the canvas chair as it went past and just as Matt made it out the door, the chair tipped and she fell off of it sideways and landed flat on her behind in the sand and gravel. Jumping back up, she ran to him and then around behind him.

He turned and tried to get her to let go of him, but she was still trying to hide against him as he said, "Taya. It's okay. It's gone. You're all right. Sweetie, let go." He took her hand from where it gripped his arm. "Taya. Taya! Look at me! It's gone. You're okay, honey. Calm down. It's just a mouse." Finally, he simply picked her up and carried her over to her swing and sat down in it. "Girl, how in the world did you survive living out here before I came?"

She leaned against his chest and sighed. "I don't know. I'm okay with everything except the mice. They scare me."

Dryly, he said, "I gathered that. Lay on me and calm down for a minute. You'll be okay." He pushed the swing with one foot gently, and ran one hand down her back. "Did you get all the cactus thorns out of your foot?"

She nodded against him. "I think so. I'm sorry I woke you up. Thanks for coming to save me. I'll ask Zan if he can look under the trailer and see where they're getting in so I don't keep bothering you."

He gently smoothed her hair. "You're not bothering me. I'll look under the trailer. I don't mind helping you at all."

Snuggling against him, she said, "Thank you. You're always my hero. I truly am so glad I found you in the desert that day."

"Me too." She could hear him smile in the dark. "Life is far more interesting with you in it."

She leaned to look up at him. "Are you teasing me?"

"Yes. I always tease you just before I kiss you. Remember?"

****

The next afternoon in the light, she did look at the dress and thought it could be cleaned and would be okay. The beads on the jacket would need to be mended, but the very nature of them hid any damage. She was worried she would be too little for it after toning up this summer and she decided to try it on, but she had to rig a string through the zipper to pull it up and down alone.

She finally got it zipped up and found that although it was looser, it still fit fine. She would rework the beading one of these nights and it would do nicely. She slipped back out of her shoes and went to pull the zipper back down and the string she had rigged pulled right out without budging the zipper. For over an hour she struggled to reach it with everything she could think of and finally resorted to waiting for Matt to come and rescue her again. She would never live this one down.

Feeling like an idiot in a beaded evening gown in the middle of the desert, she made dinner and decided she was going to wait to go get the sheep even if she had to bring them in in full darkness. Cooking was bad enough. There was no way she was venturing after the sheep in this thing!

Of course it was dark and then some when Matt finally came home. She could tell he was trying not to laugh at her, but it wasn't working all that well. Finally, she just busted up with him when he asked, "Is there any thing else I could help you with ma'am before I hit the showers?" Life with him was much more entertaining than it had been before. She wondered where he was going to go when he was done here.

****

It was only about three days after the second mouse crisis that she got into a corner that had Matt sweating, but to her seemed no big deal. She had moved the trailer that day and then gone back out on Horse with the sheep. The terrain had become much more rugged and hilly near the foot of the mountains and there were times that he'd look up and see that she had sheep in three different little valleys at one time.

Matt's crew had run out of gear and the helicopter was bringing them in before dusk for once and he was looking down to find her as they flew over. He could tell she was having trouble with Horse and wondered why the typically sweet and gentle animal was acting up until he noticed a huge mountain lion crouched just up the hill on a rock from where she was.

Zeus was clear across the herd for once and Matt was at a complete loss as to what to do. They couldn't buzz the lion with the helicopter without spooking Horse. He didn't have a rifle with him and didn't think a hand gun would even come close to hitting anything except maybe her or Horse. She wasn't close enough to camp for him to be of any help once he was dropped off. Finally, he resorted to just trying to call her cell phone in time to warn her, while he had the chopper stay right there near her.

Wondering if any second the cat was going to spring, he waited for what felt like an interminable time for her to be able to answer the phone and still handle her horse.

Finally, he heard her hello, and burst out, "Taya, there's a mountain lion in the rocks above you! Get out of there! Now!" He held his breath as she put her heels to Horse and bolted away from the rocks and then spun the horse to turn and look back.

She had her rifle out and was aiming while he began swearing at her silently for not getting clear the heck out of there. Then he heard the faint rifle reports right inside the chopper because she was so close below him. She hit the cat with both shots and it tumbled from the rocks and into the trail where she had been sitting her horse just seconds before. She held her gun on it to see if it was going to move and when it didn't, she finally looked up at the helicopter above her. He could have sworn again as she calmly turned her horse and headed down the trail to her sheep, without so much as glancing back at the lion behind her.

An hour and a half later when she finally brought the sheep in, he still wasn't sure whether to hug her or cuss her for turning and shooting the cat instead of running. She came into camp carrying her saddle, set it under the edge of the trailer and turned to feed the dogs before going inside. Matt was sitting on her swing and for the first time, he was a little disgusted with her. Apparently she wasn't aware of the damage a full grown mountain lion could inflict. She could have been killed!

He'd made dinner, but he'd been too up tight to even eat it and his plate was sitting on her table next to hers untouched. She poked her head out of the trailer and asked if he wanted something to drink with his food, and then he really decided he was mad. She was acting like nothing had even happened! She came out the door with a jug of milk and two paper cups and sat down at the table and bowed her head waiting for him to pray. Maybe that was a good idea. He needed some of the Holy Spirit right now. They said amen and she started to eat and finally stopped and said, "All right, Matt. Out with it. What's going on?"

"What do you mean, what's going on?"

"Why are you ticked off at me tonight?"

"Because you acted like you thought you were in a John Wayne movie out there today instead of using your head and getting the heck out of Dodge!"

"What did you want me to do?"

"Run!"

Calmly, she said, "Matt, I'm a sheepherder. I wasn't just going to leave it there to wipe out my sheep tonight. I had to turn around and shoot it."

He tried not to snap, "Well, you could have at least gone far enough that it couldn't have still attacked you."

She asked him quietly, "Are you saying that I didn't shoot it the way you wanted me to?"

More gently, he said, "I'm saying you scared the crud out of me, Taya. I thought that cat was going to jump you. You could have been killed!"

She looked honestly penitent. "I'm sorry, Matt. I've never had to deal with a mountain lion before. I did the best I knew how. I didn't mean to scare you. I just didn't want it to tear into the sheep."

He looked at her like she had grown horns. "That was your first time dealing with a lion?" She nodded. "And you stared it down and shot it like that?" He ran a hand through his hair and sighed and then got up and came over to her and pulled her up into a hug. "Girl, you took ten years off of my life out there today. How can you face a mountain lion but not a mouse?"

She ducked her head. "I don't know. I'm sorry."

Gently, he raised her face. "No. I'm sorry. I shouldn't have been upset with you. But Taya, next time you see a mountain lion, get further away from it before you turn around to shoot it, okay? They're dangerous. They're not just another coyote. They'll attack, even on a horse."

She nodded and softly said, "Okay. I didn't know I was being foolish. I'm sorry."

He hugged her tight. "You never fail to amaze me. You are quite a girl, you know that?"

In the quietest voice he had ever heard her use, she said, "You've never been mad at me before."

"I'm not mad anymore. I'm sorry. You just scared me."

"I thought you'd be glad I was able to shoot it okay."

He leaned back and said, "I am, Taya. I am. You're a ripping shot and gutty as . . . " Pulling her close again, he continued gently, "I'm royally proud of you. Just don't take a chance like that again, okay?"

She nodded her head against his chest, and he hugged her for a long moment. If she'd have been hurt it would have killed him.

Chapter 24

Because of the hilly terrain, and where she'd put the trailer, Mac was having a hard time deciding where to drop Matt. That first night after the mountain lion, he had brought him in and dropped him where it looked relatively flat, but it hadn't been a very good spot, so the next night he tried to put it down in the only other spot that looked promising. It was closer to camp than they'd ever dropped him and as Matt hopped out and the chopper lifted off, Matt heard Taya scream.

At first it scared him and he looked around trying to locate her, wondering what was wrong. He didn't think it would be a mouse at this time of day. It took him several seconds of looking around before he realized she was in the shower and that the helicopter had almost blown the whole rig over and was, in fact, still in the process of blowing the shower curtain with all the force of it's powerful rotors.

Before it had finished lifting off, it had completely ripped the curtain off the wire that held it and the only thing holding it was Taya herself. As Matt watched, the force of the helicopter completely ripped it away from her and blew it off like a kite into the sage. She gave another scream as it launched and Matt couldn't help himself. He turned his back to her, bent double and belly laughed. He couldn't stop laughing all the way to his tent. He'd have to make it up to her later, but right now he'd never in his life seen anything so funny.

He had no idea why she was in the shower at this time of day, because she usually showered in the morning and left the water for him at night. Something must have happened today. He stayed in his tent for more than half an hour reading to let her make it safely back to her trailer, get dressed and calm down. He was going to have a hard time facing her tonight without busting up laughing and he didn't think that would go over all that well after what she had just been through.

When he finally dared to come out, he got in his Jeep and bounced over the sage to where the shower curtain had landed and brought it back home. It was a little the worse for the wear and he decided buying her a new one would probably be in order after tonight.

He finally dared to approach her table and was glad she had a great sense of humor because there was no way he could keep a straight face. Once she cracked a smile, he totally cracked up again and she joined him. They laughed together until she had tears in her eyes and even several times during their spaghetti dinner he caught himself smiling at the thought of her standing there in the sage screaming in the buff in the wind. That was the all time funniest thing he'd ever seen in his life!

The next morning, he left her a bouquet of wildflowers and breakfast before heading out at dawn, hoping she'd know he truly was sorry even though he'd laughed so hard and that night he went to buy her another shower curtain.

The only one he could find within fifty miles of their camp had huge bright pink and orange and green and yellow flowers on it and they laughed again just like the first time when he unveiled it. There were a lot of things about this summer he would never forget. Life with her was turning out to be an adventure. He wished he knew what she was going to do after this. He wasn't sure what he would do if she said she was going back to Washington D.C.

****

September had come and gone. The nights got positively cool and the hillsides far up on the mountains turned russet and gold. Matt was working twenty hour days to wrap up his contract and Taya came to do all the cooking and rarely if ever saw him except when he stopped by before dinner. Their travel arrangements had been made and the FBI had set up security for when she was there. She had worked on her dress and had it cleaned and had decided to wait patiently for Matt to finish whatever he had to before she was going to bother him about his tux.

She'd been moving the trailer more frequently in order to find feed for the sheep, but she thought that would be a good thing as far as not being able to be located. They hadn't seen or heard another thing from John Channing or anyone else from Maryland. She had begun to think maybe they were going to let her and the past go, so she was doubly surprised one evening a week or two into October. After moving the trailer and setting things back up, she had walked back across the flat to get Matt's Jeep and bring it around. She didn't realize until she was almost right into camp that another vehicle had pulled in in her absence. Hesitantly she got out of the Jeep hoping that whoever this was, it wasn't someone from back east.

It was. It was one of the same men who had come the last time. She decided to try to make him think it wasn't her camp as he calmly walked up to her and said, "Hello, Taya. It's been a long time. You've been hard to locate."

"That would be because I didn't want to be located. Is anyone here in camp yet?"

"What do you mean?"

"Is the guy who lives here, back yet?"

"I just got here but, you're who I came to see. I'm to take you back with me. There are some people back east that miss you. And the diamond you walked with."

She could see her rifle sitting there under the edge of the trailer, but she didn't think she could get to it and pull it out in time to pin this guy down with it. She was still racking her brain for ideas of how to get away when she heard the approaching chopper.

She wasn't out of the woods, and maybe she had just gotten Matt into a lot of trouble, but she was still more relieved than she could even say. Somehow he would help her. She knew it. "I'm not going back. I live here now. John doesn't order me around like he thinks he does."

He gave her a smile that made her skin crawl and said softly, "It wasn't John that sent me."

Almost wanting to panic, she glanced up as Matt hopped out of the helicopter and she knew he instantly saw that there was a problem as he came striding across the sage flat. He walked into camp with a gun in his hand that Taya hadn't even known he possessed, but she was incredibly grateful for his second amendment rights just then. He held the gun on her visitor as he asked, "Is he a friend of yours, Tay?"

In disgust, she said, "No, he's no friend of mine." She went across and got out the rifle and held it on him too. "Can I borrow your rifle for a second, Matt?"

He glanced at her and then said, "Sure, make yourself at home."

She looked at him pointedly and asked, "You wouldn't have any nails in your trailer would you, that I can borrow?"

He'd caught on that she didn't want this guy to think it was her camp, but he wasn't sure what she wanted him to do. "I don't know. Do you need nails?"

"Yup. I need to borrow some nails. I'll bet there's some in your trailer in a drawer or a bottle or something. Would you mind checking while I keep a gun on this guy?"

Inside the trailer she could hear him digging through drawers and cupboards. He came out of the trailer with the peanut butter jar of nails and asked, "Will these do? These are the only nails I think I have."

Without even glancing up, she said, "Perfect. Can I ask you a favor? This guy is going to want to follow me. I'm sorry to do this to you, but make him sit there for about ten minutes and don't let him contact anyone while he does. Sorry I can't take time to visit. See ya around." She took the nails and Matt sat down in her chair and cocked the gun as she jumped back into his Jeep and sped away.

Just before she hit the highway, she got out and quickly put a thick layer of nails across the track behind the Jeep and kicked dirt and sand over it. She got back in and drove like a mad woman until she was out of sight of their camp or anyone on the highway and then she quickly pulled the Jeep back off the road and down into the stream bottom and hid it deep behind the brush and willows. Pulling out her secure cell phone, she tried to call the FBI and was stunned when no one would answer. *Great. Just great.* So much for taxpayer funded high technology.

She sat in the driver's seat for a few minutes trying to decide what to do. Part of her brain wanted her to think she had fooled him and that he would believe it wasn't her camp and look elsewhere, and another part of her brain was telling her that her days as a sheepherder were over a couple of weeks earlier than she'd thought and that she needed to truly get way away this time. She'd never planned where she would go other than away from wherever they found her. And now that she had gotten close to Matt, she had hesitated to plan anything because she had been hoping to go in the same general direction he was headed in the next couple of weeks. Wherever that was.

In a way that was foolish and might be putting him in danger, but she wanted to be with him if she could. She'd been hoping that was what he wanted too. She should have simply come out and asked him what his plans were, but she hadn't dared.

As darkness fell around her, she locked the Jeep and began the two or three mile walk back up the valley to the trailer. When she got close, Zeus materialized out of the darkness and came up to her and she whispered, "Where were you when I needed you an hour ago, huh?" She petted the shaggy white head and kept on up the bank toward camp. Near the rim, she paused and listened. All was quiet except the sheep in the valley and the tiny, odd click of Matt's key board where he sat at her table working. He lifted his head to listen, put out the lantern and then sat back in her chair and she came up into the camp.

Standing, he came over and hugged her tightly to him. "Are you okay? Where did you go? Where's the Jeep?"

"It's down the valley a couple of miles hidden in the willows. Sorry I took it without asking. I had just gone and brought it over and didn't realize he was here until I was right into camp. Did he give you any trouble?"

"No, he didn't give me any trouble, and I kept him fifteen minutes instead of ten, but he went out of here to find you again. They know where you are now for sure. What are you going to do?"

"I don't know. My original plan was to go anywhere they weren't, but lately I've put off making a decision, which was a bad idea. First off, I need to talk to Zan about getting someone to watch the sheep. Then I need to go somewhere for another week until we head back east."

She went to get out her secure phone again to call Zan, but Matt stopped her. "Don't use the cell phone right now. Most cell phones are easy to tap into and these guys are probably pretty sophisticated. If they have any electronic stuff going to intercept calls out here, they might intercept your call."

She stuffed it back into her pocket and said, "No one answered earlier anyway."

Matt gave her a sad smile. "Figures. Let's get you hidden out in the brush somewhere for the night because I'm sure he's watching to see if I leave here. Tomorrow we'll find a way to keep you hidden until we can sneak you out. Maybe we could get you onto the helicopter when Mac leaves and have him smuggle you out. In the mean time, you need to disappear out here and I need to make it look like this honestly is my camp. What would you think of going to stay with my parents until you decide what you're doing?"

She shook her head. "No, Matt. I don't want to bring trouble to anyone else. I've already gotten you and the Bears involved."

"Taya, if I stay here, they won't think I'm involved and my parents live behind two and sometimes three locked gates with a cop on the premises. They'll be fine. And you'll be safe and I won't worry about you."

"But I'm sure they have your Jeep's license plate. Won't they be looking for you and then check your parents' place? You need to call and warn them."

"I already did. And I called the local police. They'll be here shortly."

"I think I should go someplace away from everyone until this is over. These people could be bad, Matt."

"They are bad, Taya. There's no could be about it, so let's get you away from here. Take my tent and sleeping gear and let's load up Horse and your gun and whatever you need. We'll take you and Zeus back further into the hills for the night and tomorrow until Mac gets here and I can get you out of here. Will you be afraid in a tent all night?"

'No. I'll be fine with Zeus and my gun as long as I can zip the mice out. Let me grab some clothes. Oh, and thanks for getting the nails."

"Why did you want nails? Can I ask?"

"I poured the whole jar full in a row across the track onto the highway up there to ruin his tires, so don't drive there until I get a chance to get them cleaned up. And we'd better tell the police."

He shook his head and chuckled. "Get your things, I'll catch Horse."

She went down across the valley on the other side of the sheep and climbed to the far side of the rim before she set up his tent. There was no way a vehicle could get to her at all as far as she knew and she even decided she could just do this for the remainder of the week if she made a trek back to the trailer at night to shower and pick up food.

Chapter 25

In the first light of dawn, she got up, saddled Horse and went and got the sheep and moved them further up the valley and away from the trailer before it was light out. She pushed them in the direction Matt's crew had been working so that worst case scenario, at least she would be near someone in case of an emergency. She hadn't touched base with either Matt or Zan after what Matt had said about using the cell and decided she'd try to talk to Matt sometime during the day if she could get close enough to him. No one could intercept her plans if she told them to him face to face.

Taking the sheep as far away from the highway as she could that morning, she tried to keep them in a steep and rocky small side canyon that was almost invisible from camp and the road. It would be harder to know when she could talk to Matt, but she would be a trick for a city guy to find.

She was just getting ready to stop and eat lunch and decided to circle the sheep one time on Horse to make sure she had them all. Three quarters of the way around them, Horse started to act fidgety again and Taya looked all around her to see if there was another lion nearby. She was relatively out in the open this time and there didn't seem to be anywhere for a big cat to hide, but she whistled to Zeus to come to her, just in case. If there was a problem nearby, he would be aware of it before either she or Horse would. As he approached her, she could see that he began sniffing around and became increasingly cautious and she finally thought to look for something other than a mountain lion or coyote that would intimidate the dog.

She heard the telltale rattle at the exact moment that it occurred to her to look for a snake and she spotted it just as Horse came unglued under her. Horse spooked straight sideways for three fast steps and then reared back and spun at the same time.

Taya stayed with her up until the spin and made a wild grab for the horn as she felt herself thrown sideways out of the saddle. She was relieved that at least she was falling several feet away from the snake and she tried to catch herself as she tumbled into a pile of rocks and boulders. She was doing okay until Horse began to scramble for footing in the rocks beside her. Taya could see the hind hoof coming but there wasn't time to get out of the way. All she had time to do was duck her head so at least she didn't take the metal horseshoe in the face. She felt the solid thunk and everything went black.

****

For some reason, switching into her trailer for the night after talking to the police had thrown Matt's whole system into a tailspin. The entire trailer smelled like her shampoo and he hadn't slept well. It had taken him twice as long as usual to get ready this morning and then there was a mix up with their equipment at the last minute and he had to repack all of their gear.

They were in the air and heading out before he had made a solid decision about how they were taking Taya out of here today. He finally figured out that it was because he didn't really want her to go that he had been dragging his feet and he forced himself to remember that it had to be this way to keep her safe. He looked for her as they flew and was almost ready to panic that he couldn't find her or her sheep until he saw a few of them on the rim of a little rocky canyon.

After the rest of the crew had gotten out of the chopper, Matt went and talked to Mac and asked him to come back and get him in the early afternoon. He'd find Taya and fly her out then and hopefully that would still leave him time to do what he desperately needed to get done that day as well as leave Zan enough time to bring someone in to protect her sheep.

He worked feverishly through the morning and then when his guys stopped for lunch, he climbed to the highest point he could find and glassed to see if he could find Taya. If she was still in that little canyon, it was going to be a trick to find a place to put down the helicopter.

After searching, he located a few of her sheep still near the canyon, but he couldn't find her and hiked closer to get a better look. Taya was nowhere to be seen, and even catching glimpses of all three dogs wasn't helping. Finally, he spotted Horse in a tangle of a dead cedar tree about halfway between where he was and the canyon with the sheep nearly a mile away. Taya wasn't with Horse and Matt looked all around trying to figure out where she had gone when she had tied Horse to the cedar.

As he was searching he noticed Horse was moving around a little and was dragging the cedar tree along behind her. That was really weird. He couldn't picture Taya tying Horse to something that wasn't solid.

He looked back to where he had seen Zeus and wondered why he and Horse weren't in the same general vicinity like they usually were. Usually, Taya was on Horse and the dog was their shadow. Troubled by the unusual circumstances, he headed their way, cussing the fact that today of all days he needed things to be going smoother than this. It was October eleventh. He had four more days to package this deal up and turn it in and it was going to take every second of those four days to do it, but Taya's safety eclipsed it all.

He was almost to the cedar tree and Horse when he noticed the broken rein on the bridle and began to truly wonder if there was a problem. He looked all around as he approached the horse. John's men couldn't have found her clear out here could they?

Horse wasn't tied at all, the bridle was simply tangled in the dead tree branches. Catching her up, he improvised a rein and lengthened the stirrups and jumped on and headed for Zeus. If the dog was still there, then Taya was there somewhere. He went over the ridge and down into the little canyon and headed for the massive, shaggy white dog.

When Matt had first seen him a few minutes ago he had been walking around, but now he was lying near some rocks with his head on his front paws. Matt urged Horse to travel as fast as possible in the rough terrain, but it still took more than twenty minutes to get to Zeus.

He didn't get up when Matt walked close to him and Matt knew something was terribly wrong. He got off Horse and this time tied her up and went to Zeus to see what was going on. The huge dog wagged his tail gently and gave an almost inaudible whine as Matt talked to him. This was getting more and more weird. He and Zeus had finally called a truce and acknowledged being on the same team, but it wasn't like Zeus to lay there and not even get up. And where was Taya?

Then Matt saw the snake. It lay a few feet in front of Zeus and still gave an occasional twitch although it was obviously not in any shape to live long. He glanced at Zeus understanding now what was wrong with the great, white dog. He'd been bitten by the snake. He'd have to get medical attention for him just as soon as he figured out where Taya was.

He went past the dog and saw the heel of her boot lying behind a nearby rock and tried not to think the worst as he vaulted the boulders between them to get to her. She was breathing. Her heart was beating, and he couldn't see any evidence of either a snake bite or any other trauma, but she was out cold.

He knelt beside her and began to talk to her as he unstrapped his water bottle from his pack and splashed some on her face. Leaning down, he picked her up to gently move her out of the rocks so he could look at her better. As he set her down she moaned and he had never in his life heard such a good sound. He kept talking to her and splashed the water again and she finally opened her eyes to him.

She looked at him like she was confused to see him for a minute and then she panicked and gasped and grabbed at him. "Matt, there's a snake! We need to get away from here!" She went to jump up and then groaned and put a hand to her head, still struggling to rise.

"It's dead, Taya. Zeus killed it, but he's sick. Were you bitten?"

She hesitated for a moment while she thought about it. "No. I don't think so. Horse panicked and spooked and we kind of had a bit of a tussle in the rocks. I think she caught me in the back of the head with a hoof on the way up." She put the hand back to her head again. "Where did you come from? What are you doing here?"

"I came to get you to fly you out. Now we're flying Zeus out too. We need to get him to a vet as fast as we can. Are you up to riding out of here?"

"I think so."

"If I lift him into the saddle in front of you, can you hang on to him to get him to the helicopter?"

"Yes, I'll do whatever I have to do."

"Then come on. We need to hurry. We may already be too late if he was bitten more than once."

It was all Matt could do to get the behemoth canine onto the horse. At least once he was settled up there in front of Taya he didn't act like he was going to make a fuss. Simply the fact that he was so docile about the whole thing made Matt less hopeful about saving him. This wasn't the Zeus he knew.

Jaclyn M. Hawkes

Somehow they made it to the ridge above the little canyon where Matt had arranged to meet Mac. Matt took the saddle off Horse and turned her loose, hoping she would either stay with the sheep or go back to the trailer. As soon as Mac landed, they lifted the huge dog into the door and set him gently on the floor and buckled in and took off. Matt still wasn't sure where to go with them and Taya finally encouraged him to take them to the airport. John's men probably weren't watching the smaller port that Mac flew out of and they could rent a car and go straight to the vet. At this point, Mac offered to let them use his own vehicle in order to expedite the trip.

Neither one of them was sure if it was safe to contact the FBI or Zan, but at some point they decided they would have to. They had Mac call Zan and ask him if he would meet Zeus at the veterinarian's, hoping that if any one was listening in they wouldn't associate the call with Taya.

Apparently Zan understood part of what was going on. He met them at the veterinary hospital with an extra car and driver. While Zan was with the vet, for several minutes Taya and Matt had an intense conversation about who was going where. She finally agreed to go to his parents' complex until she got hold of someone from the FBI, but she insisted that Zan take her so Matt could go back to the desert to help his guys.

He struggled with that and finally agreed, knowing she would never forgive herself if she caused his whole contract to default and he honestly would have to spend every single minute between now and the fifteenth to finalize things. Even that was being optimistic. If he only had a few more days or a few more guys. One of the two. He borrowed the vet's office line to call Drew at the Routt County Sheriff's office and tell him what was going on. At least she would have that protection around her.

Matt was the one who asked Zan to help make sure Taya was safe. It galled him to do it, but he did it anyway. Telling her goodbye killed him. He knew that if everything went as planned it would only be a few days before they saw each other again, but he hated not being able to make sure for himself that she was safe. The long hug as he got in the car to leave wasn't nearly enough. It was good that so many issues had to be decided right away because he had to have more control of things in their lives than this and soon. Much of this would make him crazy.

Jaclyn M. Hawkes

Chapter 26

With Matt safely headed back to the desert, Taya went in to see about her dog. Over the last four and a half months he had been her constant companion and had become like her left arm or something. This time, he had probably saved her from being bitten by the snake.

It had taken all of her self control to keep her composure until Matt was headed back to his project and when she went back inside the vet's, seeing Zeus laying there seemingly lifeless just after telling Matt goodbye for who knew how long had her breaking right down and crying.

Zan came and put his arms around her, and the vet tried to help by saying they had a better than fifty percent chance of saving him. To her right then, that felt like they were telling her it was half likely he was going to die and she hugged his white head and sobbed.

Zeus had to stay in the hospital and Zan lead her out and to his truck like he was afraid she was going to break. She hadn't been this much of a mess even when she had arrived here last spring in a cast and with stitches and she knew Zan was at a loose end as far as what to do with her. For his sake she tried to get more control of herself and gave herself a pep talk.

For the next several days, she was probably going to be with strangers, in a strange place, without any of her things including clothes, and without any of her animals or even Matt, and she had no way of knowing how she could safely contact anyone. That was without even thinking about the fact that there were some rather unpleasant people who wanted to find her and keep her quiet in any way they could. She needed to get a handle on the emotion now or she was going to embarrass herself in front of Matt's family.

Before they made it into Steamboat, Taya asked Zan if he would pull over at a rest stop and give her a blessing. She needed that extra help in her life right now more than he could know. Or maybe he did know her needs. His deep, dark eyes seemed to understand when he looked at her after he finished. As Matt's brother let them through first one locked gate and then a second, Zan assured her he would arrange to have some of her things brought in to her one way or another and that he would contact the FBI for her. Sue Maylon's sweet familiar face was what saved her as she watched Zan's big truck pull away to head back home without her.

Even though Sue hadn't been around her much, she seemed to know exactly what Taya needed just then. She hugged her, and then fed her, and then sent her to the shower with a pair of borrowed sweats and the promise to let Taya use her washer until they were able to get her some more clothing.

Drew was enough like Matt that he made Taya even more homesick, but Matt's dad helped her lighten up with his easy laugh and teasing sense of humor. They were wonderful to her, and she felt guilty for feeling whiny and sad.

The fact that Taya had been kicked in the head and knocked unconscious that afternoon had been completely overshadowed by all the other issues that day, until Drew came in and asked her if she had seen a doctor yet. Sue had looked from one to the other and was horrified to find out what had happened and that nothing had been done about it. She was all for taking Taya to the emergency room immediately, but Drew stopped her.

He looked at her with a glance much like Matt's and turned to his mother. "Mom, maybe just some rest would be better. She doesn't look like she's up for a trip to the hospital. It might do more harm than good. Let's keep her here where it's safe and quiet. She's probably not used to so much stuff going on out in the desert."

It wasn't only what had happened for the last day or two, it was the emotions that had gone with all of it that had worn her out as well. Sue offered to let her stay right in their home with them or in one of the guest cabins either one. Taya opted for the guest cabin in the hopes of keeping everyone safer and not being such an unexpected intrusion into the Maylon home front, but that night as she tried to go to sleep it felt incredibly lonely and she cried for Zeus again. Then she wondered where Matt was and if he was okay after all that had happened. She still didn't even know if they were going to able to be together after all of this was over.

He must have realized how she was struggling because first thing the next morning Drew delivered a beautiful bouquet of wild flowers with a note that simply said. "I miss you, Matt"

That sweet bouquet helped her make it through the next day of living in limbo and when on the third morning Zan showed up with clothes, toiletries, cosmetics, and her lap top and then brought in her huge, white buddy, she broke down and cried again on both Zan and the dog.

Zeus was a little unsteady on his feet and limped on the leg he'd been bitten on, but he had enough gumption left in him to let Matt's dad know in no uncertain terms that he was in charge of Taya, and no one was to get near her. Having Zeus there with her helped immensely and Zan stayed long enough to tease her into being in the best mood she'd been in since she'd last seen Matt. Just before he left, he hugged her and whispered that the FBI and the Steamboat police were working together for her security.

After Zan left, Zeus was with her constantly and seemed to understand that she needed him almost under her feet to feel okay. Even though he obviously didn't feel all that hot, he dutifully picked himself up and dragged himself from room to room with her whenever she moved.

Her laptop proved to be more than simply a way to do her work so she could stay busy, and keep her mind occupied. Sue told her Matt's Email address and she was able to send him a short message that night that he returned almost immediately. Taya knew he was busy, so she didn't send more, but just knowing he was okay and took the time to reply helped her.

The next night when he woke her up at two o'clock in the morning because he couldn't wait until morning to see her helped even more. She heard his knock, and at first it scared her until she noticed Zeus was standing at the door wagging his tail. Taya flew to the door and ripped it open and ran into his arms. Even as tired as he was, he laughed at her. "Did you miss me?"

"Yes! I missed you terribly! What are you doing here?"

He ran a hand through his hair and took her hand to lead her into her living room and pull her onto his lap on her couch. "I finished that darn contract and sent it all in and then I had to see you."

"You made it okay, then?"

"Yes, you'll never guess who helped me."

"What do you mean? Who helped you?"

"Zan showed up the day after he brought you here. He had five guys with him and for two days they worked their tails off and helped us finish in time."

"Zan did that? Oh my gosh! What a sweetie. When I see him I'm going to kiss him."

Matt looked at her steadily and said, "Don't you dare, Taya. He honestly is in love with you. You shouldn't toy with him."

"He's not in love with me, Matt. He's more like a brother."

Shaking his head, he cautioned, "Taya, you think of him as a brother. He does not think of you as a sister. If you kissed him it would be mean. Don't lead him on. Plus, I don't want your mouth near anyone but me."

She laughed up at him. "Did you miss me?"

He sighed and leaned his head back. "I shouldn't even answer that. I missed you so much it could incriminate me. Living without you and wondering if you were safe was like . . . I don't even know what it was like. It was awful. The whole four hundred and something thousand dollars wasn't worth living without you for four days."

She laughed. "Dang, that's a hundred grand a day! That might be exaggerating just a little, Matt."

Smiling tiredly, he said, "Okay, maybe it was worth four days, but definitely not five."

"So now what are you going to do?"

"Sleep. I'm going to wake up only long enough to get a tux and climb onto a plane with you."

Disappointed that he hadn't touched on the future, she said, "You probably shouldn't have driven all the way here tonight. You look like heck. I would rather have had to wait to see you, than have you drive when you were too tired."

He put a hand into her hair and tugged it gently as he kissed her. "I had to come. Sorry. How are things going here?"

"Good. You're family has been wonderful to me. Zeus came from the vet yesterday morning and he's helped me not be so homesick. He's not moving too fast, but he's here and I love him. When you knocked, I knew it was you because he was standing at the door and wagging. I think he missed you too."

He reached down to pet the huge, shaggy head. "How has he been with people here?"

"He loves your mom, he tolerates Drew, and he wants to eat your dad. All in all, that's better than I expected."

Matt looked at her. "How have you done with them?"

"I love them, but I hate to be an imposition. And I feel like I'm putting them in danger. I've been trying to stay busy so I don't drive them nuts. The first couple days that was hard because I had nothing to do. Yesterday Zan brought my laptop and it's been better."

He took her hand and wove his fingers through hers. "You're not an imposition, Taya. They love me, so they love you. Don't you understand that?"

She considered that and had to admit, "Honestly, no. That kind of unconditional love is a little hard for me to fathom."

Touching her cheek, he said, "I'm sorry it is. That's the kind of love you've deserved to have your whole life."

She looked off into the distance and said, "That's how I want my children to feel. I want them to know I love them no matter what they do, right or wrong."

"They will. I'm sure they will." He rubbed the back of her hand thoughtfully. "What are you going to do now that you're not the sheep princess?"

It was hard to face him to answer when she only wanted to be with him, but she squashed her self doubt and simply said, "Make it through this trial and then the election. After that I don't know. It's difficult to know what to do until I know how careful I need to be about someone coming after me." She wished she could say she wanted to be wherever he was going to be, but she didn't dare. She still didn't even know what he wanted from her. He had driven here tonight, because he needed to see her, but he never talked about the future with her. She wasn't sure what was going on with the two of them.

He rubbed the little bone behind her ear, and she laid her head on his chest and wished for those nights back on her swing again. She already missed the simplicity of the sheep camp. They hadn't had to figure out things like the future back then. She looked up at him and he touched her mouth with his thumb and she wondered what he was thinking.

Sighing, he gently pushed her off, stood up and then pulled her up beside him. He wrapped his arms around her tightly and bent and kissed her like he never wanted to let her go and when he finally drew back, she was more mixed up than ever. She knew for the first time in her life she was in love, but she didn't know if he felt the same about her and he wasn't a member anyway.

He walked her to her door and said, "If I had my way, I'd be sleeping between your front door and your bedroom door until this trial is over, but that's probably not all that wise, and you have Zeus anyway. I'm in the cabin on this side and Drew is in the one on the other if you need anything. Thanks for not being mad at me for waking you up at two in the morning."

Leaning against his shoulder, she reminded him, "I'm actually still several nights down on you for mouse rescues and sitting with me when I was sick, remember?"

Smiling, he assured her, "I will always remember those mice until the day I die, Taya. You were far too entertaining to ever forget. If we ever make it back to that sheep trailer, I may plant one occasionally just so I have to rescue you. Kiss me, so I can go to sleep before I'm completely brain dead."

She reached up and kissed him gently and he hugged her tight and said, "On second thought, I don't care if I'm brain dead. I think I'll just stay here and kiss you instead of sleep."

That made her laugh and say, "Your mother is really sweet, but I don't think I'd want to get on her bad side.

Something tells me she's tough under that gentle exterior and I'd hate to bring out the mother tiger on your first night home. You'd better go to your own cabin and come kiss me tomorrow."

"That's probably a good idea. And you're right. She's tough." He leaned and kissed her again. "I missed you, Taya. I'm glad you're here and safe. Good night."

"Me too. Night, Matt."

She slept late the next morning. It was almost as if now that she knew he was there and done and okay, she could relax.

Zeus finally made her get out of bed to walk him or she would have slept even later. She got up and dressed and took him outside and walked the path through the compound behind the cabins with him. Where she was now was much higher in elevation than the sheep camp had been and there were conifers and aspens, instead of the cedars and sage and the mid October morning was cold. She was going to have to either pick up some of her winter gear when she was in Maryland next week, or buy new.

As she walked, she thought about what her plans were for the future. Joshua was already talking like he thought she was coming back as soon as the trial was over, and other than Matt, there was no reason not to. But except for her work, there was nothing back there she wanted to return to.

She wondered what Matt was going to do. She knew he had closed his apartment and put his things in storage after Stacy, so she assumed he would get another one when he decided what he was going to do professionally. He'd been working here in Steamboat. Maybe he'd want to go back to his old job, although she didn't really think so.

She and Zeus walked for over an hour, but she still didn't know what she wanted to do with her life, so she went back to her cabin, had a banana and a glass of milk and went to work on her lap top.

It was after noon before Matt knocked on her cabin door and let himself in. He came in and pulled her up from her seat to hug her and then kiss her, still looking tired, but much better than he'd looked last night and she asked, "Did you get all of your sleep stocked back up already? You look better."

He shook his head. "No, but enough for now. Are you up to going into Steamboat with me to see if I can find a tux? I'll take you out to lunch. We'll have a real date. What do you say?"

Hesitantly, she asked, "Is it safe?"

"Drew thinks it is. He checked in with the FBI and he's been watching for anyone hanging around. Steamboat is a resort town that's almost dead this time of year and they've seen no one so they're going to let us go. We might not even find a tux. We might have to drive almost a hundred miles into Denver. Drew and some of the others will hang out near us. Will that make you feel more comfortable?"

She smiled enthusiastically. "Yes. I'd love to go. Can I leave Zeus? Will he be okay?"

"Is he house broken?"

She glanced at her white friend. "He has been while I've been with him these last couple of days, but while I've known him, he's never been inside. I simply don't want him to bite someone, so I've kept him inside with me."

"He'd probably be happier outside than left in. Do you think you can talk him into not eating my dad if we leave him?"

Nodding, she answered, "Yes, but what about anyone else who comes?"

He yawned and turned toward the door. "I'll ask my mom if they're expecting anyone else. I'll be right back."

Taya shut down her computer, got up, and combed her hair and put makeup on and then went to change her clothes. She had brought almost nothing with her to

Colorado from Maryland, and for the desert she had only bought jeans and casual clothes, but she did have a couple of outfits that were nice from when she'd visited Madeline and she put one on.

When she came out of the bedroom, Matt stood there and stared at her and she asked, "What? Is something wrong?" She looked down to see if there was something wrong with her clothing but couldn't see anything and asked, "Why are you looking at me like that?"

"Wow, I've just never seen you in anything but jeans and your church dresses, and even then you didn't wear much makeup. You didn't need it, but you look great! Maybe I should go back and start over."

Shaking her head, she said, "No. You look perfect. Jeans fit you. Don't change for me."

He rolled his eyes and grinned. "Taya, we're going to get a tux."

"Well, you know what I mean."

"You didn't have to change either."

She took both of his hands and asked, "Will you still like me if I tell you that sometimes I wear nice clothes?"

Releasing her hands, he held her waist. "Do you honestly doubt me?"

"No, but it might bother some guys."

He kissed her slowly. "I'm not some guys, Taya. I'm just Matt. I'll like you in whatever. Always."

That made her smile as he opened the cabin door for her. "I think I knew that. What kind of food do they have in Steamboat?"

He helped her into his Jeep. "A little of everything. What do you like?"

"Seafood. I'm from Maryland, remember? I grew up near the ocean."

Coming around and getting in, he assured her, "I think we can find seafood. We can eat lobster to celebrate surviving the desert. We'll have to see what we can find open. Some places in town close in the spring and fall between seasons."

As she buckled in, she commented, "Your Jeep is so clean. What happened to it?"

He laughed as he started it. "I celebrated the end of the contract by washing and vacuuming it this morning. No sand is a beautiful thing."

She was thoughtful for a second and then admitted a little sadly, "I miss Horse. I'll bet she's lonely."

He backed the Jeep out. "I think she's okay. Zan took her back to Joseph's with the sheep. He'll watch over her for you."

Glancing at him, she asked, "What happened between you and Zan that you're all buddies now?"

He smiled across the Jeep at her. "That's a good question. And I'm not sure what the answer is, but I think he finally figured out that he can trust me as far as treating you decently. It had something to do with me asking him to take care of you while I finished in the desert."

She shook her head at him. "That's still a little strange to me. For some reason, I never pictured the two of you getting along all that well. You're both too used to being in control or something."

He reached for her hand. "But we're on the same team as far as you're concerned. If it wouldn't kill him, I'd take him to D.C. with us. I wouldn't mind having another guy along to watch over you."

"What do you mean, if it wouldn't kill him?"

"I know you don't believe me, Taya, but he truly is in love with you, and I'm the one who's going to be at the ball with you. It would be mean to take him."

After considering that, she said, "You're a surprisingly nice guy. You know that?"

"I'm getting better. That doesn't mean I wouldn't like to take a punch at John Channing some time. I'm still working on that one."

Looking out the window, she quietly said, "He's honestly not worth your hassle, Matt. I feel more sorry for him than anything anymore."

"Why sorry?"

She shrugged. "Because in the big picture, he simply doesn't understand. When he dies, he's gonna have an ugly wake up call."

He rubbed his thumb across her fingers. "Are you nervous about having to testify next week?"

"A little. I'm not even sure how much I can help. I didn't know much about what he was into, but if I can help I should, even if it makes me nervous."

He gave her hand a squeeze and reminded her, "We'll be there with you. You'll be fine."

She looked across at him again. "I bought your tickets to come back here to Colorado before the trial. I'm sorry. I didn't know you wanted to stay any longer."

"I'll change them. Do you mind if I stay longer?"

She shook her head. "Of course not. I'll love it, but it might not be a very fun time. I'm probably going to have to stay put to be safe back there."

"So we'll sit in the hotel pool a lot." He shrugged. "And order seafood from room service. You probably have great lobster out there don't you?"

"It's marvelous!" Her enthusiasm made him smile. "And bigger than you can even eat. Well, bigger than I can eat. I'm not sure about you."

He laughed at her hesitation. "I have never yet met a lobster I wouldn't try to eat." He paused for a few seconds and then asked, "Are you going to go see your parents?"

She looked up and met his eyes. "I don't know. I don't know what to do about them. I'm trying to forgive them and move on, but my dad was indicted too. Somehow, whatever I saw with John incriminated him too. They may hate me forever after this. I certainly don't think they're going to want to see me."

He concentrated on driving for a second and then encouraged her, "You simply need to do what you think is the right thing to do, Taya. And then you need to be okay with that. Just don't keep hard feelings against them forever. That would hurt you far more than it would hurt them." He reached across and took her hand.

Sadly, she admitted, "I know that. But unfortunately, I'm human. It's been hard. I've thought I was past it a hundred times now, and then I realize I'm still bitter. I don't know how long it will take me to learn to be a better Christian."

He rubbed his thumb across her hand again. "There's no such thing as a better Christian than you, Taya. You've been a wonderful example for me."

"Thank you, but you didn't see me tell off Stacy that time. I was terrible. I still feel guilty. I have an awfully long way to go."

"Did you accuse her of anything that wasn't true?"

She shook her head. "No, but I told her to get out of my camp and wait in her car. Jesus would never have said something like that."

He laughed at her face. "I still think I'd liked to have seen that. I'll bet you were a hoot!"

Guiltily, she smiled. "But it was rude. I shouldn't have done it."

"So if you ever see her again, apologize. If you don't, then don't worry about it." He turned off into a parking lot. "This is it. I think this is the best seafood in town. Bring your coastal pallet and tell me what you think."

They ate their lobster and she thought it was as good as any she'd had back east. Then they went in search of a tuxedo. They actually did find a place there in Steamboat that had one and Taya was surprised. It didn't seem like that big or fancy of a town. They were strolling down the street hand in hand carrying the long suit bag, headed back to the Jeep when Matt gave a low chuckle and squeezed her hand. "You know how we talked about apologizing to Stacy when you saw her? That's her and Justin just up ahead, headed our way. Now's your chance. Have at her."

Taya looked up the street and almost felt a little bit nervous. She hadn't truly thought she would have to be ready to apologize this quickly. As they got closer, the other two recognized them and Taya became more confident when she saw their little moment of panic. As they approached she glanced over at Matt and almost laughed at his "I dare you" look. He was the first to say something. He nodded and simply said, "Justin, Stacy. How's it going?"

He probably would have kept on walking, but Taya pulled on his hand to stop him and turned to call back to them, "Oh, Stacy. I'm glad I saw you. I've felt guilty ever since that second time you came to my camp. I was rude, and I'd like to apologize. What you had done truly wasn't any of my business and I should have nosed out and been more polite. Please forgive me."

For a second Stacy froze and then she looked up at Justin guiltily before she said, "Sure," to Taya.

As Taya and Matt walked on, behind them they heard Justin ask her angrily, "You went to see Matt since then? Twice?" He obviously wasn't happy about that and Matt laughed and Taya put a hand to her mouth to swallow her own smile. So much for apologizing. She had probably just opened an awful can of worms for the ever deceitful Stacy. Every once in a while Matt would shake his head and chuckle on the way home, and Taya laughed with him. Poor, stupid girl.

That night Taya got to meet all of Matt's family when Sue had a dinner to celebrate Matt's coming home and invited all of her children and their families. There were thirteen people around Sue's big table and a couple of them were very small and very glad to see their Uncle Matt home again. He was so gentle and sweet with them that Taya had a hard time not staring. She knew he was gentle, but she hadn't ever seen this side of him.

Taya was glad she had had so much experience at official dinners with her parents. Her automatic manners kicked in and she forgot to be nervous at meeting them all.

Later that night, Matt had her on his lap again, this time on his mother's porch swing. It was so cold out that he was in his coat and she was wrapped in a blanket, but it was still nice to be back in a swing with him. He must have understood that she missed those nights with him in the desert already. Those had been sweet times. They didn't stay out too long and then went over to Drew's cabin and watched a movie with him before Matt walked her back to hers. He didn't go in this time and simply kissed her goodnight on her porch. Even though she was tired, she missed him when he left.

She read her scriptures before going to sleep and then lay there with Zeus on the floor beside her. She was still wondering what she needed to be planning for her life. She'd been trying to pray about it, but she wasn't coming up with many answers. Chiding herself for being so wishy-washy about making a decision, she set a goal to have a definite plan for the near future within the week. She didn't know what she was going to do, but she knew she needed to make some decisions. Finally, she dropped off to sleep thinking of Matt's sweet good night kiss.

Jaclyn M. Hawkes

Chapter 27

At two-twenty-eight a.m. Matt heard Taya scream in the cabin next door and jumped up, threw on some jeans and ran. He met Drew on her porch with his gun drawn. When Matt told him to put it away and knocked loudly Drew was alarmed and said, "Matt, what are you thinking? What if there's an intruder in there with her? Get out of the way!"

Matt gave Drew a grin. "Oh, there's someone in there all right. Or rather something, but it's not an intruder. If it was, she'd have shot him and Zeus would just now be eating the body. I'll bet you twenty bucks it's a mouse."

He'd hardly finished speaking when the door flew open and Taya came running out and hid behind him. He took a second to calm her and then sent her to sit on the hood of his Jeep. Turning to Drew who stood by looking at them like they'd lost their minds, he said, "You'd better come help me, Drew. This is a seriously big cabin to hide a mouse in, and she'll never get back to sleep if we don't find it."

As they went in and shut the door behind them, Drew whispered, "Why doesn't she just have Zeus look at it? That dog could simply scare it to death and then we could merely go in and pick up the body."

"Zeus sticks to things like coyotes and lions. I don't think a mouse would ever occur to him."

"Gees, if she screams like that when she sees a mouse, what does she do when she sees a mountain lion?"

Matt shook his head at remembering her first mountain lion. He told Drew what had happened and how upset he had been at her about it, and Drew looked at him to see if he was being serious. He raised a hand to defend himself. "Dead honest, Drew. She goes out in the middle of the night with a thirty-thirty and blams yotes without blinking an eye and then stays out there with her sheep for the rest of the night. I used to lay there in my tent and feel guilty for not going out to save her even though I was working like sixteen hour days. She's a dead shot, and I don't think she'd ever touched a gun in her life until this summer. In D.C. they don't even let you hardly keep them, do they? They have the strictest gun laws in the country."

"So what's up with this mouse thing? Why do they bother her?"

Matt shrugged. "I don't know, but she comes unglued every time. She's actually so darn funny I almost get into trouble laughing, but then afterward I'm her hero, so it's kind of handy."

Drew laughed and said, "You're disgusting. So what do I get out of this?"

"Hey, you're a peace officer. And you're certainly not going to get any peace with a mouse in her cabin."

"Are you going to tell her how many jillion mice are likely to be in here?"

Matt shook his head. "Nope. I'm going to get her a cat and arm wrestle Zeus into not eating it. Even heroes have to sleep occasionally."

Drew chuckled. "Good luck with that one. He probably doesn't even chew cats before he swallows them."

"You'd be surprised how easily that dog can be bought with a good steak."

It took them a while, but between the two of them and a broom and a mop, they approached her with the offending trophy at which she promptly stood up on the hood of Matt's Jeep to get further away from it and screamed and swore. Then she slapped her hand over her mouth in embarrassment. At that point Drew threw the mouse out into the trees and Matt came to help her off his Jeep before she dented the hood and asked her forgiveness for scaring her into cussing.

The next half hour on her couch was so nice talking to her to get her back to where she thought she could sleep again, that he hoped she found another one in there before morning. He walked back to his cabin wondering how he was going to break it to his mother that he was in love with a Mormon.

Back in his bed, he made the decision to get serious fast about checking into her church. He'd read the Book of Mormon she'd given him and believed it to be authentic and he'd felt better at her church and being taught by the missionaries than at any other church he'd been to. He wanted to become a real member, but he needed to make sure it was the actual teachings he felt strongly about, and not the beautiful girl who had shared it with him. He knew how much it all meant to her, and he had to be willing to take her beliefs seriously.

His thoughts made him get back out of bed to pray once more, something she had helped him to be able to do again. Prayer had been the main impetus that had helped him keep on keeping on with the Herculean contract he had just finished. Right now, he needed to know for sure what God wanted him to do and believe in this situation.

Somehow, even after searching his soul, he still fell asleep to dream of a girl in a Washington Wizards nightshirt standing on a red Jeep.

On the way into his mother's kitchen for breakfast the next morning she planted a kiss on the top of Drew's head for his part in rescuing her in the night and Matt smiled at Drew's blush. Sitting next to Matt, she reached for his hand under the table and gave it a squeeze as she leaned to kiss him and thank him as well. She smelled heavenly and he decided that mice were one of God's greatest gifts to the male of the species.

They spent the morning on-line where she ordered several outfits from some local department stores and then in the early afternoon, he ran downtown to pick them up. That afternoon she modeled for him. He'd never been much of a shopper, but it was a great day simply helping her find clothing. He probably encouraged her to buy too many things, but she looked great in them all.

Chapter 28

Early the next morning they flew out for D.C. and she asked Drew if he would be a liaison of sorts between the FBI agents who would be watching out for her as she flew and was transferred to their hotel. Originally, they had arranged for two others, but on talking to the agents after checking in, that was beefed up to nine so there would be at least three other armed men with her around the clock. During the fundraiser and on the way to and from the courthouse there would be even more.

Matt had known she would be at home with the glitzy, high rolling type of party this was going to be, but he was still a little overwhelmed with the beautiful, queenly woman who walked out of her hotel room at his knock that evening. Even in the security crush, she stepped into the sleek limousine that was waiting for them outside the lobby without batting an eye. He and Drew and the others with them got in beside her like it was all in the course of a day's work.

Matt was her date, while the others were only there to protect her, but on the way into the building it felt good to be there for her and know the others had her back in case of a problem. Inside, Drew stayed close, but the others spread out a few yards and Taya talked and mingled like this was second nature to her.

She absolutely sparkled with her crystal beads in the lamp light. Even her up-do had glittering pins woven through it, and he honestly felt like he was the prince and she was the princess at the ball. They got some of the elegant little canapés and finger sandwiches and a fluted glass of fruit juice at the long buffet tables, but Taya didn't actually eat anything after she got it and eventually merely set it aside.

After she mingled for a while and had had innumerable photos taken with the candidate whose night it was, she took Matt's hand and whispered, "Would you dance with me?" He gladly led her out onto the dance floor. Here they didn't have to talk to anyone they just danced. Even in her heels, she fit perfectly against his chest and he wrapped her in his arms and inhaled the smell of her perfume and wanted to stay like that forever. It was incredibly nice to hold her against him in the low lights. There on the dance floor it almost felt as if they were insulated from the rest of the party and socializing. It was only the two of them and the music and the night's magic.

They danced close and talked until finally she sadly whispered again, "Much as I hate to say it, we probably needed to take another turn around to face some more cameras. Are you game?"

With one last spin, he whispered back, "Absolutely. Anything for you, Taye." She smiled and stepped off the floor and he had to respect that she took the fact that she could sway this vote very seriously.

He was a little flabbergasted a moment later when he realized just how seriously. She stopped at a table and took out a beautiful pen and a check and was in the process of writing it out when she was interrupted by a news reporter covering the event. He asked her if she would answer some questions on camera and when she agreed, he starting rolling.

The first thing he did was introduce her as the former fiancé' of Congressman John Channing who had had him arrested for assault at his own major fundraiser and had then pressed the charges and testified at his trial. He went on to make a big deal of the fact that she was now here in support of the opposing candidate, James Livingston, and asked her if she had anything to say about that.

Matt was totally proud of her when she replied, "I *was* engaged to Congressman Channing, but at the time I didn't know the kinds of things he was involved in and capable of. I'm afraid I had to find that out the hard way and am still paying for that." She indicated the brace on her left hand. "I can't say anything about what John is being tried for, but I can tell you I believe James Livingston is by far the more honorable candidate, and he is who I will be voting for on election day, and it is to his campaign that I am contributing."

The camera zoomed in on the check she was writing and Matt was surprised when he realized she had just written a check for twenty three hundred dollars and handed it to the gentleman who was there to take it. Matt didn't even know it was legal to donate that much. She smiled one more time at the camera man and then calmly took Matt's elbow and they went on to mingle again.

A little later she whispered to him, "Dance with me one more time, Prince Charming? Then can we go back to the hotel and order a pizza?"

Slipping a hand around her waist he replied, "Absolutely, Princess Taya. I would be honored." He led her onto the floor once again and took her into his arms. Black tie parties would probably get old fast if you had to do them all the time, but once in a blue moon it was ridiculously fun to dress up and escort a princess. The chance to dance with her in all her finery was far more than merely fun. She looked like a beautiful, magical fairy princess tonight, and felt like heaven here against him. Even having to have his picture taken this many thousand times was worth it to hold her like this.

The clock struck twelve and they told their host goodbye to another spate of cameras and then they and their entourage headed back out to the waiting car that security had already checked out. On the way back to the hotel, Matt was surprised to see that they had more intimidating black SUVs on both sides of them. Instead of reassuring him, it was more nerve racking. What was Taya up against here?

At any rate, the pressure had to dissipate soon. The news reports had probably already started to air the footage of Taya and it wouldn't take long to fire up the spin doctors and political experts who would be all over this like a pack of wolves. Matt was sure the fact that this fundraiser was scheduled for the day before the trial wasn't coincidence. And with the election just over two weeks away, Taya's appearance here tonight could very well be devastating to John Channing's political career forever.

Drew apparently didn't think the escort was normal and he leaned to one of the agents and asked what was going on. Several of them looked at each other before the agent answered stoically, "During the security sweep at the venue, explosives were found under the limo."

Matt was horrified and turned to the agent and all but snapped, "And when were you going to mention this little detail to us?"

The agent didn't even flinch when he returned, "It's under control, Maylon. We caught it, and telling her would only upset her." He gave Matt a stony look and continued, "Which won't help anything."

Taya put a manicured hand gently on Matt's arm and he swallowed his desire to tear into the guy. This was all nearly unfathomable to him. He'd had no idea Taya had been in this much danger out in the desert.

All of them were feeling the tension, as they disembarked from the limo and hurried through the hotel lobby to their section of rooms. Matt and Drew were together in a suite that adjoined Taya's with the others' on both sides and across the hall from them. Even the hotel security was on alert and for the night tonight they would have a man in the hall constantly and the hotel itself would be watched closely as well until after Taya testified and flew out.

Taya wanted a pizza, but in light of security, two of the guys went downstairs to the hotel restaurant and brought back food instead. Matt took Taya to her room, but he stopped her before she went into her bedroom to change. He hadn't had her to himself for one second all night and he wanted to kiss the princess before the night was out. He knew she was tired, and he held her to him gently as he bent to kiss her pretty neck where the long sparkling earrings barely brushed it. That was all he wanted, but he'd wanted to do it all night.

"You were great tonight, Taya. I was proud of you. You made a difference when you had the chance. It took a lot of guts, but then that's always been your strong point." He nuzzled her skin and kissed her again. His voice was husky when he finally said, "You look so beautiful tonight. It was fun to be with the princess. Thanks for bringing me."

He kissed her again for a long, long moment and then let her go into her room to change back into the Taya he was used to and he went into his own room. He had gotten as far as taking off his tie, when she knocked on his door.

Looking a little embarrassed as he opened it, she said, "I forgot I can't get out of this dress alone. I had Allie help me get into it when she did my hair, but in light of the security issues tonight, would you help me with the zipper?"

"Of course." He smiled at her, remembering when she had gotten stuck in this same dress that night in the sheep trailer. She turned her back to him and he bent to find the pull. He had to lift up the hem of the jacket to find it, and when he did, his finger nail caught on something sharp in the beads. He lifted it to see what it was and was surprised to see that one of the beads was huge and clear instead of black like the rest and had metal prongs instead of simple stitching. He looked up at her in amazement, as he reached to pull her missing huge solitaire from the threads in the lining of her jacket and said, "I think we found your diamond."

"What?" He pulled it free and put it into her hand and she looked up at him incredulously. "You're kidding! Where was it?"

"You weren't joking about it being obscene. Did he really expect you to wear that thing?"

She looked up at him with big eyes. "Oh my gosh! This dress has been through an ambulance ride, the hospital, flown to Colorado, and dragged all over the desert. It's been to the dry cleaners! And we danced all night in it. I can't even believe that thing wasn't lost somewhere!" She finally heard his question and she looked down at the brace on her left hand, and sighed. "I wanted a simple gold band, but it wasn't about symbolizing an unbroken circle of love. It was about status." This time when she looked up at him, her eyes were sad. "Now what do I do with it?"

"I don't know."

"I don't want it, but I don't want to give it back to him and help finance his campaign. Is it mine or is it his?"

"You've got me. Maybe Drew would know. At any rate, put it somewhere really safe. I don't even want to guess how much that thing's worth."

She sighed and then laughed. "Ah, what's money? I spent twenty three hundred dollars tonight to try to make a difference in an election. I can't even believe I did it. The only other time I've written a check that big, was when I bought a car."

"I was beginning to wonder if writing checks like that was everyday stuff for you. I guess it was merely another Taya surprise. You'd think nothing would surprise me by now, but you still keep blowing me away."

She patted his cheek. "You say that, but you always deal with whatever. You're my most durable friend ever, do you know that? Thank you."

He grinned. "Yeah, but what you don't know is that you ought to charge me admission for all the interesting entertainment."

"Then you should charge me for all the services rendered."

"Like?"

"Coming to camp by me. Helping me survive the fever from Hades. Rescuing me from mice, mountain lions, rattle snakes and slippery men. Saving my dog. Even like helping me unzip this dress. Twice now I would have been stranded in it without you."

He laughed and unzipped it. "You do owe me, don't you? I'll have to think of a way you can repay me. Hurry and change and come eat with me. I'm starving."

Jaclyn M. Hawkes

Chapter 29

Security was uppermost in their minds on the drive into the courthouse and getting into the court room itself, even with the media everywhere, was almost anticlimactic after last nights' bomb threat. The first day of the trial was a total waste of all of their time. John Channing wasn't even there that day and it was a bunch of legal maneuvering and bologna. By that afternoon, nothing had been accomplished other than that they were all bored stiff except during the drive to and from, when they were all tense.

Taya had been afraid her parents would be there, but they hadn't been either and she came back to the hotel much relieved. She knew she needed to go see them while she was in town, but it was going to be hard. Matt mentioning it had been a good thing. It had helped her to be more willing to face them, but she was half afraid to. Even after all these months, she still felt betrayed, and she knew they were going to be mad about her involvement with John's trials.

The trial started on a Friday, so the week end was a bust because of security, but Taya decided she was going to her home singles ward to church Sunday even if it wasn't all that prudent and she dragged Matt and Drew and the others along with her. Who could tell? Maybe it would end up being a good missionary moment. At any rate, she needed to go to help her deal with the anxiousness she was feeling.

She was already in the church building when she realized she hadn't thought about Relief Society and it being all women. She had to decide whether to kill an hour, or make the five of them wait outside the room for her, send them all to the elders' quorum, or make them sit with her in a room full of women. She turned around to look at all their faces knowing it was up to her, because she was the only one who had a clue what was going on. She and Matt had always skipped the first hour to avoid being conspicuous.

The elder's quorum president walking in the door behind them helped her decide. She took him aside and explained what was going on and asked him to take Matt and Drew and one of the others and show them to the elder's quorum and she would keep the other two with her for the first hour. That way, at least Matt and Drew would be spared from sitting through Relief Society and she would still have two men right with her. If there were to be a problem, the others would be right next door. Matt was comfortable with church because of the other times he'd been with her and he took this turn of events in stride with his usual unruffleability.

The rest of church went relatively smoothly until after Sacrament meeting when they were on the way out. One of the local guys from her ward who had always had a thing for her, rushed up to her in the lobby and went to throw his arm around her shoulders. Almost instantly he was shoved up against a wall with the arm wrenched up behind his back and Taya had been literally surrounded by her entourage. Taya diffused the situation as quickly as she could, but not before the poor guy had been traumatized and her ward had had their moment of excitement for the year. As they quickly exited the building, she tried to laugh. At least if she ever came back to this ward that particular guy would never bother her again.

Back at the hotel they ate and then Taya settled onto the sofa in her sitting room to read the Book of Mormon. She was feeling like she was on this crazy amusement park ride that had her happy and then anxious and then smiling again.

She hardly knew her own mind, and was hoping for some peace of mind and spiritual guidance.

Within just a few minutes, Matt knocked on the adjoining door and came in to sit with her. "Whatcha doing?"

"Studying the Book of Mormon. What are you up to this afternoon?"

"I don't know for sure. I guess I just want to come and be with you. Do you mind?"

"Of course not. Come in. What's Drew doing?"

"Napping. He's a firm believer in Sunday being a day of rest. Later he'll want to watch football. What are you studying?"

"Captain Moroni. He was one of the great leaders and prophets in the Americas hundreds of years ago."

"Captain Moroni of the title of liberty?"

She smiled. "Hey, how do you know that? You've been reading the copy I gave you."

"You asked me to, and I said I would."

Surprised at how he always took things in stride, she asked, "Have you already finished it?"

"Yes and I'm going through it again. It's a seriously wild read. Some of those battles are outrageous."

She nodded sadly, "You'd have thought they would learn, but they never seemed to for long. We're just like them today, I think. We don't seem to learn to stay on the right path for long either."

"Some do, Tay. Some people are truly trying to do their best. Don't discount everyone."

"You're right. I'm sorry, that was negative. You're good for me. You're always so wise."

He took her hand and chuckled softly. "Not wise, just Matt. I was thinking about you when I said some people are trying to do their best."

"Well, I mess up a lot, but my intentions are basically good. And the longer I work at it, the better I get, but it's a good thing we usually have a lifetime to work out the kinks. I'm going to need it as slow as I learn. I'm incredibly grateful that God is patient."

He looked at her with the most intense look and asked, "How do you know?"

"How do I know what?"

"That God is patient."

She had to think about that for a few minutes and then answered, "I guess because I know that no matter how many times I make mistakes, He still hangs in there with me. Why? How do you know God is patient?"

"I'm not sure I do understand what God is like. I know I don't understand Him like you do. I'm still trying to figure all this out. I'm a late bloomer I suppose. It's only been lately that I've even realized how important all of these concepts are. Maybe that was one good thing that came of dealing with Stacy. I learned that being without God wasn't good. Before that I was a little luke warm. My relationship with God wasn't all that vital to me until I didn't have one and realized how much I was struggling. But now, even though I'm trying to get serious, I still find myself wondering what He's like. You seem so sure about so many things that I need to know how you know. How does anyone know for sure?"

"I guess the best way would be to study about Him and talk to Him a lot."

"How do you truly study about God? I mean, a lot of the Bible is pretty nebulous, and no one can even agree on whether He's a spirit or what and to some He's kind and to some He's all fire and brimstone. How do you know?"

This time she looked right at him and thought. *Well, this is it.* "Actually, that's easy, Matt. This is going to sound simplistic, but it works. You kind of have to work backwards. All you have to do is decide if the Book of Mormon is true. Which takes some work on your part. But if it's true, then Joseph Smith really did translate it and he truly did see the Father and the Son in the sacred grove, and the church truly is Christ's original organization headed by Him. And the prophet really is a prophet. It all has to be right.

"At that point, you can know for yourself that God has a prophet on the earth who is speaking for Him and all you have to do is find out what the prophet says. If you know Joseph Smith was truly a prophet and saw and spoke to God, then you can believe that God looked and acted the way he said He did."

She smiled up at him encouragingly. "On the flip side, if you know the Book of Mormon isn't true, then none of it's true. I say that because I honestly believe it is true and that if you truly want to know for yourself, you'll find that out as well. This is one of those things that the more you really check it out, the more solidly you're convinced. The ones who don't believe are the ones who haven't thoroughly checked it out with honest intent. And the nice part about that is that when you do check it out, it all makes sense. In some ways, the whole thing is simply a lot of no brainers. It's like, no duh, if you're nice, you'll be happier than if you're grumpy. Or if you are clean living, you'll feel better physically and emotionally than if you aren't."

She shrugged. "For me. Once I knew for sure, then I could follow the prophet's counsel, knowing for sure that it was right, without ever having to question the validity. But that only works when you've found that knowledge out for yourself. Now all I have to do is research whatever my question is at the time. Usually, one of the prophets has made an official statement about whatever it is and I can know that that's God's word, not some human being's take on an eternal concept. And yeah, there are always going to be some funky things we don't know for sure, or at least there's not an official doctrine. Some things are too sacred to reveal or no prophet has ever made an official declaration about it. But, some things we know for sure. God and Jesus are two separate beings who have bodies that resemble us and they look exactly like each other. Some things we know.

"As far as how patient God is. I believe the only way we can truly know Him is to study all we can and spend a lot of time visiting with Him, just like getting to know any one else."

She hesitated. "You're kind of giving me that look. Did I just make you think I'm an off the deep end wacko?"

"Mm. No, but only because I know you're not an off the deep end wacko from living by you in the desert."

"Oh." She looked a little confused and after a second or two she asked, "What does that mean?"

"Well . . . You just summed up the subject of God in two matter-of-fact minutes. And you did it in a way that makes me go, 'So, okay, I'll buy that.' Now what do I do about that? How am I supposed to fit the rest of the world into your little nutshell?"

She laughed and rested against his shoulder. "Please tell me you don't expect me to have all the answers."

"I don't. But you have enough of the answers that I'm going to have to hurry to catch up. I hate feeling like a light weight compared to you. I guess my male ego keeps intimating that as the guy, you should be able to lean on me occasionally if you needed to. I'm talking intellectually or spiritually or something."

"I know what you mean." She wove her hand with his. "And you're right. I do need that. More than occasionally. All women need that sometimes, even if they're too feminist to admit it. Strong women need even stronger men. God intended it to be that way. He actually wants men to be the heads of families and the spiritual leader and always has, with some qualification of course. But whether or not that works out is up to each of us individually, isn't it? Isn't our own level of spirituality and eventual eternal salvation up to each of us personally?"

"I'm sure, but it seems like having someone to encourage each other back and forth would make it much more attainable."

She smiled up at him. "There you go again with that incredible wisdom. I think you're right. A partner would be key. You are definitely not a light weight compared to anyone."

He glanced at her. "You're not fooling me, Taya, but I'm working on it. So is there a trick to finding out for sure if the Book of Mormon is true or not for myself?"

"Uh, no." She reached up and put a hand on his cheek. "Sorry. I mean, there's Moroni's promise at the end. But it's not a trick. You simply have to ask for yourself until you get an answer."

He shook his head. "That's not what I wanted you to tell me. I wanted the two minute, matter-of-fact deal so that I didn't have to rely on my own ability to figure this out. What's Moroni's promise? Same title of liberty guy?"

"No, this is a different Moroni. This one is the one who's Mormon's son and is only mentioned at the very, very end of the Book of Mormon. Remember after that last great battle where both sides creamed each other and there was only one Nephite left and he had to spend the rest of his life hiding so that the Lamanites didn't kill him?"

He nodded. "Okay, I remember him."

"There's a place there where he makes a promise to people who want to know if it's all true. Moroni 10:4 He says that after you've read, if you will ask God if it's true with faith, and a sincere heart, and real intent, God will 'manifest the truth of it unto you by the power of the Holy Ghost'. The Holy Ghost, the Spirit, is the only way any of us truly know anything. You have to ask and then listen for that still, small voice that brings the peace and warmth to your heart. That's how you know for yourself. And honestly, sometimes it's hard to hear. At least for me it is. It took me a long time to figure it out when I was seventeen. Of course my brain was still missing at the time, like most seventeen year olds."

He laughed at her. "Really? There was a time in your life when your brain was missing?"

She rolled her eyes. "Completely. In retrospect, I realize it's hard to survive with no brain. I almost didn't survive that time period. My lack of judgment was truly phenomenal. Thank goodness for Madeline. She's the one who found it—my brain. We found it barely in time for me to come to understand that the Book of Mormon is true before I'd made too many poor decisions."

"I think mine was still missing until about four and a half months ago. I told you I was a late bloomer. Justin definitely did not help me find my brain."

"Good friends are important. I can't imagine how different my life would be without Madeline and joining the church. My parents weren't nice, Christian people like yours. I mean they were okay, but I hadn't been given any kind of a spiritual foundation or value system other than the culture of society around me. And in D.C. at least, that was whatever I wanted to pick and choose."

He squeezed her hand. "You must have picked and chosen relatively well to have come to where you are without guidance."

"Oh, of course I've had guidance since Madeline. That's the great part of the church. If you really want answers, you couldn't ask for a better deal. Look, I'll show you." She went to the desk to retrieve her laptop. "There are two great websites. For beginners, the best place to start is mormon.org. It's the official church site for people who want to know more about what the church truly teaches. Then when you're a little further along, there's lds.org. Watch this."

She pulled up the internet on her laptop sitting on the coffee table in front of them. "Anything you want to know about anything. You can pull it up by topic . . . or which prophet . . . Or if it's in the scriptures. It's totally slick and easy. The most computer illiterate grandma in the world can check it out. I never have to go without guidance now, even when I'm not able to go to a steady ward where I have friends and help. It takes a little more self discipline when I'm by myself, but then when you're alone with a herd of sheep there's plenty of time to contemplate the things you miss in the chatter of society."

After looking thoughtful for a moment, she went on, "As crazy as going from here to the sheep seemed, it was a good change for me in lots of ways. It was very grounding. You can see things more clearly when you're at a little bit of a distance."

He thought about that and then said, "After getting a glimpse of what your life here must have been like, I can't even believe you ended up out there with the sheep. Looking back on when I first met you, I never dreamed you were Taya, the Washington D.C. socialite."

"Socialite isn't truly the right word. And it *was* a good place to hide."

He nudged her with his elbow. "You were marrying a congressman, Taya. I'd call that a socialite and then some."

She closed her computer and set it aside and lifted his arm up so she could turn to him and lean on his chest. "I'm simply me, Matt. Just Taya. No matter where I am."

He pulled her up onto his lap like he had gotten in the habit of doing when she was so sick and she lay against him. "I'm really glad about that. I'd have never gotten to know you as the woman in the evening gown being interviewed by the news."

She spoke without raising her head. "Madeline called and said she saw us even on the news in Denver. I thought we would only be a local story."

He wrapped an arm around her. "A congressman being arrested at his own fancy shindig for assaulting his fiancé' was far too juicy of a story to stay local, and you've kind of snowballed from there with the corruption allegations and then supporting the opponent. And I'm sure looking like a supermodel can't have hurt."

She laughed right out loud at him and wacked him. "You are such a gumbah sometimes. You'd better go watch football with Drew so I can try to take a nap. I'm already starting to get up tight about testifying tomorrow."

He rubbed her arm. "You're not going to be up tight at all tomorrow. You're a total cool cucumber. I know you."

"A second ago I was a supermodel, now I'm a cucumber. I'm deteriorating fast this afternoon."

He smiled and shook his head. "Oh, I don't know. I love cucumbers. They taste delicious." Leaning down, he bit her gently on the lip.

She kissed him for a few seconds and then broke it off to laugh. "That is the all time worst segue into kissing I have ever heard!"

He gave her his mellow smile that went so perfectly with his soft drawl as he said, "Hey, it worked. Quit giggling. I'm trying to taste you here."

Chapter 30

When he left almost half an hour later, she did try to nap, but as soon as she laid down there seemed to be a million thoughts going around and around in her head. The happy spirit she had felt in Matt's arms began to dissolve into wondering why when they were such good friends; they couldn't talk about their future. What was up with them? She honestly didn't think Matt was the kind of guy who was just stringing her along, but they had no plans beyond getting through her testimony at the trial.

Realistically, that was probably tomorrow, and at most another couple of days. She turned over and smacked her pillow almost roughly, as she tried to focus on something other than her and Matt's lack of communication about the future.

She was going to have to face John again tomorrow and this time, knowing that she had openly worked to destroy his political career. She knew if any of the people who wanted him elected wanted to keep her quiet, they had only the next eighteen hours or so to do it and that was a scary thought.

She wondered if her parents would be there tomorrow as well. She knew she needed to deal with them and her feelings toward them, but everything in her wanted to run away from it. And Joshua had spoken to her a number of times about coming back to work full time at the office again. It made sense, but her heart wasn't in it.

Mostly, the problem was that she was feeling like the sand was running out of her hour glass with Matt. Maybe that was a good thing, because he wasn't a member, but it didn't feel like a good thing. Which didn't really matter anyway, because as much as he acted like he liked her, he hadn't said so much as word one about them being together in the future except in a completely casual way.

They had so much fun when they were together. Even when they weren't having fun, they had this easy friendship that felt so much like home. So why was there no plan beyond the next day or two? In a way it made her want to panic. She wasn't sure she wanted to face the future, wherever she was going to end up, without him. No, she was sure. She definitely didn't want to face it without him, but she didn't know what to do about it. For some reason, trying to decide about him made her so confused.

She got up and knelt to pray again. She'd been doing that a lot lately. She wanted to do the right thing, but what was the right thing? She lay back down again to listen after her prayer, but it was impossible to feel any peace with her kaleidoscope of thoughts going round and round and round. She got up and went to the window to look out into the late afternoon in the city, and then decided maybe that wasn't such a good idea. The view was dreary even for all the hustle and bustle, and the police had cautioned her to not be any more exposed than she absolutely had to be until after she had been a witness and the danger would be over.

Just looking for a minute or two had been enough for her to know that this wasn't what she wanted anymore. She closed her eyes and thought back on the purple dusk of the desert and the sweet smell of the sage after the rain. She hadn't liked the dust and the heat and the dry, but she had loved the peace and the wide, open spaces. She should go back out west, even if things didn't work out between her and Matt. Although maybe that was foolish when she was in a good market and owned part of the company here. Wasn't it?

She found herself walking her hotel suite and tried to make herself sit down and relax, but she was incredibly tightly wound.

Matt knocked and she opened the door between their rooms. "It doesn't sound like napping; it sounds like pacing in here. Are you okay? Not sleepy?"

She came into his arms and leaned her forehead against his chest. "Not sleepy. My mind won't let the rest of me rest."

"Drew and I were thinking about food. Would something to eat help?"

She shook her head. "No, why don't the two of you go down to the restaurant and actually sit and eat. I'm not hungry anyway, so there's no reason for you to have to eat up here with me. Maybe I'll eat later."

"What is it you're thinking about? Can I help you?"

She looked up into his warm, brown eyes and wished she could come right out and ask what was in his head about her, but she couldn't do it. She shook her head and turned away from him. "I'm thinking about anything and everything, and all intelligent reasoning has escaped me. I don't think you can fix that. But thanks anyway. Go eat. I'll be fine."

He looked hesitant and studied her face for a moment and then sighed. "We won't be gone long. I'll bring you something."

After he was gone, she paced again and then sat back down and absently turned on her computer, but she didn't work on Sundays. Finally, she picked up her cell phone and called Madeline. She knew she was probably busy with her two children, but she wanted to hear her voice anyway. Madeline had always been able to make sense of things that were nuts to Taya.

At first Taya simply small talked and Madeline visited back and then she paused and asked Taya what was really going on and Taya surprised them both by starting to cry. It took her a minute to get some composure and then it all came tumbling out in a rush.

Madeline listened and asked a few questions and then in her sweet, patient way reminded Taya, "In all the struggle, Taye, don't forget your Father in Heaven is watching over you and that He *is* in control and will help you with your struggles and decisions." She ended with, "I'm sorry, Taya. I can't tell you what to do, because I'm not there to even know what you're going through, but He can. Have faith in Him and trust your gut feelings here and you'll be fine. By this time next week, this will be all resolved, I'm sure."

"Thank you, Mad. You're right, I'm only overreacting. Thanks for letting me call and bawl on you. Kiss those babies. Love you. I'll call you in a few days."

Just as she was going to push end, she heard Madeline say, "Hey, Taya?"

"Yeah."

"Call your old home teachers and get a blessing."

Taya sniffed and smiled. "I believe I will. See you, Madeline."

"Good luck tomorrow. By Sweetie." Taya closed her phone and the tears started up again and she went in search of a tissue.

As she came back into the sitting room, Matt poked his head around the door to offer her food. When he saw her face, he advanced into the room and put the Styrofoam box on the table. He took her hand and then sat down on her couch with her again, and she leaned on his chest and tried to stop crying while he rubbed her back. Finally, he asked, "Are you sure I can't help you with anything?"

She wiped her nose and hid her face in his shirt. "I'm sorry. I don't know how you can help me. I'm not even sure what's wrong. I feel like the roller coaster queen this afternoon. One minute I'm laughing and the next bawling.

I'm worried about the trial and my parents. John's going to hate me forever and he probably should. Joshua wants me to come back to work here. I'm afraid and I don't even know of what and . . . " She looked up at him and then shook her head and looked back down. "I don't know. I'm just really confused. I'm sorry."

He kept rubbing and kissed the top of her head. "It's okay. But I do wish I could help."

"You are. I wish we had brought your guitar."

"Sorry, no guitar. We could find some music though." He picked up the remote and fiddled with it until he found music and then found some soft rock and turned it down. "There, that will feel you better."

Taya raised her teary face to look at him and he said, "That's what my niece says. It seems to work."

It did. Taya laughed, and Matt smiled down at her and hugged her. "You're okay, babe. Now you've cried and you'll feel better and can get back to being a supermodel and a green vegetable. And have I got a deal for you. Drew and I were able to procure a fine set of Uno cards in the hotel gift shop. How's that for exciting? There were face cards too, but we decided not to buy those on the Sabbath."

She shook her head and laughed again, and wiped at the tears that were still on her cheeks. "What did you say you ate for dinner?"

He raised his hands in his own defense. "Hey, you know me. I've learned my lesson. The most dangerous substance that goes into this body is buffalo wing sauce. Well, and all kinds of ice cream toppings, but some of those have fruit in them, so I get veggie points."

"Can I trust you two at Uno? I'm not going to get rooked, am I?"

"Can you trust us? Listen to you! I am the most honorable cardsharp you've ever had the good fortune to be rooked by. Come on, I'll show you."

"Okay, but first I'm going to call my old home teachers and see if I can talk them into giving me a blessing sometime before the trial in the morning."

"What's a home teacher?"

"In the church, every family, or in my case single, has a pair of priesthood holders who are supposed to visit them from time to time and sort of watch over them in case they need something. The women also have visit teachers who are ladies. It's God's way of making sure all of His sheep have someone looking out for them so no one falls through the cracks."

"I keep being surprised by how organized everything is with the church."

"God's house is a house of order. Just a minute, I'll call and then be in."

Her home teachers agreed to come as soon as they could get to her hotel and she let the other guys know to expect them and then went in to play Uno with a little more hope of getting a handle on her emotions than she had been having. A priesthood blessing would help her to at least have some peace of mind with all of this.

****

Matt had known even before she decided to try to nap that something was bothering her. It bothered him too even though he didn't know what it was because she was so not talking to him about it. Most of the times they were friends as usual, but every once in a while these last few days there was this invisible, silent elephant sitting between them. Worse than that, he didn't know what her plans were after this trial and when he'd tried to ask her about them, she hadn't really answered him. It had made him wonder if she was hedging for some reason.

He loved her and he was relatively sure she liked him. At least she acted like it, so he wasn't at all sure what was going on here. He wasn't even going try to deal with her one time revelation that she didn't think she'd ever fall in love if she hadn't by the time she was twenty-four. He loved her enough to want to be with her even if she couldn't fall madly in love with him.

Theoretically, she'd know after tomorrow if she was free to go or not as far as testifying against John, and he knew her old boss or partner or whatever he was, was pressuring her to come back to work here, which made Matt want to reach through the phone and throttle the guy. And the heck of it was that he didn't even know what his own plans were professionally or where he was going to be living because, he was hoping he could go in the same direction as her if she'd let him. Much as he didn't want to completely leave home and family to move to a huge metropolitan area in the east, he'd do it if she acted like she wanted him to. Which led back in a circle because they didn't seem to be able to talk about any of this.

Then he'd known she was pacing. And now she was crying and calling for some men he'd never even heard of to come and give her a priesthood blessing. She was obviously struggling, and it killed him that she wouldn't even truly talk to him about what was going on and then turned to someone else who she hadn't seen for more than six months for help, instead of him. Which she couldn't because he didn't have the priesthood she needed. Gees, it made him confused.

He pasted on a smile and played Uno, trying to help her to find her own smile again. When two sharp, polished young men showed up at the hotel in expensive suits an hour later, he was more frustrated than ever. These were not the fatherly type priesthood holders he had envisioned.

Taya excused herself and took the two guys and went into her own suite of rooms and left Matt and Drew sitting at the table with their cards. Drew looked at him and asked, "Who are they?"

"Two guys from her church. She's seriously uptight tonight and asked them to come over and help her."

Drew looked at him for a minute and then asked him out right, "Why are they helping her instead of you?"

"She wants something called a priesthood blessing. I don't hold the priesthood you need to give that to her."

Drew fiddled with his cards for a second and then said, "Dude, if I was you, and felt the way you do about a girl like that, I'd be for doing whatever it took to get her what she needs. Those two pretty boys seemed more than happy to see her. You'd better get a little more serious or you're going to be kicking yourself for a long, long, long time."

"I'm trying Drew, but it's not that easy. To hold the priesthood, I have to become a member of her church, which I'm going to do, but in the mix of all this contract and hiding mess, I'm not getting there fast enough. And since we've been back here, there's something else bothering her that she can't even talk to me about. I don't know what's going on."

"When are you flying out?"

"Same as you. Supposedly first thing day after tomorrow if she's through."

"Is she coming, or is she staying here?"

It about made him sick to say it right out loud, "I don't know."

Drew was looking at him, but Matt didn't even want to look up to meet his eyes. He finally did, and Drew said, "Once you find her man, don't walk away."

For a while they could faintly hear voices through the adjoining door, and then they heard her see the two home teachers out about a half hour after they arrived, but she didn't come back into his suite. Finally, at after ten o'clock, he had to know if she was okay and knocked quietly on her door.

She said, "Come in," and he let himself in, but there were no lights on, only the radio, and it took him a second to see that she was standing in front of the window in the dark looking out at the city lights spread out as far as you could see below.

He came up behind her and she backed up to lean against him. When she did, he put both arms around her shoulders and hugged her and put his chin on top of her head. "Did the blessing help you?"

"Yes. Not as much as I'd hoped. I guess I'm not having enough faith."

He didn't know what to say to that, so he didn't say anything, just continued to hold her. In time, she moved in his arms and when he went to release her, she turned to him and put her arms around him and came back close to him. He wrapped her back into his hug and was torn between basking in holding and being held, and hating the fact that he had no idea what was going on.

When she finally looked up at him, he studied her trying to see if he could figure out what was in her head, but he couldn't. All he could see was that she was unhappy and needed him. He bent his head and tentatively kissed her and then after a minute kissed her with all the pent up feelings and frustration that had been building up in him. She met him half way, and pressed closer to him still. When he finally ended the kiss with almost a groan and rested his chin against her hair, he had definitely been the one to pull back. Crimony, she was so hard to figure out right now.

He didn't know what she was thinking, and he didn't know what she needed and when she looked back up and then pulled his head back down to hers, he went with it and kissed her again. She was obviously as frustrated as he was, and just knowing that helped his heart. He'd give about anything for that funny, little trailer porch swing right now and a good, desolate patch of desert to go along with it. Friendship had come so easy there. He kissed her back until she took a little shuddering breath and hid her face against his neck. Holding her like this, even when they were upset, was heaven.

After several more minutes, she took a long, deep breath and let it out. He knew she was tired and she had a big day tomorrow. Just when he was going to suggest she go try to rest, she said, "Kiss me one more time, Matt. Then send me to bed."

He searched her eyes again. How could she look at him like that and not want to talk about their future? He gathered her so tightly in his arms he felt like his emotion would crush her except that somehow he knew she needed this. His kiss strengthened her. He could feel it, and he could feel her frustration dissipate under his mouth. He finally understood that she didn't know what she needed anymore than he did. Together they could figure it out. Maybe this wasn't something that talking fixed. Kissing had helped. Kissing had helped a lot. He'd have to remember that.

He raised his head with a sigh, brushed her bottom lip one more time and kissed the pink scar above her brow. "Good night, Taya. I hope you're able to rest. I'll pray for you, okay." He gently touched his mouth to hers one last time and left her standing there in the dark. Man, he'd have liked to have kissed her for about another hour.

Chapter 31

When she emerged the next morning looking like a million bucks in her conservative slacks and blouse and heels, he looked at her intently, trying to see how she'd done last night after all. She looked a little tired, and a little nervous, but she wasn't afraid of him in the least and met him with a long, sweet kiss.

He searched those striking blue eyes again and then gently kissed her on the forehead this time and offered her his breakfast. She took a bite of his toast and drank some of his milk and said that was all she could face for a while and then she dug through her purse and freshened her lipstick while she waited for them to finish.

They piled into three cars, with her riding in the back seat of the second one between him and Drew. Matt let out a huge sigh of relief when they were safely inside the courthouse. Hopefully, today would be the last day she would have to feel like there was a possible price on her head.

She gripped his hand as they walked down the hall, ignoring the media and he knew exactly when she saw her parents. She broke stride just for a split second and then her grip tightened slightly. He had to hand it to her. She truly was one cool cucumber. She greeted the handsome, dark haired couple who stood in the hall with perfect grace, "Hello, Mother, Daddy. How have you been?"

Her mother didn't answer, merely stared at Matt, but her dad responded like a world class politician, "Good, thanks. How have you been, Taya honey?"

"Excellent. I should introduce my friend, Matt. Matt, these are my parents, Stan and Evelyn Kaye."

"It's good to meet you." He extended his free right hand to shake theirs before Taya continued on into the court room surrounded by five men who looked like secret service in their dark suits and ear pieces. *Holy smokes! That was their first meeting after walking out on her, broken and bleeding on the floor? No wonder she was struggling with facing them.*

He and Taya and her entourage found seats off to one side and sat in a tight group to start what would prove to be a long day. When John Channing came in Matt looked him over. He looked what he was. Wealthy, confident and almost pretty he was so smooth. John looked hard in their direction, but had eyes only for Taya and Matt at once doubted her prediction that he would hate her forever. Matt had assumed the guy had to have disliked her to have hurt her so badly, but that wasn't the way he was looking at her. He bent and whispered, "I thought you said John Channing wasn't in love with you."

She whispered back, "He wasn't. And he isn't. I was just a pretty girl who had a big trust fund. He's a good actor." She glanced at John and then continued to look around the court room.

A big trust fund. Yet another Taya surprise, only this one didn't feel all that fascinating. He wondered what her definition of big was and if she would have ever mentioned that except in this situation. It kind of hit him in the pit of his stomach like a one two punch after just having realized that this congressman was in love with the same woman he was. Did she really not know it?

He saw the two men come in who had shown up at her camp those months ago. They were still snakes, even if John honestly was in love with Taya. The one he had held the gun on gave him a malevolent stare. *What a warm guy.*

The morning dragged on, even with the ridiculous theatrics of the attorneys, and Matt had never been so grateful for a lunch break. He'd been hoping for a reprieve, but it turned out miserable between the hostiles around them and the crowds. He could tell Taya was still uptight and she ate almost nothing, in spite of basically no breakfast, and was glad to get back inside away from the reporters to get this over with.

When she was called to the stand, she truly was questioned about having seen and heard a miniscule amount that seemed suspect. It was no wonder she hadn't figured it out before hand, but what she had seen, dovetailed right in with the rest of the evidence compiled to prove John's guilt, so her testimony had been necessary. The defense attorneys tried to jerk her around and Matt was totally disgusted, but Taya handled them like a queen and, in fact, made them look petty she was so gracious about it.

At least at the end of the day, they were through with her and she could go where she wanted now in relative safety.

As they exited the court room and were caught in the crush, John and his attorneys caught up with them, surprisingly, with no media for a moment. John went to touch Taya on the arm and the latent warrior in Matt came out fast. He stepped right between them and literally froze John with his cool glare even before any of the FBI people could intervene. John dropped his hand to his side and Taya put her hand inside Matt's elbow to gently get him to back off a little. "Its okay, Matt. I'll talk to him."

Matt stepped back and John looked up at him and then to Taya he said, "Hello, Taya." She nodded silently and he went on, "I wanted to tell you I'm honestly sorry for everything. I'm sorry I hurt you that night. I was such a fool. And I'm sorry you had to have surgery and go away and feel like you had to hide. I'm certainly sorry for the way those attorneys treated you in there. In looking back, I know now what I lost when you left me, and I think I understand some of what that night cost you, and I'm sorry for it all. I know you probably hate me, and I don't blame you, but I want you to know I'll always love you anyway. I know you've done what you felt you should. And I don't hold it against you. I guess I'm simply trying to say I'm sorry. I wish you the best in the rest of your life."

He went to turn to go, but Taya caught his arm. He looked down at her left hand that was still in a splint and then up at her face as she said, "We found the diamond, John. Only a few days ago. It was still caught in the lining of my dress. I'll send it to you."

He put a gentle hand over hers on his arm and said, "Keep it, Taya. Maybe it can start to pay for some of the things I've cost you. It can be my first act of trying to get my life back on track, and making things right. You were always a good example for me. Maybe I'll get it right yet." This time he did walk away, and they let him go.

Taya looked up and met Matt's eyes. "Wow. I almost think he was being sincere."

Matt nodded. "I'm sure he was. He might have ended up okay, even as a congressman if he'd actually married you. You have a way of straightening people's kinks out."

She searched his eyes for a minute. "I'm never sure what to say to you when you say stuff like that."

He didn't look away as he said softly, "You don't have to say anything. Just know you're appreciated."

She put an arm around his waist. "Thanks, Matt." She glanced past him and then said, "I guess it's my turn."

He looked behind him and then went with her to where her parents were coming out of the courtroom. She stopped them and said, "Mom, Dad. I need to tell you something. I know you're disappointed in me. And I'm sorry for that. And honestly, I was disappointed in you too, and I'm sorry for that as well. I just want you to know that I love you, and I always will. I'm sorry we didn't turn out better friends." Neither Stan nor Evelyn seemed to know what to say to her, and after a moment her face fell a little and she turned away from them to continue on down the hall. She'd done it and made it through, and he was proud of her.

He put an arm around her shoulder and squeezed and said, "Don't give up on them, Taya. Some day they'll figure it all out. Don't let it hurt you all over again. Let it go."

She reached up and wiped away a tear. "I am. It does hurt a little though. I'm sorry."

"You're doing fine, honey. Don't apologize. Let's get out of here, shall we?"

Drew drove with an agent in front with him and as they rode in the back on the way to the hotel Taya's phone rang. It was Joshua again. Matt could tell from her answers that he asked how her day had gone at the trial and if she was done, and then he wanted to know how soon she would be coming back to work with him. Matt knew that was what he was asking even before she started to answer because she turned and looked at him before she decided what she was going to say. He met her eyes steadily and she told Joshua she needed some time to think about what she was going to do before she committed to him.

When she closed her phone, she turned her head to look out the window, but Matt knew she was crying again, because she reached up occasionally to wipe her face.

Not ten minutes later, Jim Horrocks called Matt's phone, and he took the call wondering if something had come up wrong with his final submittal of the project. Actually, Jim was calling to say they had been completely pleased with his work. So pleased, that they were offering him another contract for an even bigger project in southern Colorado this time. It would be better money, but the timeline would be much more reasonable.

Matt looked up from the notes he was taking to see Taya watching him with teary eyes. It was another dream project, but he had to make some serious decisions before he could commit to something right now and he knew it. He asked if he had to decide that second or if he could get back to Jim on it later and got off the call before looking back at Taya to see that she was crying toward the window one more time. *Man, we're a pair aren't we? Both of us are a mess.*

Back at the hotel, the rest of the security team packed up to leave and the three of them decided to get out of the hotel for dinner for once. Taya took them to the seafood place that had always been her favorite and Matt ordered a lobster that he truly wasn't sure he could eat in honor of her part of the trial being over.

Both of them were trying to make it a festive dinner, but no matter how hard they tried, neither one of their smiles reached their eyes. Matt couldn't finish the whole lobster even with Taya taking a couple of bites, and Drew generously offered to help polish it off before they went back to the hotel.

As soon as they got there, even though it was only a little after eight, Taya pleaded a head ache and went in to go to bed after the barest minimum of a good night and Matt's heart felt like it had been run over when he heard that adjoining door shut. She'd never said whether she was staying or going and he got a definite impression that he would be getting on that plane without her in the morning.

He changed his clothes and went down to the hotel pool and swam laps until he threw up his fancy lobster dinner in the nearby restroom. He didn't even care how he felt and went back to the pool again. It was this or go out in down town Washington D.C. alone tonight, or the hotel clubs which held no allure for him whatsoever. Drew was back in the room, but Matt couldn't face him there or on the town so he simply stayed in the pool and exercise room until his body ached and his mind went gray. At eleven, security came and locked up and he headed back up stairs. He decided he wasn't going to pack tonight and face Drew, so he pulled on a pair of pajama pants and set his phone alarm so he could do it in the morning.

Even after swimming and exercising for that long, sleep eluded him and he laid there remembering all the different times he and Taya had been through on the way from that first meeting in the desert to this lonely, luxury hotel room. He searched through each little moment trying to find when it had been that their sweet friendship had gone from treasured to not worth the hassle for her.

After hours, he couldn't find that defining moment and gave it and sleep both up to get up and go look out the window of the room the way she had been the night before. He either wanted to break something, or break down, but he couldn't do either one without waking up Drew and having to face him in utter defeat. He went out into the sitting room part of the suite and began to pace in front of the TV in the pitch black of two a.m. Twice he got down on his knees. First to ask for more guidance, and secondly to ask for help in dealing with this discouragement and loss that hurt so much it was physical.

He thought back to when he had been discouraged about how his life was going when he'd been living with Stacy and he was completely off track spiritually. It had been depressing, but nothing like this. Nothing in his whole life had come close to despair like this.

Finally, he sat down in a chair in the dark and simply tried to empty his mind of it all. The only thing that happened was that for some reason, he kept remembering that sweet peace of the night his mother had gone back home and Taya had woken up on his lap in the swing. The tranquility of that night had been more tangible than he could fathom. In twenty-six years, he'd never known he could feel like that. He'd give anything to have just five minutes of that back with her. Thinking of her made him start to hear her in his mind walking around on the other side of that stupid door that felt like the Grand Canyon between them. He could almost picture her over there making the floor creak from the weight of her steps.

He ran a hand through his hair and sighed. It felt like this night had already lasted a month. He didn't think he could get through it, but then he didn't want morning to come because then he'd only have to leave her. He'd never even told her how he honestly felt about her. He should have. Maybe if she'd known, it would have made a difference in her decision of whether to go or stay. He thought she had known even without him saying it out loud. And if she didn't get the hint from that last, desperate kiss, then telling her right out wouldn't have made much of a difference. How much he cared had been blatant. He'd wanted to breathe her in like oxygen.

After about forty five minutes of him thinking he was imagining her pacing over there, he finally realized that he truly was hearing her walk the floor. It was almost three o'clock in the morning, and he wondered why she was up pacing this time. Her part of the trial was over, and she'd faced her parents.

She hadn't given Joshua a final answer as far as he knew. Maybe that was why she couldn't sleep. He wished he had the guts to just knock and tell her he loved her and couldn't live without her and beg her to at least agree to let him move here so he could be by her. He still couldn't understand what had happened to their close friendship. Only night before last they had been kissing like they truly mattered to each other, and when they had started out this trip, he'd thought they were a couple. What had changed all that?

He got up and paced too. He couldn't merely sit there when he knew she was up. She used to turn to him for help, but apparently not any more. He didn't understand how something as good as what they had could disappear like a whiff of smoke. Why? She at least owed him that, didn't she?

He listened to her pacing and knew she must be only a few feet from him here struggling to make it through the night too. He'd gone from hurt to mad at her because that emotion was so much easier to deal with, but listening to her now, he felt only that he wanted to do what he could to help her with her troubles, whatever they were. He loved her enough that even if she wasn't going to be with him, he'd do what he could for her. He stopped in front of the door to figure out what he was going to say to her when he knocked.

He never got the chance because as he was standing there, she quietly pulled the door open and leaned her head into the room and started to whisper, "Matt. Matt."

She was looking toward the bedroom door and didn't even see him standing there right beside her in the dark and she jumped when he whispered back, "Taya, what's wrong?" She brought a hand to her chest and gasped and then came right to him and buried her face against him as he lifted his arm to embrace her. "What's wrong, Tay? There's not another mouse in a place this nice is there?"

She shook her head against him. "No. No mice. Just monsters that are keeping me up."

Still whispering, he asked, "What kind of monsters?"

"Lonely monsters." He knew exactly what she was talking about.

"They've been camping out in my room too. Nasty, little suckers aren't they?" He wrapped both arms around her tightly.

After a couple of minutes he said, "I can fight lonely monsters for you, Taya. I'll volunteer to forever, in fact.

Anywhere you need them fought. D.C. or Colorado or South America. I'll help you herd those llamas."

She looked up at him in the dark. "What do you mean?"

"I mean I need to know why you're pulling away from me, Taya. Because if it's something we can fix, then I need to fix it. I don't think I can get on that plane in a few hours without you."

She looked up at him, questioning and whispered louder, "What? What are you saying?"

"You heard me, Taya. I love you, and I want you to be honest with me and tell me what's wrong. Our friendship at least deserves that. Why the distance since we've been here? Have I done something? Or is there something else here that's bothering you? What's going on?"

He couldn't tell for sure, but she looked confused there in the dark. "Why are you asking me what's going on?" This time she forgot to whisper at all.

He sighed and looked up at the ceiling and then back at her. "Taya, I need an answer. I deserve an answer. We've been good friends. The best of friends. Why is planning beyond today not even an option for us?"

She opened her mouth, but nothing came out. She just stood there looking up at him and he went on, "Is it the church? If it's the church, we can work with that. I'll see the missionaries again. I want to be baptized, I just haven't had time. Is it the church?"

She shook her head at him. "Matt, I'm not the one who won't talk about the future. I haven't made a single plan because I was hoping I could plan to be where you are. You're the one who won't let us plan anything. Are you just done with me or what?"

He was shocked. "Am I just done with you? I'm never going to be done with you. I love you. How can you be done with someone you love?"

She looked at him and completely forgot to whisper again, "Matt . . . What? What are you telling me?"

"You heard me, Taya. What are you telling me?"

She shook her head. "I don't know what I'm telling you. I guess I'm simply telling you I don't want to be without you and I'm sad that we don't have any plans to be together anymore." She looked down and hid her face on his chest.

He was just going to ask her to look at him and repeat that so he could understand what she was saying when Drew came out of the bedroom and glanced at them there in the dark on his way into the bathroom. He paused before he shut the door and said, "Please tell me you're talking about getting married and not about leaving each other." He shut the bathroom door and Matt took Taya's hand and led her back into her own suite of rooms. He turned on a small lamp and pulled her to the couch with him.

When she was sitting there beside him, he looked at her and said, "Say that again."

"Say what again?"

"What you were telling me in the other room."

She looked up and searched his eyes for a few minutes and finally asked, "Can we talk about getting married? I don't want you to leave me."

He lifted her up onto his lap and hugged her against him. "Oh, Taya. I'm not going to leave you. I mean, I thought I was going to have to leave you because you didn't want me to stay with you, but I would never leave you willingly. I'd love to talk about getting married. I just haven't known what you were thinking about me. What do you want from me, Tay?"

"I . . . I don't know exactly. I didn't honestly think you would be willing to talk about getting married, but I know I want to go with you wherever you decide you're headed."

"And I haven't made any plans because I was waiting to find out what you were going to do before I could decide. Are you going to stay here and work with Joshua?"

"I don't know what I'm doing. Are you going to stay in Steamboat, or take this new contract? Or both?"

"Taya, I won't take the contract if you're not going to be in Colorado. I can come here if that's what you want. I could find work here if you need me to."

She leaned into his neck and took a deep breath. "I'd rather not stay here unless you feel strongly about it. I think I'm a wide open spaces kind of girl now, but I can work out of a sheep trailer if I need to, so I can go wherever you need to be. I only want to be by you."

He paused. "Like how by me?" He didn't breathe while he waited for her answer.

She hesitated. "Uh, pretty close."

He pulled her back so he could see her face. "Come on, Taya. Talk to me here. You're killing me. How close is pretty close?"

Her blue eyes were huge and then she snuggled back into him so she wasn't looking at him and asked, "Would this close be too close?"

He pulled back again. "Yes, unless you honestly agreed to marry me. Having you this close is too tempting for long. Could we truly talk about getting married?"

"I would really like to."

"We haven't known each other all that long. Are you sure? Do we need to be engaged for a long time so you don't have any doubts?"

She smiled up at him shyly. "How could I have any doubts about you, Matt? I fell head over heels in love with you in a sheep camp. The only thing I questioned was how you felt about me and what to do about falling in love with a truly good man who wasn't a member. If you want me, you're stuck with me forever. And I don't want a long engagement unless it's important to you. I just want you."

He looked at her steadily. "I thought you said you didn't think you could fall in love."

"I had never met you when I thought that. You came and I was history. I'd follow you to the ends of the earth now. All you'd have to do is play your guitar and promise me you'll hold me on a swing occasionally."

He rubbed a hand down her back, "That swing was heaven. But there are a couple of other things we'll need eventually. I have great memories of this summer, but wouldn't it be nice to have an indoor shower this winter? With no sand or cactuses nearby? I want you to be comfortable and secure and have a place for Zeus and Horse.

Her face lit up. "Really? You'd let me have Horse?"

He put a hand into her silky hair and tugged on it. "Taya, I'll be your husband, not your parent. I'm not going to tell you what you can and can't have. But the first time I saw you on that ridge in the desert, you were on Horse. I thought you were the purest form of art. You should have Horse. And Zeus isn't even a question is he?"

Her forehead creased for a minute. "Technically, he's Joseph and Zan's, but he thinks I'm his."

"And it's wonderful to know he watches over you. I don't know where this contract is for sure, but whether we go there or only hire a crew and check on them occasionally, we'll be glad to have Zeus. That being said, we'll have to have a house where we can keep him without him eating any of the locals."

After thinking for a minute, she asked, "If we're going to have a real house, could we have room for a real office in it?"

He tipped her face up to look at him and said softly, "We can have whatever we want, Taya, but I thought that eventually you wanted a nursery instead of an office."

Her eyes flew to his and stayed there for a while. She nodded. "I do. I've always wanted that in general. Now the babies I want have brown hair and brown eyes."

He rubbed a thumb softly across her bottom lip. "We may have to negotiate that one. I want dark haired ones with blue eyes and perfect lips." He leaned to kiss her.

Eventually he continued their conversation. "We probably should decide on some other things before we worry about babies. We need to decide about this contract for sure and let Joshua know what you're going to do."

"And sometime I need to do something with all my stuff in storage here and my car. Most of it can just be sold, but I should make sure there aren't any things I want to keep and get it taken care of."

"I think I might sell a lot of my stuff too. I'd like to keep making a new life with you. You've been so good for me."

"Is your family going to be upset that you're getting baptized or marrying a Mormon?"

"I don't know. I don't think so. I think they all loved you, but I don't know. I'm going to guess that they've seen what a good influence you've been on me and are thrilled about you. Before you I didn't really know much about the LDS church so they probably don't either. I think they will love you because I love you and I'm the one who's marrying you."

She looked up at him and asked, "Why didn't you tell me? I've been miserable for days because I didn't know if you were moving on without me."

"Taya, I tried to ask you several times about your plans after the trial and you evaded the question. I thought you were the one moving away from me. But I was going to follow you if you'd have let me."

She laid her head against his chest. "I didn't mean to evade the question. I just didn't know what this trial was going to take or how the election will play out. I even wondered if I would be putting you at risk if John appealed forever or somehow got off on a technicality and then won the election. He still might for that matter. I might be way more hassle than you bargained for."

He shook his head and hugged her. "You've been the best thing that's ever happened to me, Taya. You're the good woman behind the man I can be. You're the one helping me to reach the greatness waiting on the other side that my mom was talking about. You could never be too much hassle. I'm just incredibly thankful for you. And I want to take you somewhere nice and propose to you with a real ring and . . . Wait." He searched her eyes again and asked gently, "Do you want a ring? Or is that a bad question?"

Putting her hand to his cheek she asked, "Do I have to have a diamond?"

"Honey, you don't even have to have a ring if you don't want. I'll understand."

"I would love a ring, but can we just have a band that truly does symbolize love? Because I do love you, and I do want to be with you forever, and I'm so grateful that you have nothing to prove with a big diamond."

"I'm a simple guy, Taya. Are you sure that won't get old after the life you've led?"

She shook her head. "You're not simple. You're unpretentious. It's one of your best things, Matt. We'll both get old. We'll do it together and be incredibly happy as great, great grand parents. What do you think?"

He pulled her close and kissed the pink scar above her brow and then her mouth again. Finally, he breathed, "What I think is that you are a gift from heaven."

The End

About the author

Jaclyn M. Hawkes grew up with 6 sisters, 4 brothers and any number of pets. (It was never boring!) She got a bachelor's degree, had a career and traveled extensively before settling down to her life's work of being the mother of four magnificent and sometimes challenging children. She loves shellfish, meat lovers pizza, the out of doors, the youth and hearing her children laugh. She and her adorable husband, their younger children, and their happy dog, now live in a mountain valley in northern Utah, where it smells like heaven and kids still move sprinkler pipe.

To learn more about Jaclyn, visit www.jaclynmhawkes.com.

Author's Note

Down on the highway between the little valley we live in and the next valley down the mountain on a ridge overlooking the river, there stands a little old sheep herder's trailer with a sign draped across it that says, "Nightly Rentals". Now, I'm sure someone put the sign on it as a joke, but to me, it was absolutely thought provoking. Sometimes, when that centrifugal force of life makes you start feeling like your just about to go winging off, wouldn't that life of a sheepherder be amazing?

Except for the mice. If they just weren't so dang fast maybe they wouldn't be so scary. Thank goodness for husbands, Jaclyn

www.ingramcontent.com/pod-product-compliance
Lightning Source LLC
Chambersburg PA
CBHW070307260626
47160CB00003B/759